ALL THE WAY HOME

Mariellen Langworthy

SR
Stillwater
River

Visit our website at **www.StillwaterPress.com** for more information.

First Stillwater River Publications Edition

ISBN: 1-946-30027-6
ISBN-13: 978-1-946-30027-0

Library of Congress Control Number: 2017951318

1 2 3 4 5 6 7 8 9 10
Written by Mariellen Langworthy
Cover design by Dawn M. Porter
Published by Stillwater River Publications, Glocester, RI, USA

Publisher's Cataloging-In-Publication Data
(Prepared by The Donohue Group, Inc.)

Names: Langworthy, Mariellen.
Title: All the way home / Mariellen Langworthy.
Description: First Stillwater River Publications edition. | Glocester, RI, USA : Stillwater River,
        [2017] | Interest age level: 012-018.
Identifiers: ISBN 978-1-946300-27-0 | ISBN 1-946300-27-6
Subjects: LCSH: Lesbians--Fiction. | Interracial dating--Fiction. | Runaway teenagers--Fiction. |
        Blacks--Segregation--United States--Fiction. | Murder--Fiction. | Kentucky--Race rela-
        tions--Fiction. | BISAC: JUVENILE FICTION / LGBT.
Classification: LCC PS3612.A54 A45 2017 | DDC 813/.6--dc23

To Elda, my wonderful wife—our journey together has been filled with love, excitement, travelling, kindness, writing and so much laughing. I would not have missed this time for anything.

For Maizie Smith whose heart was always bigger than her troubles.

Thank you to my writing group for their support and great ideas—Rebecca Maizel, Tracy Hart, Maggie Hayes, Rebecca DeMetrick, Linda Melino and Ashley Bray.

PAINE HOLLOW
1932

CHAPTER 1

My bare feet slip, olive-brown silt squishes through my toes and thin branches sting my face as I half slide, half stumble down the path to the river. A big black crow caws and flaps off across the water. My eyes follow the crow to Booker who's in his rickety flat-bottom skiff with a fishing pole, a catfish struggling and twisting in a fight for its life. He yanks the pole backwards and that catfish lands between his bare brown feet. The grin on his dark face means his pa won't whack him tonight.

I lose the struggle to keep my balance and slip slide down the mud. One of them wooden buckets whacks me on the shin. It's 1932 and you'd think there would be a water pipe running up to Granny's cabin. Guess we're not worth the trouble.

"Damnation," I yell. My arms jerk and I toss the two hateful wooden buckets toward the water. I'm seventeen and still fetching water. But not for long, you can bet your life on that. The purple bruise against the pale skin of my arm twitches as I grab at a branch to break my fall down the slippery mud path. I screech as thorns tear at my fingers and Booker flops onto the bottom of the skiff for all the world looking like he's scared to death. That catfish keeps flapping at his feet. Scrambling to my feet, I wipe mud off my raggedy flour sack dress I sewed myself and take a few steps forward.

"Booker!" I holler across the water.

If possible, he presses himself tighter against the bottom of his boat. As I bend and pick up them damned buckets, out of the corner of my eye I see him raise his head. I fill each one slowly, acting as if I can't

1

see him. Then his brown, nearly black eyes peek over the rim of his boat. Even from here I can see the fear. Setting the buckets on the muddy shore, I holler.

"You got yourself a big one." We been friends for maybe a month or so. He's not actually supposed to fish in white people's water, so usually he meets me along the rails where I walk to work.

Sitting up, he takes his fishing knife out of his belt and smacks the flapping catfish on the head, then he drops it in a bucket in his skiff.

"Maisy. Don't be hollering." His whisper skitters across the water. "Your granny around?"

"Nah. She's in the cabin. She won't hear you."

"Well," he smiles at me like the morning sun coming up over the hills. "I ain't taking no chances." Grabbing his thick paddle he whips it through the water as fast as he can. He looks back once, but keeps on going. The rope handles of the buckets bite into my hands as I fill each one. I don't blame him for running from my granny.

Someday I will too.

* * *

"I seen you with that colored boy," Granny Wharton screams at me as I lug the two buckets sloshing with water over the ridge of the pathway. She's standing on the step of her wooden house, her normally white, wrinkled face the color of raw meat. Her shack isn't like the houses I seen in *Life* Magazine, with windows that open, big porches and electricity. Her broken panes are covered with cardboard and it'll be a hundred years before we get any electricity way back here in these Kentucky hills. And it don't help being mixed in with the coloreds in them shanties by the water because they don't have money for electricity any more than we do.

"I tole you about talking to them coloreds," Granny Wharton shrieks waving her broom. I set the buckets on the bare ground. That broom and me have seen too much of each other. Gently touching the bruise on my arm, I back away knowing what's coming. Stumbling on a rock, I lose my balance. Before I realize what's happening, she is down the stair and swinging her broom handle at me. It hits my ear. I'm sure my skull splits open as I wrap my arms around my head. She brings the handle down on my back three times making my ribs vibrate with pain. I have to run. That's all to be done when she's like this.

Run.

So I do. I run through the brambles that surround our little patch of land. They prick my skin and little dots and lines of blood pop up on my forearm. Least, old Granny can't follow me to my chickabiddy, my very own secret hiding place. Granny wasn't always so mean. She wasn't sweet and kind like a granny's supposed to be, but in the beginning she'd tell me stories and sometimes fix a special treat for me. I let myself believe we might make a home together. But that hooch finally caught up with her and now she's meaner than a snake. She might as well live under a log.

I burst through the undergrowth of my chickabiddy which is a clearing with tall trees standing around them two big boulders I can lean against or sit on. The pricker bushes discourage anyone from wandering through. This is where I hide until Granny comes back into her right mind. My ma always called me her little chickabiddy. She'd hold me on her lap, wrap her arms around me and sing me a song she made up about me being her chickabiddy, her sweet little thing. When I was snuggled right up against her warmth, I never imagined I'd be anything but safe.

I sit on the patch of cool green moss surrounded by the smell of dampness, my back against the rock, letting out a long weary breath. Slapping a mosquito on my arm, I flick its dead body into a patch of fiddlehead ferns. The sun rests on the horizon and splinters of light shoot through the branches of my favorite hickory tree. Seems I'm always running away from somebody aiming to hurt me.

The sharp, pointy edges of the rock poke at my back. I stretch, then kneel at my hidey hole. I hid a piece of wood I found floating in the river one day under some low hanging branches. Reaching until my fingertips touch the grey stone sitting on top the wood, I roll it off, lift the wood and take out the old piece of tar paper I found by the train tracks. The tar paper keeps my magazine dry for exactly times like this.

I love magazines and newspapers, reading them over and over. Anything that tells me there's a world beyond this sorry place. This one is a year old. A 1931 *Life* that Elwood tried to bribe me with just the other day. If Granny weren't his second cousin and her thinking he's doing her a big favor by paying her rent and slipping her money now and then, I'd never step foot in his stupid restaurant again. That's one nasty man.

I run my finger over the big white letters. LIFE. Being seventeen and sitting here surrounded by prickers and leaning against the rough bark of this tree sure isn't going to be my life. I have plans. I open the magazine right to the very middle and squint at the full page picture and story about the fancy roadster that looks like a race car. Mr. Ford, in Detroit, is making it special. Why anybody needs a car like that, I surely don't know. Old Seth in his Model T is just fine. Then I study the man standing beside the car, his leather cap and goggles, his fancy suede jacket and slick black pants. He probably lives in one of them brick houses in Detroit I saw pictures of and his wife probably wears a silky dress that flares around her calves and has one of them big white collars.

Detroit.

Everybody must be rich in Detroit.

That's where I'm going as soon as I can get out of here. Going to get me a job at Mr. Ford's car factory and have myself a real good life. My ma told me you have to dream big to get what you want and I surely don't want to be stuck here. I want that good life. My ma talked about Detroit like it was the promised land and said anything was possible there. You can be anybody you want to be and life would be a comfort there. Not like the hardness here. My ma was saving every penny for train fare. The two of us were going. Least I think it was for the two of us. She never said exactly that I was going. But, I'll never know, seeing

4

as how she got shot in the head and Granny Wharton, my dead father's mother got me and all the money. It wasn't much and it was supposed to be for me, but Granny took it and that was the end of that.

What I do know for sure is I'm getting myself to Detroit even if I have to keep working for that nasty man, Elwood. Every pay day before I get home, I take all the change and hide it in my pocket and only give Granny the one dollar bill. She'd beat me good if she knew I had a stash of coins under my mattress on the floor of my room. Every week it gets a tiny bit bigger.

I flip the page and run my palm over the wrinkled picture of a woman wearing a ruffled apron, a big old smile on her face, cooking on a stove. You just turn it on instead of chucking it full of wood. The refrigerator next to her runs on electricity. And there's an electrical mixer-upper behind her. That's going to be me with not a cast iron skillet in sight.

Or a broom.

CHAPTER 2

The sun's up over the hills as I walk along the railroad ties between them long shiny tracks that disappear into the woods. The soles of my shoes crunch on the stones. My toes were curling under themselves so I cut the top out of my old leather shoes. I could walk these rails with my eyes closed seeing as how I walk them twice a day to and from Paine Hollow which is a good three miles each way. Paine Hollow's the only town hereabouts for maybe twenty-five miles, and it's where Elwood runs his restaurant. I don't know why they got electricity in town and we don't. They say we're way too far up in the hills. No use thinking on that. Instead I think about the $10.53 I saved. It's not much but it will eventually be enough to get me to Detroit.

And, truth be told, I'm also listening for Booker to slip out of the underbrush like he's been doing for over a month now. Booker helps his pa deliver the fish they catch in the river. We got to be friends because one day when they come to Elwood's, a big old catfish slid off the counter and flopped on the floor. Booker and me both leaned down at the same time, bumping our heads. He grinned at me and whispered. "They's both crazy." We been friends ever since. Least I got me somebody to talk to. And that means a lot.

The dirt road to town is considerably shorter than the tracks, but if me and Booker walked that road together, some of them folks might get riled up. That's why I walk along the tracks hoping to see him. We're just learning about each other. He's really my only friend since

Granny took me out of school three years ago to work. Except for Lucymay. But she got married and has a baby girl already and her husband, Bucky, don't like us to get together with each other. He says it's a waste of time lollygagging around with me when Lucymay has plenty to do especially with another baby on the way. So I'm glad for Booker. It gets real lonely living with Granny.

The bushes rustle and Booker slips out, quiet as a rabbit, and steps beside me. His bare feet walk on these rocks like they were soft as cotton.

"How'd you get away from your pa *this* morning?" I ask.

"Tole him I didn't catch no fish, but I knew a real good spot I was heading for." Something crinkles as he fusses with his pants pocket.

"What'd you do with that big old fish you caught this morning?"

"Hid him in the water on a stick. I'll get him later." More crinkling. "Look," he unfolds a page of newspaper and holds it up for me to see.

"Pa was wrapping fish and I seen this." He grins and his shiny brown eyes dance. "Remember you read to me about her in that magazine? I knowed you'd be interested."

He hands me the page and points to a picture under the headline in big, bold letters.

EARHART CROSSES ATLANTIC ALONE

Booker's finger touches the picture of Amelia Earhart, that leather helmet with her short blonde hair escaping around the edges, standing on the wing of her airplane.

His finger moves along her blonde curls then he glances over at me.

"Look at that. Your hair's just like Amelia's, only long," he says smiling at me like I could be Amelia herself. He reaches out to touch my hair but whips away his hand, shoving it in his pocket. His fishing knife, hitched on his rope belt, flaps against his hip.

"I don't think she wears no flour sack dress like me," I say, bitterness sitting on my tongue.

"Someday," Booker's eyes shine on me. "You'll get out of here."

"I will," I say. "If she can get herself across the ocean, I can get myself to Detroit."

"Read me every word of the story," he says settling into my stride, his shoulder brushing mine every so often.

* * *

"You're late," Elwood hollers as the door closes and that damn bell tinkles behind me. My eyes fly to the old clock by the register and it says 7:02. Knives and forks clank against plates and voices sound like a hive of bees. The radio blares the news so loud you'd think everybody was deaf. Beau, Elwood's old coon hound, shoves his graying muzzle into my hand.

"I'm taking a nickel off today's pay." The wattle on his neck covered with tiny stubs of white hair wiggles. He's a mean old man.

I open my mouth to argue, but he grabs me by my upper arm and pulls my face up close to his. His breath smells like the outhouse behind the store as it hisses between those yellowed teeth. The voices in the room go still and the clinking of forks on plates stops.

"I ain't payin' you to keep company with them coloreds. You hear me?"

"I-I-I..."

"I seen you with Amos' boy, what's his name? Bookie or something. I seen you out the back window coming off the tracks just now. Amos brings me good fish cheap. You're not messing that up for me." He gives me a shake then pushes me backward. I stumble over my feet but catch myself on the sticky corner of a table. Coffee sloshes over the edges of Mr. John's heavy white mug as murmurs of agreement from the customers ripple through the restaurant.

"Git in the kitchen 'fore I fire you." Beau slips between us, his eyes following Elwood's every move. Without even looking, Elwood ruffles his fur and scratches his ears. Beau relaxes and sits at Elwood's feet, his tail thumping against the wooden floor.

Even though I want to spit in his face, I hustle into the kitchen and grimace at the piles of dirty pots and pans left for me from this morning. I kick a sack of flour. Hard. I don't even care that it hurts my toes. It don't hurt as much as keeping my mouth shut to that nasty old man.

I run water into the sinks then reach for the scouring powder and the scrub brush muttering to myself. Sure's not his business who I talk to. Not for three cents an hour. Anyways, my friends are my friends and he sure's not my daddy to tell me what to do.

* * *

I finish scrubbing the last wooden table in the empty restaurant, picking a stubborn glob of food off with my fingernail. It's just me and Elwood. Sweat drips off the end of my nose and my skin's like I'm covered in pig grease. The radio's on. Elwood plays it all day long. Bing Crosby sings 'Brother, Can You Spare a Dime?' Kind of depressing. At least I got more than a dime. I glance at the clock. 3:42. Soon I can get out of this hateful place.

Plus today's pay day. I wipe the table dry and lift each of the two chairs upside-down onto it, scraping off a dried piece of egg or something disgusting stuck to the leg of one chair.

I feel him before I see him. My back hairs rise and I turn to get across the room from him, but his hand clasps my shoulder and then slowly runs down my back until he touches my behind, his fingers pressing into my flesh.

9

"Git your hands off me." I yank away from him and head toward the broom so I'll at least have a weapon.

He laughs. Not one of them happy laughs, but more like a snicker. He is one nasty man. But like he says, nobody'd believe me anyway if I told, what with his good works for the town. Elwood chuckles to himself all the way to the counter. Beau follows, wagging his tail against Elwood's leg and waiting beside him until Elwood scratches his ears. Then he lies down. Elwood's register ka-chings when he opens it to count his money. He's probably the only person along the Kentucky River that's got money what with this depression going on and no one having any work. Every once in a while he loans money to folks about to lose their home. And he does pay Granny's rent, but still, he's got piles of money for himself.

I reach for the broom standing next to the rack of magazines like *Time, Modern Screen, Life, Saturday Evening Post* and *Good Housekeeping* plus six or seven pulp magazines. There's a new Tarzan one I wish I could buy for Booker. He loves me to read to him. Leaning against my shoulder, he'll point to different words and ask what they are. There's also the *Ashland Times* and the *Detroit News* too. Boy, I'd sure love to have a copy of that *Modern Screen*. I love them movie stars, but I'm not spending my money on that. Specially not if Elwood's getting it. I grab the broom and start sweeping the floor. Sweat drips off my chin and I'm hot as spit on a griddle. Sure would love one swallow of that Coca Cola that Elwood's sips while he fingers his money. He looks up at me like he can read my mind, taking a long draw on that bottle. He grins at me and winks.

"Don't even think of leaving early. I ain't paying you 'til four o'clock. Maybe two minutes after." He laughs then squats and nuzzles Beau face to face, the dog licking Elwood's ugly mug.

The broom swishes against the worn wooden floor as I gather up crumbs, bits of food and stuff I don't even want to think about. Ten more minutes. Then, like every day, I sweep beside the table at the front window and my eyes follow the outline of the big brown stain that's sunk into the wood. Looks like someone spilt a whole pot of gravy,

10

wiping it up but couldn't get the color out of the floor. But it wasn't gravy.

It was my ma's blood.

I was eight years old and me and Ma was having a special Saturday breakfast together. I was just biting into my bacon when Sheriff Judd, her boyfriend—I seen them kissing all the time and heard them bumping in the night—came through the door, not even calling her name or nothing. She looked up at him, her eyes wide open, her hand raised in front of her. That's all I remember. Not remembering makes me think she's going to come and get me any minute. I don't believe she's really gone. It's impossible she'd be dead. I was sitting right there and I would have remembered. I miss her, but I've never cried when I think about her. Not once. I won't cry until I know she's truly gone.

The only thing I remember after my mother's hand paused in the air is Miss Charlotte rocking me on her lap and holding my head against her chest. We were sitting on her parlor sofa. Her finger with red fingernail polish, just like my ma's, ran along the silky yellow and green stripes as she told me my ma was dead and had gone to heaven. Even though she said those words, I never believed it was true. Not once, not even now, do I believe it.

Ma's waiting for me somewhere. I know that's true as true can be. Maybe she's waiting in Detroit.

I know she's alive because nothing ever happened to Sheriff Judd. Everybody knows he'd be in jail if she was dead.

"I'm locking the door," Elwood's voice smacks into my ears. "Here's your week's pay."

I hold out my hand and he lays one dollar bill in my palm and counts out fifty-seven cents. He did take my nickel, that cheap son of a bitch. But now I got $11.10 all together.

"Put that broom away and git outta here," he says holding the door as his empty hand reaches for my breast. I whip my body sideways, clutching my money in my fist. He pats my bottom.

For all the world I want to whack him with my broom. Instead, I slip the coins in my pocket and return the broom to the corner. I glance

11

over my shoulder and see Elwood fiddling with the door so I slide a copy of *Modern Screen* up under my dress and hold it with my arm.

"See ya' tomorrow," he says scratching Beau's head.

"Yeah." I smirk and call him son of a bitch in my head again.

CHAPTER 3

The corner of Granny's mouth does a tiny twitch as I walk toward her. I miss her smiling at me. She used to call me her little muffin. Now she complains about me day and night. There's nothing I can do right in her eyes.

"That skin flint still paying you two cents an hour?" She gripes as I hand her the dollar. I nod my head in a lie. "Cain't you get more money out of him?"

The imprint of his hand still burns on my behind as she looks at me with her rheumy eyes and, for half a second, I truly think she's going to grin at me. She used to laugh and tease with me before she and her jug got to be best friends.

"No, Granny. I asked, but he can't afford it." Lying this time with words.

"He is a cheap skin flint," she grumbles sipping her afternoon moonshine. "I,,f you worked harder, he'd pay you more." The rasp in her voice warns me to shut up. Ain't never worth arguing with Granny when she's already started drinking. That little brown jug sitting next to her wooden chair in the shade of them red oak trees near our front step tells me to keep my big mouth shut. Real tight.

"I'm gonna wash up," I say turning toward the open doorway.

"Don't you be lazin' around 'til you get your chores done." The slur in her voice is all too familiar.

"But, Granny—"

She spits in disgust on the front step and hands me the mop. "Git the floor mopped. It's filthy dirty."

"Granny," I moan, my mouth parched and begging for a Coca Cola. "I got to have a drink of water first."

Something snaps in her eyes and I know she's coming after me again. I know it wasn't easy for her to take me in and raise me. She's not exactly the motherly type but at first, she'd tell me stories and teach me about wild berries and dandelion leaves. Now she beats on me in the flick of a second.

"You spoiled little brat. You're a spittin' copy of your mother. You just had whatever you want to eat and drink at Elwood's while I eat stale bread and moldy cheese." She lurches for the mop. I whip it out of her reach and grab a bucket for water, taking the mop with me to the river. She's right about getting what I want to eat. Long as it's left on somebody's plate after they're done. If she weren't so hateful I'd bring her something. She'd never know somebody else slobbered on it first.

Stumbling down the path to the river, I fill the bucket, looking to see if Booker's fishing in his skiff, but he's not. I dip my hands into the water and drink until my stomach hurts. Then I splash the cool river water on my arms and face, letting it dribble down my chin and in between my breasts. My back aches and my arms are about to fall off, but that don't matter. If Granny Wharton wants her floor mopped, she gets it. Now. Makes me wonder if my pa was as mean as she is. Or if she got mean when he died.

Once inside I pick up the tiny braided rag rug that I made. It lies next to my mattress. Then I drag the other wobbly chair for our table outside. Before I start mopping, I slip my fifty seven cents into my sock between my mattress and the floor. If Granny hears it jingling in my pocket, she'll take it and beat me good.

I'm plumb tired and what I want to do is to sit real quiet in my chickabiddy, leafing through my magazine, imagining myself living in Detroit. Instead, I wet the mop, wring it with both hands and scrub Granny's floor, then mine. At least we each got a bedroom. I'd probably kill her in the night otherwise. Just as I'm finishing up the kitchen and sitting area, neither of which is very big, she yells at me.

"When you're done, clean out the outhouse. It stinks like hell."
I hear the hooch in her voice as the words slur together.

Maybe my daddy died to get away from her.

* * *

I finally get my chores done and head for the woods to get some time to myself. The evening air is cool and long shadows cut across my chickabiddy as Booker and me look through the magazine I stole from Elwood.

"Um-huh, she is beautiful," I say looking up at Booker, my finger on the picture of Jean Harlow in my stolen *Modern Screen*. "Don't you think?"

He tips his head to one side, looks at the picture then looks at me. And smiles.

"What?" I tease him. The sun's almost setting making the trees in my chickabiddy reddish and orange.

"She ain't as beautiful as you."

"I know *that*," I say slapping him lightly on his knee. "I'm waiting for my movie contract to arrive by parcel post." I flip the page. "What about him?" I hold up the page with John Wayne.

"He ain't my type."

"Mine either."

"But look at this," I tap my finger on a young boy. "You won't believe this." Booker leans against me, his eyes holding me in that special way.

My cheeks warm and confusion shrieks through my chest. I don't know whether to say something about him and me. I choose not because it is too hard to talk about.

"Look at this boy named Jackie Cooper. He's nine years old," my voice rises. "He's getting an Academy Award for being in a movie. A nine year old. Can you believe it?"

"A little kid gets a prize for having his picture took?" Booker is aghast. Then he grins at me. "You should get a prize for being so beautiful."

Dozens of crows flap above us in the trees, cawing and arguing with each other before settling down for the night.

We sit quietly, the air crackling between us. My mind is all at sixes and sevens. I want to explain how I feel different about him than he seems to about me, but I can't find the right words as I surely don't want to hurt his feelings. I like him, a lot, but not in that certain way. Instead, I stare at my lap.

"How come your granny so mean? She drink like my pa?"

"Probably because of getting stuck with me," I laugh, relieved to talk about something else. It must be true, though. When my ma was here, my granny used to pat me on the head once in a while and buy me penny candy for my birthday. I skim through a few pages of the magazine and tap a picture of Bette Davis. "That's what Granny used to look like."

"Sure. 'Cept your granny ain't got no teeth."

"Your pa drinks?" I ask. Booker don't say nothing but pokes at the ground with a stick. "Not supposed to because of Prohibition," I say. "He'd be breaking the law."

"Him and every man I know. Even Reverend James. And some womans too." His eyes twinkle. "They have to arrest the whole country, I guess."

"Granny, too."

"Yeah. That'll make her mean like my pa." He stretches his legs out and leans against a fallen log that's covered with moss. "You got a daddy?"

"He died of the influenza when I was two," I said. "The only memory I have of him is from a picture my ma had. But it's so tiny I can barely see his face." I don't feel sad or upset about not having a pa. Guess that's normal if you never really knew the one you had. But my Ma, that's different. I miss her something fierce.

I leaf through my magazine as mosquitoes buzz around our heads. Booker slaps one on his arm.

"Seems like we been friends forever," he says.

"Yep." I flick my eyes off the magazine for a second. "Only a few weeks though."

"Hope I know you for a long time," he says, poking his stick into a rotten log.

A blush creeps from my chest to my face as I study my magazine.

"Look at this picture." I tip it so Booker can see. "Every one of them men in Detroit always wear their Sunday-go-to-meeting suits. Just every day. Look at that." I tap my finger on each man crossing an intersection. "And look at them lights on the tall poles. It must never get dark there."

"When do they sleep?" he asks.

"Maybe they're too busy." I turn the page.

"Look. Here's a picture of that Mr. Roosevelt. I heard he's running for President."

Booker leans in to see, his shoulder pressing against mine, warmth holding us together. He quickly pulls back, slumping against the boulder.

"You going to be eighteen by voting time in November?" I ask.

"Just barely."

"You can vote for FDR. That's what they call him, you know." Getting to say who's going to be your boss seems mighty important.

"Probably not." He snaps the twig in two pieces.

"You got to vote."

"I can't read or write and I ain't got money for the poll tax." He runs his finger over the skin of his forearm. "So I cain't vote."

"What? We studied the Constitution and it says you can vote. There was a special amendment."

His mouth puckers and his eyes wander the tops of the trees. He looks at me and shakes his head.

17

"It might say we can vote but not many of us coloreds can pass them tests or pay that money."

"You don't have to take no test or pay money to vote. It's free."

"We coloreds do," he speaks so softly I almost think it's the leaves rustling.

"That's not right."

We sit for a long time. Real quiet. Finally I can't think of what to do so I leaf through my magazine.

"Hey. Look." I hold up the magazine. "Tarzan the Ape Man is a movie."

Booker laughs. "All we need is a movie theater."

"If we lived in Detroit...," we say at the same time. We both laugh. Then he stops laughing and stares across the clearing.

"I bet in Detroit," Booker says, "we could go to the movies together, 'stead of separate."

"I bet you're right."

"Would you go to the movies with me if we lived in Detroit?" he asks, looking straight at me. "We could sit next to each other." His eyes get real shy. "Maybe hold each other's hands."

My stomach flip flops because it surely seems he likes me different than I like him. I don't know what to say about him liking me and I don't want to hurt his feelings. Besides, the words I want to say are all scrambled up in my head. Talking about being colored and being white is real hard.

I listen to the crows and watch a beetle burrow under the rotten log while I wait for the right words to come. But they don't.

"So." I say instead. "You don't have a ma?"

His face gets still and sadness washes into his dark eyes, so I wait quietly, looking at the picture of Johnny Weissmuller playing Tarzan hanging from a vine in midair with a little piece of something across his middle.

"She passed on three years ago." He takes a deep breath. "She was sick after..." His voice fades. "It's been hard for my sister 'cause my pa expected her to be the ma and she was barely thirteen then. Plus she works at Miss Lizzie's."

"I never met your sister."

"She ain't got time. Actually," he says looking around at the sinking sun, "I gotta get some nets and barrels set on the river."

He stands over me for a moment, his eyes kind of sad with some hurt in them. Then he turns and disappears into the bushes, and I can't even hear his foot steps.

CHAPTER 4

It's almost 4:00 and I'm done with my sweeping. Elwood's counting his money but as usual he won't let me go 'til the very minute of four o'clock. I lean the broom in the corner by the magazine rack and smile to myself as my eyes flit across the magazines and land on the single issue left of *Modern Screen* sitting there all by its lonesome. I liked showing Booker about Jackie Cooper.

I've been wondering about Booker. It's been six days since I seen him and every morning I walk along the tracks expecting him to slip out of the bramble. But no Booker. I haven't seen hide nor hair of him. I expect he's mad because I didn't say yes right away about going to the movies, but I couldn't find the words fast enough. Mostly I hope he isn't sick or that his pa didn't beat him bad. Truth be told, I miss him.

Elwood seems mighty happy stacking his coins in little piles. Beau lies at his feet, his head on Elwood's shoe. I slip into the kitchen so I can peek out that tiny back window. Just in case Booker's waiting for me which I hope he is. I miss talking to him. I'm on my tippy toes stretching to see if he's down by the tracks when Elwood's arm wraps around my waist. His other hand fumbles with my breasts. Stupid. Stupid. I should of known better than to let myself get cornered in the kitchen. His sloppy wet lips are on the back of my neck. His whiskers scratch my skin and something hard presses against my backside. Vomit churns in my throat. I make myself take two really slow breaths while I look for something to clobber him with. My fingers wrap around the cold iron handle of the frying pan. I swing it over my shoulder toward his head as hard as I can. I hit something and his grip on me loosens. I twist away from him and run like hell. Right out of the kitchen, across the dining room. I stop with my hand on the door knob. Beau jumps up and wags his tail at me.

I scream in my loudest voice. "You ever touch me again, I'm telling 'til someone listens. I don't care who knows."

Beau whimpers and Elwood leans against the kitchen door jamb, holding his head. A tiny line of blood runs down the side of his face. He laughs.

"Nobody ain't never gonna believe you, girl. I'm deacon of my church and president of the Chamber of Commerce. They'll laugh in your face."

"If you think paying Granny's rent makes you a good person, you're wrong." I holler as I pull open the front door, the bell jangling. I run half way down the dusty street, my breath making ragged hiccups before I stop. He's right. Nobody will believe me.

Except Miss Charlotte. She held me and rocked me for days when my ma got shot. If anybody believes me, she would. I got to tell her about Elwood before it eats me up.

Miss Charlotte's Dry Goods Store is three stores down from where I am standing in the middle of the street. She's been real good to me. The ladies from her quilting circle save denim overalls or dungarees that are too worn out to pass around again and give them to me. A horn honks and I jump backwards as Seth and his Model T rumble past. He waves and I cover my nose with my hand and shut my eyes for the dust. There's been talk of paving Main Street with that black tarry stuff, but the men jabbering at breakfast say there's no money for it.

After walking through Seth's dust cloud, I swing the door open to Miss Charlotte's store. The smell of new cloth surrounds me and my shoulders relax. I breathe real deep. Long bolts of fabric lean up against every wall real neat and straight. A rack of thread with the colors of the rainbow hangs next to a shelf of scissors, needles, and embroidery hoops each in its place. Miss Charlotte steps out from behind her cutting table laying down a big pair of shears when she sees me.

"Maisy." Her arms wrap around me and I let myself sink into her soft bosom. She must be about as old as my ma. Gently she pushes me out at arm's length and smiles like the moon rises in my face. If you look quick, you think she's a movie star with her curly red hair tied with a ribbon and her eyes as green as moss. But then you notice that her front teeth are bucked and there's always a smear of red lipstick across them.

"How's that quilt coming?" she asks letting go of me and straightening the sash to her swirly skirt.

"More'n half way. I sewed some of them fake pearls you gave me in the corners of some squares and it looks real nice."

"Here," she says reaching behind her cutting table. "I got a pair of overalls for you." They're folded nice and neat. I take them and hold them up against my chest.

"Oh!" She wiggles her fingers telling me to come behind the table. "Ta da!" she says with a grin that makes her teeth stick way out. She's holding up a shimmery square of red satin. She hands it toward me and nods her head. "For you."

"Me?" I never had anything so beautiful. It's a little more than a foot square and I'm already planning where I'll sew it into my quilt.

"Take it." It ripples in the light as she hands it to me.

My fingers graze across the silky surface. "Thank you, Miss Charlotte. It's so gorgeous." Ever since she held me on her lap that day my ma got shot, I half sort of thought maybe she'd be my ma one day and I'd have a nice home down Main Street. But, I guess running her store and taking care of her mother kept her too busy to be my ma.

She smiles at me then reaches under the top of her cutting table. "One more thing. I know you love these and I finished reading this cover to cover. My mother did too." She tucks a pulp fiction magazine between the folded overalls and my chest. I peek, hoping it's *Tarzan and the Ant Men* so I can read it to Booker, but it's one of her favorite detective magazines.

"Thank you, Miss Charlotte. I really appreciate you passing these on to me. You know how I love to read." I'm thinking now might be a good time to tell her about Elwood.

She beams at me like she just gave me one of them fancy Henry Ford cars.

"So Maisy." Her voice changes to being kind of nervous. "You're not seeing that boy Booker, are you?"

"No ma'am."

"It's just that there's talk you been seen being familiar with him lately."

"I.... we...."

"It's just that people would not look kindly on you. You know?"

"I do, ma'am." Sweat drips from my armpits along the edges of my ribs.

Her red fingernail picks at a bolt of green material with little yellow flowers while she waits for me to say something. I don't know what she expects.

"You see," I mutter, "I, um, I'm helping his sister. You know. Since their mother died it's been too much for her. Just helping out a little now and then. Not really seeing him, just helping out."

She raises up her hand for me to stop. "Oh yes. Promise."

"Yes. I promise it's his sister I'm helping."

Her green eyes are riveted to mine like she's detected the lie and is waiting for me to blab.

We stand looking at each other. A wagon creaks outside and the rhythm of horses clomp clomp along the street. Miss Charlotte's clock ticks mighty loud.

She blinks and a kind of hardness floats into those eyes. Then she takes a deep breath.

"You two being seen together? Don't forget, is especially dangerous for Booker." She pauses. "Remember those colored boys on trial in Scottsboro, Alabama last year?"

I nod.

"Assumptions get made," she says. "And then there's trouble."

One second.

Two seconds.

And all my insides crumble on top of each other.

* * *

The light from my kerosene lamp makes shadows flicker across my wall. I wet the thread with my tongue and push it through that tiny eye of the needle, pulling the ends even with each other. Miss Charlotte says you stitch with a single thread, but I worry it will fall apart so I wrap the doubled thread around my finger and roll it off into a knot. A mosquito buzzes in my ear. I flick it away and run my hand over the half finished quilt spread out on my mattress and study the uneven denim squares. Some have pearls, some have them belt loops or leg seams and I made two by cutting out a pocket, even keeping them little copper rivets. That makes me smile because I never saw a quilt with pockets. I trace my fingers along the flour sack strips holding all those squares together. I got a few different patterns so it's real pretty. Specially with those little pearls Miss Charlotte gave me.

My brain is real confused by her talk about Booker and me. I'm not thinking that I want to kiss Booker and all that or be his girlfriend. I've never liked a boy in that special way or had one like me. That I know of. There was Harlan McCoy in third grade who tried to kiss me but I punched him in the nose. I laugh out loud remembering.

But, it might be possible that Booker feels that way about me. I don't want to lose him as a friend because he's a good friend. Besides, right now he's my only friend. But I don't want him to mistake my feelings about him. Every time I try to explain, the words get scrambled and stuck inside my head. I'm not sure if that happens because he's a boy, or because he's colored. Or both. Whichever, I really like him for a friend.

Miss Charlotte's voice threads through my brain. My face gets hot thinking about how can it be dangerous to be friends?

Actually I *know* why....it's all them hateful feelings people have sitting in their hearts....but I sure don't understand. Me and him laugh and talk and dream. How's that so bad? He's the only person that knows about me and Detroit. I don't want to give that up. But I surely don't want no harm to come to him either. There's enough trouble going on with Elwood. Speaking of hateful.

Something scrambles outside my window. Probably a skunk or raccoon. I reach for the red satin and fold it along the top edge of my quilt. When I'm done patching I'm going to cut my red satin into strips and sew it along that very edge so it's against my face when I sleep. Just to see what it'll feel like I slide the satin along my cheek. It feels like when Ma would press her cheek against mine and say good night. A tiny shiver sparks in my chest. I slap that piece of satin onto the mattress. *Ma. I really miss you. I want to cry for missing you, but I got to keep my heart hard from all the meanness going around.*

Some of that meanness is why Booker and me can't be friends. I read in the newspaper what those colored boys did in Scottsboro. It was real bad. Them boys are saying they didn't do anything and got blamed because they're colored. That might be true what with so many people hating colored people, but how can you get arrested if you don't do anything?

But Booker would never hurt me.

Enough. I gather up my quilting stuff and blow out my lamp. Tomorrow's pay day and I'm not being late. That cheapskate Elwood's not taking any more of my money. And he's not touching me.

Not one more time.

CHAPTER 5

Twenty more minutes 'til I get my pay. All day I stayed at least ten feet away from Elwood. He looks at me now with one of them conniving glints in his eye while he ruffles Beau's ears, and then smiles down at him. He probably loves that dog more than anything on earth. Except his money. Just the same, I keep sweeping the dirt out the front door and off the step. The sky is real blue, but it's not boiling hot so the three mile walk home will be nice. I'm hoping Booker shows up so we can talk. I got lots to tell him. Closing the door behind me, the bell jingles as I go to put the broom away. Elwood must of gone in the kitchen since there's no sign of him here. The register is closed up tight as a tick otherwise I might help myself to my pay and just leave.

I lean the broom in the corner. I'm done, but I know for sure Elwood's not paying me until 4:00, so I run my finger over the slick covers of the magazines. I pull out the new *Life* because I like the pictures and then collapse onto a wooden chair. Beau wanders over and lays at my feet. I always open up a new magazine right to the middle. There's an ad for one of them electric washing machines that's got that wringer thing attached right to it. Boy would that make my life easier. I bet they got them in every house in Detroit. I turn the page and there's a picture of a bunch of people with signs. Looks like they're pushing and shoving. Squinting, I try to read one of the signs. *Give Us Back Our Jobs.* I read the words under the picture and it seems Henry Ford took these people's jobs from them. Shut his factory down, just like that. Wonder if that's the same Mr. Ford who makes that fancy roadster in

Detroit. I flip the page. On the radio Cab Calloway's singing *I Got the World On A String.* My foot taps without me even thinking about it.

"Maisy Wharton! You git in this kitchen this instant," Elwood yells at the top of his lungs like maybe he got his hand caught in the meat grinder. I can only hope that's true. Beau startles and lifts to his feet, heading toward the kitchen.

"I'm not coming in the kitchen when you're in there." I flip to the next page. There's that Lucky Strike advertisement. That girl grinning and selling them cigarettes and standing in them fancy high heels.

"I said." His voice turns nasty. "Git in here."

"I told you, I'm not coming in that kitchen."

"You broke my big mixing bowl. So git your butt in here."

"I did not." I know that's a trick, but I hate him accusing me of something I didn't do.

"You come pick up the pieces or I'm takin' it outta your pay."

My knee starts jittering up and down and I can hardly pull in a breath of air. I don't answer him.

"You son of a bitch," I whisper to myself.

Suddenly he lunges out the kitchen door and snatches at me with one hand, a rolling pin raised above his head in the other. Beau barks and Elwood pats his head as he stares at me. He's got that tiny white bandage on his forehead where I hit him with the frying pan, and his lips are grey they're pinched so tight together. I jump up and back away. The magazine slides to the floor.

His eyes are as steely as ball bearings. "You little whore, flaunting yourself all the time," he hisses in my face. The smell of bootleg hooch fills the air.

I keep backing up, then look down real quick at my flour sack dress and my shoes with the toes cut out. I wonder what part of me I flaunted. I glance at the clock. 3:59. I got to calm him down so I can get my pay.

"Listen Elwood. There's just been a misunderstanding."

"This ain't no misunderstanding. You led me on, just like a whore." His arm falls from the air and the rolling pin smashes against

27

the table top. The salt shaker bounces off and shatters on the floor, salt scatters across the stain of my mother's blood. Beau whines like he's worried about Elwood.

"Now see what you done," he yells. He lurches toward me. The heavy smell of alcohol almost knocks me over. His foot slips on that brand new issue of *Life* magazine and he loses his balance, barely catching himself with the back of a chair. He straightens and looks at me, his head kind of wobbling. The hair he combs over his bald head is hanging off of the side of his head.

He points at me with that finger with the blue nail that's about to fall off.

"Just for that, you ain't gettin' a cent this week. Nothin'. I ain't payin' you. Now git outta here." The red veins on his cheeks stand out like spider webs.

"You can't do that." Blood pounds in my jaw making my eyes practically pop out of my head. I want to grab that rolling pin and smash him in the head.

"I can and I will." He slams the rolling pin down on the counter. "Now git outta here 'fore I hurt you bad." He's coming toward me with that rolling pin swinging in the air. Beau rubs against his leg, whimpering.

"Give me my money," I scream.

He swings that rolling pin toward me. "Git out." The sweet-sour smell of hooch hangs between us.

I take a couple of deep breaths. I got to calm him down. Elwood, I..."

"And don't come back. Ya hear. You come in here I'll crack your head open like a ripe melon."

"You firing me?"

"You're fired. Fired. Got it? Fired." He wobbles, then grabs the corner of a table, his hand reaching for Beau, fingers gripping his fur.

If I were the crying type, I'd be crying now. Instead I spit a big gob of goober right on his clean floor. Then I slam out the door, that damn bell echoing in my ears.

CHAPTER 6

On the way home, I kick stones along the railroad tracks thinking about what to tell Granny. She surely won't believe me about Elwood and him touching me. Prob'ly not even care. But she will care about the money. Maybe I can get in the house without her seeing me, and I can take four quarters from under my mattress and give them to her. Damn. I pick up a rock from the tracks and wing it at a tree trunk. I'm not giving Granny *my* money. That's practically two week's pay for me. But, I still got to tell her I got fired.

I stop and listen for Booker, hoping he's rustling in the bushes. But there's only blue birds singing to each other, the breeze whispering to the leaves and the low whistle of a train coming this way. I lean down and lay my hand on the steel rails warm from the sun and, sure enough, the vibrations go right up my arm. I walk a little further, and when I hear the whistle real strong, I jump off the tracks and slip-slide down into the gully, pushing myself into the bushes. Those flying rocks can poke your eye out when that train rumbles by.

I trudge up the dirt road to our cabin and there she is, sitting on that wooden chair she drags outside of an evening to have her 'tea' that smells like Elwood's breath. Maybe by now she's had enough and she won't care about nothing. Except, knowing Granny, she could be stone cold dead and she'd still care about my money.

I stand in the shadows and watch her slumped in her chair. Our three scrawny chickens scratch around her feet. Maybe they'll peck her to death. I take in a long breath because I know I'm a cooked goose. Nothing left to do but tell her.

When I come up beside her, she sticks her hand out for that dollar bill. She don't even look at me or say howdy. Or smile like she used to. When nothing touches her palm, she squints and moves her head so she can see my face.

"Granny Wharton," I say. "There's a little prob…"

"Jus' give me the dollar and don't bother me with your yappin'" She takes a sip of her tea, the heaviness of moonshine floating on the breeze.

"I don't got a dollar."

She lifts her cup to her lips and swallows every last drop then turns her watery eyes on me. "You don't got a dollar? Is that what you said?"

I nod, afraid to open my mouth. I take a step backward.

"I must of misheard you," she says. "'Cause you always got a dollar."

I stand real still, my fingers twitch against my legs, sweat running down my ribs.

"Did you lose it?"

"No ma'am." I shuffle another step backwards.

"Maybe somebody stole it?"

"No ma'am." I inch away a tiny bit more.

She places her cup on the hard packed earth. One of the chickens pokes its head inside it then looks at me with its beady eye like I tricked it. Granny stands up, leaning on the broom for leverage. Then she steps toward me until we're looking eye to eye.

"You spent it." A fact, not a question.

I step back fast knowing there's trouble coming but she grabs the front of my dress in her fist and throws me onto the ground. One of the chickens squawk as my foot kicks it. I try to stand up, but her shoe is in the middle of my back and my face is in the chicken-scratched dirt.

"You spent it." she screams. "That's my money."

I struggle to get out from under her foot and onto my knees. The pressure on my back stops. As I push myself to my feet, the broom handle smacks me on the side of my head. I bite the inside of my cheek. The coppery taste of blood seeps over my tongue.

"Git up," she screeches. "What'd you do with my money?" This time the handle hits my left eye. I scream as my hand flies up to my face. There's blood on my fingers and I can't see out of my eye. She must have broke the whole side of my head.

"Granny. Listen. Please." I take tiny steps backward hoping she won't notice.

She stops, wobbling as she tries to focus on my face. "What? You jus' kidding your granny?"

"Elwood fired me."

"He fired you?" The impossibility of that rings in her voice. Her face scrunches up and her eyes squeeze into tiny slits. Knowing she's going to whack me again, I step backward.

"Wait. I can explain." The broom handle hangs in mid-air.

"You better." It drops to her side. "He closin' or something? Hard times, these are. This *de*-pression and all."

"He," I want to tell her what he done to me. I want her to know. "When he…"

"When he what?" the handle raises shoulder high. I step backwards.

"Touched me…" Her eyes narrow and a peculiar look passes over her face. For a moment I think she knows what Elwood done and that she'll drop the broom and hug me close up to her. Instead, the whacks come fast, one after the other.

"Don't you lie." She hits me again and again, grasping the neck of my dress so's I can hardly breathe. I can't figure out where to turn. "Liar. Liar. Liar," she yells frantically with each hit. She yanks me in every direction mumbling "You let him, you whore. You dirty little whore."

31

Finally I push my hands against her chest and hear cloth ripping. I look down and my dress is torn down to my waist. She lets go for a second.

"You whore," she screeches, her eyes bulging.

I run like crazy, my feet slapping the hard-packed dirt.

"I'm not ever coming back," I spit, looking at her over my shoulder. The broom lies on the dirt and she rocks her face from side to side in both her hands.

* * *

"That's it. That's it." I yell at the fallen log and the big gray rock. I press a wad of moss tighter against my eye because it's still bleeding. "I'm not going back to Granny's. Ever. Not ever." My voice is getting hoarser and hoarser with all the yelling. I grab up some stones and throw them against tree trunks as hard as I can. They hit with a satisfying thunk. I smash a dry stick against the boulder, shattering it to pieces. I know I got to stay furious otherwise all that sadness sitting in my chest will burst out of me. Fear wobbles in my throat. I throw another rock at a tree. I hate it at Granny's, but it is my home. I have no place to go.

"Maisy?" A voice whispers behind me.

"Booker?" I whirl around and he's standing at the edge of my chickabiddy. "Where the hell you been?"

We stand looking at each other for forty days. He's biting his lip and then he smiles. His grin is kind of lopsided but I sure am happy to see it. Remembering my ripped dress, I cross my arms over my ratty brassiere and tug the torn piece of my dress up, holding everything together with one hand. I nod toward the fallen log and sit myself down tucking the loose material from my dress into my brassiere. He still stands near the briars, his hands jammed in his pockets.

"You look terrible," he says. "Your granny?"

32

"Yep."

"Heard you yelling," he says. "I couldn't not help you."

"Come sit beside me." I pat the log.

He slides to the ground, keeping some distance between us, and leans on the log where he rests his head against the moss for a second. "So what are you going to do?"

"I don't know. I'm never going back there. Never."

His lips purse and his head jiggles.

"I have to leave. I got no place to live now."

"Leave?" Alarm rings in the evening air. "Leave here?"

"Yep. I'm heading for Detroit. Buying myself a ticket tomorrow," I say wondering if I can buy a ticket for $11.10.

His hand reaches toward me, then flies back into his lap.

"Cain't do it from here. Gots to get to Cincinnati first."

My body lunges off the log, my fists clenched. "How you know that?"

"Asked my pa. Said only freight trains run along here."

I hate him for a second, then I know it's not his fault. I should have been asking and finding things out instead of just believing what my ma said.

"Where you been?" I ask.

"People are jabbering about us, my pa says." He takes his fishing knife out of his rope belt and cleans under his fingernails. The crows squawk and caw their evening complaints at each other.

"There's nothing to talk about and it's none of their business. You know it's Elwood causing trouble." The sharpness of my voice says more than my words.

"So how come your granny beat you so much?" He sits forward and peers at my eye that's swollen shut. "Nasty."

"Elwood fired me."

"He's a damn fool. Ain't nobody gonna work harder than you." He stands slipping his knife into its sheath on his belt and gathers a handful of cool moss. He holds it up to my eye, real gentle like.

"So what's your pa say the jabbering's about?"

33

"Bad things happening." He dabs the moss on my cheek, then holds it against my eye again. "Cain't see?"

"Can't see nothing. Your pa mind if we're friends?" I hold the moss myself and Booker leans against a honey locust tree, peeling a loose piece of bark off then tears the strip into two long pieces. He gives one to me.

"Said if I talked to you again, he'd beat me 'til I couldn't breathe."

I gasp, then realize I'm only half surprised.

"So that's where you been?"

"Yep. Watching you from the bushes when I could." His dark eyes land on my face and it's as if his arms fall around me. "Just being sure you're safe."

My heart does double beats, then slows.

"Your pa hate me that much, huh? To beat you?"

His bony shoulders lift and fall. "Don't know." His voice lowers so I can barely hear him. "Mostly he don't want me hanging at the end of a rope."

"Oh Booker…." I wail. I am not going to cry and make a fuss. I hate crying. I haven't even cried for my mother, but somehow hearing those words makes the tears press hard against the back of my eyes. But I will not cry.

"That's just not fair," I holler. "We didn't do anything bad."

He purses his lips.

"It ain't us," he says. "It's what everybody else thinks."

My breath comes in stutters. "Then why are you here?"

"Seems I can't stay away." His arm reaches toward me, pauses, then flops by his side.

I smile, but my knees do a nervous jittery dance.

* * *

Evening settles and a full moon rises over the edge of the hills. A breeze chills my bare arms and raises goose bumps.

"You cain't stay here," Booker says for the millionth time. "You'd best be goin' home and making up with your granny."

"I said it and said it and said it. I am not going back. I'd rather die."

"Well you might. You sure are strong for a girl. But you still a girl. You cain't be out here by yourself. There's mans in the woods. They ain't got no place else to go these days."

He stands and looks down at me, hands on his hips.

"And just what are you going to eat?" He waits. "You can't live on dandelion leaves and fiddlehead ferns."

I hadn't thought about food, but I don't tell him that.

"If I can't stay here, I'm going to start walking on the railroad tracks and catch me a train somehow. There's got to be a train that'll get me to Detroit. My ma said so."

He stares at me, doubt spreading across his face.

"And," I practically holler. "I'll eat fiddleheads, berries and whatever I can find." Mr. Smarty Pants.

He gets real quiet. And stays quiet. I wait, rubbing my hands up and down my arms. The tree frogs and crickets start up the night music.

"I didn't want to tell you about this but seeing as how you're so stubborn." Booker stops.

I wait.

"There's a broken down box car that got left somehow. It's way far into the colored woods down past where the river bends. It ain't smashed up or nothing. Just its wheels are gone and a few boards missing."

"I could live there. That's what you're thinking?"

"Maybe just while you make up with your granny. Least it's kinda hidden and you'd be dry if it rains."

I jump up and hug him quick like. For a second, our bodies are warm pressed together.

I pull away real fast.

35

"Booker, you're a genius."

His arm reluctantly slips off my shoulder and his foot scuffs the ground.

"One thing." He bites his lip. "Like I said, it's in the colored part of the woods. Maybe you don't..."

"Course I would. Can you take me there now?"

"We got to be careful not to be seen. Not likely a body's around but sometimes a man might hunt coons or rabbits of a night." He wiggles his bare toes into the dirt, looking at me with his face all scrunched up. "It's more'n twice the way to town, way out in them woods. Actually, I don't know if it's a good idea."

My excitement sinks. Seems like I'll be sleeping with the crawly bugs on the ground of my chickabiddy.

"Besides I didn't get my nets out yet tonight."

I sink onto one of the boulders, my head flopping into my hands. It's quiet between us. I slap a mosquito on my arm.

He coughs, clearing his throat. Words seem to be struggling to get out of his mouth.

"Here's what we'll do," he says. "I'll set my nets and go home while you sneak into your granny's—"

"I told you—" My head flies up.

"Shut your mouth, you pig-headed girl. Just listen for a minute." There's a long silence except for the peepers and the hoot of an owl. "You sneak in and get whatever you can from your granny's and bring it here. When the moon gets straight up in the sky, I'll come back and get you."

I reach to give him a great big hug, but I let my arms flop to my sides because I don't want to give him the wrong idea.

"Booker. You're a good friend to help me get on my way to Detroit. I'll surely miss you."

CHAPTER 7

I peek through the cracked front window of Granny's shack. The lit kerosene lamp is on the table and the flickering light almost makes our shack look like a home. I don't see Granny nowhere, though. Her 'tea' chair is back in the kitchen. Seems she got herself into the house. That's usually my job, letting her lean on me while she wobbles and stumbles with me dragging that dang chair behind. I creep up to the door and push it open a crack.

She's snoring like a bunch of wild animals fighting with each other, so I slip in through the door and close it behind me. I don't need no skunks following me into the house. I tiptoe to the kitchen to get an empty flour sack. Then I grab the lamp and skulk to my room, stepping over the planks of the floor that creak. I close my door tight, hoping she doesn't hear me.

First thing I do is spread my half-made quilt on my mattress and bundle my scissors, needles, threads, the old pair of denims and my piece of red satin into it and stuff it all in the bottom of the flour sack. I change into my other dress but fold my two pairs of underwear, two pair socks and my long sleeved work shirt for when it's chilly and roll them in my torn dress. Slipping the picture of my father into my *Modern Screen* magazine, I gather my other magazines and drop them in. I grab my comb and the gold compact with the mirror. That's all I got in this world from my ma. I open the compact and look at my eye. Swelled shut. Can't even see a tiny bit of my hazel eye. I pat a little powder on my face. Just to be close to my ma. I wonder for a minute if she'll come back here looking for me but won't find me. I snap it shut and pack it with my comb. I hope she'll know to look for me in Detroit. My room is bare, just the wooden crate for my table and my rag rug left. Rolling my rug up tight, I stuff in into my sack. Finally lifting my mattress and folding it over itself my hand goes to the exact spot where I keep my money in an old sock. I really don't want to carry it in the flour sack. What if I drop it? Or somebody snatches it?

My eyes scour my room. A pile of scraps from my quilt are in the corner. Quickly I spread them out. Here's a long piece of flour sack. I fold it over and tie the ends around my sock and slip the loop around my neck. Now I got me a purse. Probably smart to hide it under my dress. I look around my room one more time to make sure I got what I want. And to say good-bye. A little sadness flutters in my chest seeing as how this has been my home for most of my life, even though it don't feel much like a home now. I've lived here since I was eight, but my heart's pounding to get out of here. I surely do wish it was me and Ma leaving this place together. Not me, all by myself, going out into the world.

Taking the lamp in one hand and my sack in the other, I open my door. Granny's still snoring like a pig with a bad cold, so I head for the kitchen. A jolt of fear hits me. I can't steal Granny's food. She'll beat me 'til I'm dead. Then I swallow my giggle because how's she going to catch me now? I'll be gone. Gone. Yessir. No more Granny whacking me. So I take what I can. A chunk of cheese, half a loaf of bread, two cans of hash, a half of a salted fish and a handful of wooden matches. I leave the small bowl of blueberries she picked, but I take the last empty flour sack, just in case. Leaving the kerosene lamp on the table, I turn it off so it don't burn the house down. At first it's real dark, but my eyes adjust and the moon's rising anyways.

Being careful not to thunk my sack against anything, I get out the door and almost stumble over the wooden buckets. I pull the door closed real quiet and grab one of the buckets thinking it might come in handy. A quick grin at the moon and I head for my chickabiddy.

Good-by, Granny. You're not beating on me anymore.

* * *

I know Granny's yard and the woods by heart, but everything looks different at night. The moon casts some good light, but there are still plenty of shadows. The tree trunks are a shiny gray, but I can't tell what's in the dark places as I make my way to my chickabiddy. My sack snags on the briars giving me a little yank each time. I go slow, careful not to tear a hole in it. Something rustles in the bushes ahead of me.

"Booker? That you?" No answer and total quiet. I stand real still. The swishing starts again and suddenly I know what being so scared you can pee your pants means. What if it's one of them hoboes. The shuffles come closer. I don't know whether to run, scream or wait but then it don't matter because a raccoon the size of a bear with three babies following her struts across the path in front of me. The mother hisses at me, those sharp white teeth reflecting in the moonlight. I'm so relieved. Her babies scamper into the bushes on the other side of the path and mama gives me a low growl before she follows them.

When I can't hear no more scrambling, I take a careful step on my rubber legs. I don't fall down. I take another. Then another. Soon I know I'm almost there, so I keep on going. Please let Booker be waiting. I'm at the edge of the clearing now and no Booker. As I step into the place I know as well as the palm of my hand, a whoosh surrounds my head followed by a triumphant screech. I whirl around thinking I'm being attacked and spot a big owl, wings spread with something in its beak swooping out of the clearing. My heart pounds down to my toes. For the first time, I wonder if I can do this.

Still no Booker. I sit on the ground between my sack and bucket hoping I don't get bit by a creepy, crawly nasty centipede. I could light a match. No I better save them. Something else squawks and two bats take turns flitting through the moon light. I pull my sack up real close and sit real still. A soft movement comes closer. Please, please let it be Booker. My muscles turn to mush as his long, lean silhouette steps into the clearing, moon light reflecting off the planes of his face.

* * *

"We're almost there," Booker whispers.

"It's about time. We must of walked twenty miles," I snap, my feet aching from stumbling over rocks and branches in the pitch darkness. Brambles snag at my sack, and it'll be a miracle if it's not torn to shreds. My leg must be black and blue what with that bucket bouncing against it for the last forty hours. Seems like the whole world is woods. I complain about every four minutes, but Booker doesn't even answer me.

Finally, he stops and puts his finger up to his mouth to hush me. He leans over close to my ear and whispers.

"The box car is just through the thickets, but I don't know if a'body's sleeping in it or not."

"What the?" I let the bucket thump to the ground.

"Sh-h. This train track's been pulled up. But you never know where mans are in these woods."

My chin falls to my chest and I think *what the hell*. That seems like something that would've been good to know before we stumbled through the dark to get here.

"Mostly mans catch the trains outside the town," Booker whispers.

"How we gone find out?" I whisper back trying not to sound crabby.

"You stay here and I'll creep up and listen for snoring. Them hoboes always snore."

"Hoboes? This boxcar is supposed to be for me."

"Sh-h. I'll be right back."

I grab his shirt as he turns and pull him back close to me. "What are we going to do if them hoboes are in the boxcar?" I ask still whispering, even though I want to shout and run out of here.

"You think on that while I go look."

Now I wish I hadn't stole Granny's food in case I have to go back there. She'll beat me 'til my bones break. Then I remind myself, no matter what, I'm not going to Granny's ever again. I'm never living with that broom handle. Ever. I'm going where I can have a good life and make a real home for myself.

I can't hardly hear Booker as he walks through the brush. Before I know it, he's back, a big smile on his face.

"Ain't no one there. It's yours."

I don't know whether to shout for joy or be scared to death, but big jumping jitters run through my body.

Booker glides, but I stumble, through the undergrowth. Up close the box car looks huge. It's kind of tilted and vines are growing all over it. The sliding door is about halfway open and there's writing on the side that I can't read in the dark.

"So let me boost you up there," Booker says. "Then I'll come see you in the morning after I get my fishing done."

"What? Wait. You're not staying? I'm going to be here by myself? What if there's critters in there?" My voice gets louder and louder. My stomach's in my throat and I am gasping air. I'm having a heart attack. "What if someone climbs in the boxcar while I'm sleeping?"

A long stream of air escapes from Booker. It's real quiet except for all the screeching and buzzing and rustling.

"Maisy," he says exasperation rising in his voice. "What did you think?"

"I don't know. But it sure wasn't this."

"Well, this is what you got." His voice slices through the night air. "Or going back to your granny. That's the choice you got."

I walk closer and try to peek inside the open door but it's pitch dark in there.

"Just one night?" I beg.

"I'd stay, but you know I cain't."

And I do.

"You got a match in all that stuff?" His voice is jagged. I can tell he thinks I'm an idiot. After considerable digging, I find my matches and hand him one. He strikes it against the wooden door and we both stand on our tiptoes and peer into the boxcar. There's some bottles, some tar paper and an old shoe, but not much else. No spiders or wild animals that we can see. The match burns down and Booker spits on it then turns to me.

"So?"

"Give me a boost," I say swinging my sack and bucket into the boxcar ahead of me. He makes a step with his hands laced together. I put my foot in it, hold his shoulder and he lifts me up. I flop around on the floor like a fish trying to throw a hook, but finally get my feet inside.

"I'll come when I can," he says. A long pause. "You be brave."

I pull my sack up close to me and watch Booker slowly melt into the underbrush, the moonlight reflecting off his shirt. And then he's gone.

I am alone. Squeezing my sack against my chest, I pretend it's my mother. Holding me. Singing *Chickabiddy* as her soft hand brushes my hair off my forehead.

But really. It's just me. By myself in the dark.

CHAPTER 8

My eyes fly open. Why am I'm sitting up in my bed? I blink several times and remember this is not my bed. I am in a broken-down box car back in some strange hills and far into woods I've never seen, with my arms grasping a sack with all my belongings in the world. Even though I didn't want to fall asleep, I must have. It's still darkish out, the sun is below the horizon and the light is shimmery. Sounds like water rushing not too far off so I must still be near the river. Booker said the boxcar was past the bend. That's a long, long way from Granny's. Where she lives the river is slow and lazy. Hearing that rushing water I wonder if this is near the mill that closed down last year.

Putting my sack beside me, I stretch and pull myself to my feet and slowly walk around the box car. There's a hole in the floor that if I stumbled into I could fall right through. Just two other small holes in the sides where the boards cracked loose. Spider webs cling to my face. I swipe at them but they're hanging every which way. My feet scuff at the yellowed newspapers lying on the floor and I push one of the bottles with the toe of my cut-out shoe. The floor tips just a little and I walk from one end to the other, hardly noticing the tip at all. Just where I stop is a big charred spot like somebody tried to build a fire. A tin can with dried chunks of something ugly lies on its side, the jagged edge of the top bent backwards and its label peeling off. I lean down and touch the blackened spot to see if it's still warm. It's not, but the palm of my hand is dusty black. In the corner is something that looks like a rat's or possum's nest and rodent droppings cover the floor. I get the creepy crawlies thinking I slept all night with a nest of rats. Nothing seems to be moving so I go over and nudge the whole nest with my foot, jumping backwards real fast. Nothing happens. I pick up an old leather shoe that's lying on its side and toss it at the nest just to be sure. Nothing.

I push hard against the back doors, but they are stuck shut. A splintery board with knot holes that looks like it was ripped off an old barn leans up against the doors. I wander over to the open space between the front doors and look out at the morning. Just a bunch of bushes and trees except for a tiny clearing with some scorched earth where someone made a fire off to the side of the boxcar. I give the door a good push but it's stuck too and won't budge a tiny inch. It's just wide enough for me to slip through.

Booker won't be here until the sun is halfway up the sky. So, I can stand around wondering what to do or I can do something. First I got to clean this place up. But I got no broom. I sit down, hanging my legs over the edge, when I spy the bushes. I can use branches with leaves if I can only figure out how to get back in the box car once I jump out. It's pretty high and I'm thinking of giving up when I notice my bucket. I can turn it upside down and use it as a step.

I break off a branch of leaves to sweep out all the cobwebs and droppings, then I push the nest with my foot to the door and give it a kick into the bushes. Sweat drips off my nose from all the cleaning and fixing I been doing. The morning sun slashes across the floor of the boxcar. I'm thinking how surprised Booker will be when he sees all the spider webs and mouse droppings gone and that nest hanging in the bushes instead of in the boxcar. Eight empty bottles are lined up against one wall along with that nasty can and I folded up the old newspapers in case I need them. The most proud I am of myself is that I put the tar paper over the hole in the floor and I unfolded my rag rug and laid it right on top. Nobody can step on it without falling through, but them critters won't be sneaking in. I brought me in four rocks and put the board on top of them and made myself a little table. My ma's compact, my comb, the matches wrapped in my red satin square and my food are sitting on it. I lay the tiny picture of my pa against the compact.

Wish I had one of my ma, too. I touch her compact and longing tightens in my chest.

I set out my pointy scissors in case I need some protection. And, my stack of magazines. I want to fan them out like I saw once in a photograph in *Good Housekeeping*, but there's not room enough. I don't know where I'll sleep, but I got until tonight to figure that out.

I snap a piece of salted fish off, rip off a bite of bread and sit with my legs dangling out the door of my new home. I listen to the quiet. No morning voices floating through the air from our neighbors, no Granny banging in the kitchen swearing at something that only she knows and no chickens squawking at each other. Just the leaves rustling and a bird singing now and then.

I do wish Booker would get here.

* * *

The crashing in the woods sounds like a herd of horses. Probably Booker doesn't want to scare me. The sun's high and I'm hot and dying from being thirsty. Hope he brought some water. He bursts through the bushes.

"You been sitting there since I left?" He laughs. Then he holds up one arm with a bucket full of water sloshing over the edge. "Look what I brought you."

"I am parched." I jump from my perch and run toward him. He puts the bucket down.

"Help yourself." Then he grins at me. "You might be wantin' to wash that face of yours, too."

I flop to my knees drinking water out of my cupped hands and splash the cool water on my face, then drink some more letting the coldness run down my throat. I raise my eyes and there's a second pair of brown toes connected to brown feet. I look up at the hem of a flour sack dress and I keep looking up until I see the sun shining like a halo behind her head.

"This here is my sister, Promise," Booker says. "And this," he points to me, "is Maisy. The one I tole you about."

While he's talking, I hear Miss Charlotte's voice in my head. *Oh yes. Promise.* Promise. Miss Charlotte meant Promise was Booker's sister. Did she know I was lying about helping her?

It don't matter now.

"How'd you get a black eye?" I notice her lips as she speaks to me. Her hand is on her waist, hip cocked to one side. Something strange wiggles in my stomach. No words come out of my mouth. Then the oddest feeling comes over me like I've known her for a long time. I shake my head. Probably being so thirsty all morning. My heart pounds against my ribs.

"Her granny beat on her bad," Booker says.

I stand up and jiggle my shoulders. What's the matter with me? I'm not hardly ever at a loss for words.

Promise holds out her hand. "I brung you a chunk of bread I baked yesterday."

"Thanks," I squeak, squeezing the spongy softness with my finger tips as I take it from her hand. A strange feeling wavers through my chest. "That's kind of you." My voice echoes in my ears. What's the matter with me?

"Ain't nothing." She waves her hand toward the box car. "Sleep all right?"

"Yep." I turn to Booker who's grinning at me and I can tell he's glad to see me. "Come see the inside. I fixed it up."

Just as I thought, Booker is truly impressed, but I'm not sure what Promise thinks.

As we all clamor down out of the boxcar, Promise taps her foot on the bucket I'm using as a step.

"How are you going to get that up inside when you go to bed or when it's full of water?" She looks at Booker like *stupid girl*.

"I got an old ripped dress." Granny's raging face flashes through my head. "I was going make a braided rope to pull it up." I say flicking my eyes at her.

"See," says Booker. "Smart, too." Promise squints ever so slightly and a chilly look crosses her face. He doesn't notice as he scuffs at the dirt in the small clearing.

"Your fire pit can go right here. Somebody already tried a fire here." He bends over, collecting apple size rocks and tossing them into the clearing until he has a sizable pile. He straightens his back.

"Just clear this little area and…"

"I know how to make a fire pit," I say too sharply.

"Smarty pants," Booker smirks at me. He knows I get testy when somebody tells me what I should do. "Pa's making deliveries and I got to go."

"Old Elwood's?" I grimace.

"We done him this morning." His eyes drop away from me looking right to the ground.

"What?" I say.

He don't say anything. His big toe twitches and he bites the insides of both cheeks.

"Something's up. What?" My voice is even sharper.

His eyes slowly meet mine.

"I didn't aim to tell you," he pauses. "Your granny told Elwood you ran away and left the lamp burning meaning to catch her on fire."

"Liar. She's a son of a bitch liar." Little drops of spit fly into the air.

Promise bites her bottom lip and narrows her eyes at me.

"I know she is," Booker says. He squeezes my arm, then his hand flies off me like it's on fire.

"What else she say?" I demand.

Booker clicks his tongue in the back of his mouth.

I wait. Promise quietly studies both of us.

"She told Elwood 'good riddance to rotten garbage'." His voice almost disappears.

I'm relieved and furious at the same time. After all I done for her. But least she won't come looking for me. I guess I am on my own. Really on my own. No home. No family. Nothing.

Booker finally speaks. "I'll come back later. Promise can stay for a bit."

"Maybe she'll explain to me where I am in these woods," I say.

"You walked here. How come you don't know?" She says, staring at me.

"This is your neck of the woods, not mine." My eyes shift between the two of them.

Booker laughs. "Well these colored woods is famous for getting white people lost. Them trees will grab you good." He reaches to touch me, but drops his hand by his side.

Promise's eyebrow hitches up and Booker grins, tugging on one of her braids. Something special passes between them. I wonder what Booker has said about me.

He waves as he heads into the woods, whistling to himself. Crows caw, following him.

Promise barely breathes for the longest time.

"He's sweet on you," she mutters, her voice sharp as a knife.

"I can't help it," I say.

"Um. Um. Big trouble."

CHAPTER 9

"T his was a good idea," I say watching Promise's long fingers, brown on top and deep pink on the undersides, work their way down the low branches of the trees, pulling leaves off and stuffing them into my flour sacks. "I 'preciate your help."

"You can't sleep on that ole wooden floor. Least this will be some kind of a mattress. Crumpling up them old newspapers was smart too." About an hour ago she gave me her first smile and now I get another one. My chest wobbles. I don't know why.

I tie off the stitching I did across the top of the first sack, and she hands me the other one. There's something about her eyes. They pull you in, but then you bump into a whole bunch of sadness. Not the kind of sadness that you want to run from because it might eat you up. It's just there. Waiting.

"Where you learn to sew?" she asks.

"My granny showed me. She used to show me lots of things like cooking dandelion leaves and gathering mushrooms until the hooch took her over." I pull the thread through the material of the flour sack, whipping the thread along the edges.

"That quilt you made is real pretty. Where'd you get all them denims?"

"Miss Charlotte saves them for me."

A look I don't understand whispers across her face. "Miss Charlotte is real special."

"How do you know her?" I ask. Jealousy creeps into my chest. Her bony shoulders shrug. "Just do."

We stand looking at each other with the rustle of the leaves above our heads and the faint rush of water through the woods.

"Come on," she grabs one of the stuffed sacks, walks to the door of the boxcar and tosses it in. I follow and throw the other one into the dimness.

"That'll be good tonight," I say.

"Two more things. Then I gotta go before Pa misses me." She slaps a horsefly off her arm. "First, you gotta have something for privacy acrost this opening." She points to the boxcar doors standing about two feet apart.

"You're right. But I don't have extra velvet curtains lying around."

She almost grins.

"You said something about a ripped dress?"

"Perfect," I say stepping on the upside-down bucket and hoisting myself into my new home. I turn to give Promise a hand, but she's already pulling herself up onto the boxcar floor.

"Here." I whip my ruined dress from the floor where I dumped it emptying out my flour sacks. "You hold it up and I'll cut the skirt off with my scissors."

She holds the material taut while I cut the skirt free with my little sewing scissors. Then we look at the opening, figuring out how to hang it up. It fits right across the opening with a few inches on either side.

"There's a hook here," I say pointing to the wall near the opening.

"I found a nail or something sticking out over here," Promise says.

When we're done, it *is* perfect. The material covers the bottom of the opening and the top is open to let light in. And it's loose enough that I can crawl right under it to get out.

"Maybe the mayor's wife will let us decorate her big ole house on that hill," Promise stands with her hands on her hips.

"I think we're too fancy for her tastes," I snort.

"One more thing and I gotta hurry or my pa will wale on me."

"I don't want you getting hit," I say. Panic wells in my chest.

"But you gotta know where to get more water because we won't be back for a while."

"You mean that water you can hear?"

"Come on. Grab your bucket."

Promise makes a pathway through what looks like a jungle of briars and thickets. She holds each stickery branch while I squeeze past trying not to let it prick my bare arms or legs.

"You know to only make a tiny fire? 'Specially at night?" she hollers over her shoulder as she picks at the next batch of briars.

"How am I going to stay warm or cook on an itsy fire?"

"Mans be hunting for squirrels and coons or rabbits in these woods sometimes. They come way out from town for hunting. You want them to see you?" Her words are a slap. How could I be so stupid?

"I'll remember that." I duck into the pathway she has made.

"And don't use green wood."

"I'm not an idiot," I spit back, harsher than I meant to be.

The skin on my bare arm snags on a pricker thorn as we burst into the sunlight. We stand at the edge of fast moving water. It's hard to believe it's the same river as by Granny's. I never seen this old Kentucky River move faster than molasses on a cold day. I untangle the bucket from the thicket and suck at the blood on my arm. Promise points up river where water is gushing out of a skinny passageway beside the mill. A big wheel turns and turns, water dripping off each slat as it slides by.

"That's the mill they closed last year because of the depression. My pa worked there but he was one of the first that got fired. Then the whole place just up and closed down."

"Anybody live there?" I ask thinking it would be more comfortable than a boxcar.

"Just them hoboes. You do have to watch out for them. Most are just fine, but some…"

I wait for her to finish but she taps my shoulder, wiggles her hand to follow her through some bushes then she trips from rock to rock down the slope that leads to a patch of pebbly land hidden in a nook of the river bank. I lose hold of my bucket as I slip down the path and it rolls ahead of me and lands at the water's edge. Leaning down to get my bucket, I realize I can't see the mill. Just trees and river.

"This is my special place where I come sometimes. Just to get some peace and privacy." She looks at the ground, a tiny grin twitching at her cheeks.

"What?"

"What?" she says back.

"Why are you grinning? What's the secret?"

"I'll show you." She reaches for my hand, then let's her arm drop by her side. "Come on."

"How come you stopped from touching me?" I ask.

She looks at me like I'm the stupidest person alive.

"Because I'm white?" I say.

"No. Because I'm colored." Her hand is perched on her hip. She looks away from me and mutters, "That's the problem with Booker." Without looking back at me, she runs for the river, throwing herself into the water with a splash. She dips her whole head under the surface then pops up and laughs.

"Come on in," she says standing up, her flour sack dress wet against her chest.

That funny feeling in my stomach happens again as I run toward her, and before I even realize it, I'm soaking wet, dress and all. She splashes water at me, her laughter like a bird song.

I'm thinking we might end up being friends after all.

CHAPTER 10

P romise left.

My bucket is full of water but the emptiness of the woods descends leaving me feeling like the last human on earth sitting here on this rock. The edges of the rock poke my backside. It's not that I don't like being alone. God knows I spent plenty of hours in my chickabiddy hiding from Granny's wretched temper. But I always knew how to get back home. The underbrush whispers and leaves jitter up and down. I peer into the shadows as a squirrel pauses, then jumps out of sight.

Now this boxcar is where I live and, for the life of me, I can't get anywhere except to the river by myself. It's not that I don't appreciate Booker finding a place for me. But I don't want to be stuck here anymore than with old Granny because I know if I can get to Detroit, I'll find me a real home. And a job. A place I belong.

I wonder about Booker for a minute remembering the shine in his eyes when he looks at me, but I don't know what to think. I want to be his friend, but I'm not so sure that's all that's true for him. Sometimes the way he looks at me is like he's asking me if I'll like him in that special way. I do like him better than any friend I ever had, but not like I want to kiss him. I just don't feel that way about him. Besides, it would cause a handful of trouble.

What I truly have to think about is getting myself to Detroit. That's where my life is going to be.

I stand and stretch. A blue jay scolds me for disturbing him.

"You might be happy eating grubs in the woods," I say to him. "But I want a job at Mr. Ford's car factory and decent clothes, and a house the wind don't blow through with an electric refrigerator full of food." The jay flies away, not interested in me. But I'm thinking that maybe someday I'll have a Model A car to drive on them asphalted streets instead of walking on these dusty, rutted dirt roads. I want to go to a real moving picture show and not just read about them in my magazines. Mostly I want to have a life where I'm not always running and ducking from getting beat on or getting touched like I'm somebody's whore.

I squeeze my little money sack hanging around my neck. The main reason I'm stuck is not really these woods. It's the $11.10. I jingle the heavy coins. No question but I got to find me another job. But how can I find my way out of the woods, the colored part of the woods no less? I got to get Booker to show me how to get to town from here, seeing as how I have no idea where I am. Maybe he'll take me tomorrow.

Until then, I'll work on my quilt as the light fades and I'm stuck again in the pitch dark.

Standing in front of the boxcar, I realize that my bucket is full of water and I can't use it as a step to climb in the boxcar door. Well I'm sure not sleeping out here on the ground and I'm not tossing the water out and hauling another bucket of water for twenty minutes from the river first thing in the morning. I sit down again on my pointy rock and let my eyes wander around the clearing. I'm starting to think running away wasn't a good idea when I notice a couple of pretty good size branches lying on the ground.

I drag those branches over to the boxcar, stacking as best I can. Carefully I try climbing up on them. It almost works, but they get real wobbly and I slip off, my leg getting stuck between two branches. After I haul six rocks and shore up them branches, I try again. I got me my steps.

"Ha!" bursts out of my chest. I can take care of myself. So there, Granny.

The sun's setting and this little clearing changes into a dance of eerie shadows. I lift my bucket of water into the boxcar, water sloshing down my front, then I climb inside the boxcar using my new steps. My stomach growls like crazy so I eat a chunk of bread and a bite of cheese. It's too dark to read or sew so I guess going to bed is about the only thing to do.

In the fading twilight I check the curtain me and Promise fixed for the door to make sure no one can see in. Not like it's going to protect me, but it makes me feel better. Then I stretch out on the two lumpy bags of leaves and newspapers that Promise helped me make today. The picture of us pulling off leaves and stuffing them in the sacks floats through my head and makes me smile. I can see her dark eyes looking at me, kind of wary and kind of sad. And something else I don't know the name of. That jiggly feeling scampers in my chest.

Reaching for my quilt, my fingers search for each of the little pearls. I find the two squares with pockets and think they'd be good places to hide something. Stretching my legs out, I roll myself up in my almost finished quilt and close my eyes. Least I'm not sitting straight up tonight. The crickets chirp and the katydids sing making a ruckus. Then something rustles almost out of reach of my hearing and goose bumps pop up all over my body.

"Just breathe. Relax," I whisper to myself. "It's a possum or a raccoon looking for their dinner. They're sure not coming in here because you fixed that hole. Just go to sleep."

The swishing gets closer. I hold my breath, listening real hard and I think I hear a voice. And then another. I fling my arm toward my table, feeling for my scissors with the sharp point. My money sock falls across my chest clunking against my wooden table as I wrap my fingers around my scissors. Goose bumps pop up on my arms. I'm afraid whoever's out there heard the thunk. The shuffling turns to footsteps whispering through the underbrush. I leap from my bed and peek around the curtain. The curtain. The curtain. That's a red flag that someone lives here. Quickly I lift the material off the nails and throw it into the shadows of the boxcar. It's almost dark, but the sky is still silvery and the steps get closer. I know it's a hobo or a rabbit hunter like Booker said. I clutch the scissors, every muscle in my body ready to strike.

The voice becomes clearer. No. That can't be. I know that voice.

It's Elwood.

Chills run through my body. I move quietly to a crack in the rear wall of the box car almost stumbling over my bucket of water. I press my face against the splintery wood, and sure enough, on the other side of the brush, maybe a hundred feet away is Elwood and his cousin Hog with big rifles for hunting deer and a torch for light. I listen for Beau. I don't hear him. Guess he don't get to hunt for deer, only 'coons.

"That old box car been here more than ten years at least," Elwood says pointing right at me it seems.

Now I'm sure he's seen me looking through the crack and is coming to shoot me.

"How'd it get way out here?" Hog asks.

Elwood lifts his rifle to his shoulder and takes aim straight at me. My fingers hurt clutching the scissors and my heart beat is probably rocking the box car back and forth. I hold my breath, waiting.

"Used to be a spur out this way," Elwood says lowering his rifle. "But the axle broke on this car and it was just too much trouble to haul it."

"Bums stay in it?" Hog says raising his rifle. He shoots at something in the bushes. The blast fills the box car and echoes off the trees. There's no air to breathe.

Warm liquid trickles down my leg and puddles around my bare feet.

"What was it?" Elwood asks.

"Rabbit."

"Get it?"

"Missed."

"Good thing. You'd of blown it to bits with that rifle of yours," Elwood snorts as he studies the sky. "Getting late. Probably ain't nothing but coons and possum left in these woods anyways."

"You said there might be some deer left out here."

Elwood grunts.

"Why'd we haul ourselves all this way out here?" Hog growls.

"To wear down your fat ass," Elwood says laughing his dirty laugh. Hog pushes him in the shoulder and they turn back where they came from, tramping through the brush.

I stand still, leaning against the rough wooden wall, for a long time after their voices have disappeared. Stepping out of the puddle, I grab something from my meager pile of clothes and dry my legs and feet. My hands still shake and my heart beats like I ran all the way to town. Finally I lie on my mattress, leaves and newspapers crinkling under me.

I can't help but think that if I still had a ma, I'd be in my own bed in my own house, her hand warm against my cheek and her leaning down to kiss me good night.

CHAPTER 11

My eyes pop open. A ray of sun streaks right in my face. I must have gone to sleep last night because my scissors lie open on the splintered floor boards. I stretch on my mattresses, my arms flung above my head and my toes spread wide. The leaves crinkle and the sweet smell of oak and hickory makes me feel like I can get out of this old boxcar and face another day. Standing up I spread my quilt across the bags of leaves just like it's a regular old bed. Picking up my curtain from the floor, I decide to leave it down. I toss it into the corner as last night flashes through my head. Shaking myself to throw all them bad feelings off me, I wish Booker and Promise were here. I listen to the quiet. I surely don't miss Granny screaming at me, though. Not one little bit.

I change into one of my clean pair of underwear, noticing that the scratches on my arms and especially my legs look like I've been wrestling a mountain lion. Those bushes and pricker vines can chew you up, that's for sure. I need pants, like Booker. I always hated these stupid dresses, but girls don't wear pants around here. Probably not in Detroit either. Wait. I got that old pair of denims that Miss Charlotte gave me for my quilt. I grab them, hoping that they fit me.

They do. A little too big, but I cut a strip off my curtain with my scissors and make myself a belt, tugging it tight around my waist and tying it in a knot. I tug my flour sack dress down like a long shirt and roll the bottoms of the pants up so as I don't trip on my face. Grabbing a chunk of bread and the last piece of cheese which has little cracks in it from being dried out, I climb down my steps. I reach back and heft my bucket of water to the ground. I sit on a rock and eat my breakfast. The sun is high in the sky meaning it's probably more like lunch than breakfast.

Skimming the bugs off the top of the water in the bucket, I drink using my hand as a cup. Then I wash the sleepiness off my face using the hem of my dress for a towel. I try out each of the rocks that's big enough to sit on to see which one is most comfortable. The one smack in the middle of the clearing and sitting right in the sun is now my personal rock. I squat on the rock and nibble on my cheese, thinking on how to get myself out of these woods and on my way to Detroit.

As I am about to pull myself up off the rock and wipe bread crumbs off my chest, footsteps crash in the woods. Booker. That's his way of letting me know it's him coming and not some sneaky hobo or crazy man like Elwood. His thrashing makes me happy and something real heavy that's been sitting on my shoulders, rolls off me. I can't wait to tell him about Elwood. Standing, a big grin crawls across my face. He bursts out of the bushes, branches slap against his chest. I look for him to flash his smile at me, but he's not smiling. And his eye is purple, swollen and closed shut.

"Holy mackerel. What happened to you?" I jump up and rush toward him. I grab his arm and lean in close to see his eye. Dried blood is smeared across his cheek. He probably don't want to hear about last night right now.

He whips his arm away from me and stands there, so angry I hardly recognize him.

"What happened?" I reach to touch his cheek but he pulls away and squats down at my bucket cupping water in his hands and splashes it on his face. I've never seen him like this.

"Booker. What happened?" I demand, standing over him.

Maybe my tone gets to him. I've never raised my voice to him. He looks up at me. "My pa." He gingerly touches his cheek, his fingers lightly creep toward his eye. I wait. Two crows argue above us in the trees, their shadows flicker across us as they fly away.

"Your pa? Why?"

"Elwood." He washes his face again, letting water drip from his chin.

I open my mouth to tell him about Elwood and Hog, but knowing he needs to tell me what happened, I shut up and wait.

"We delivered this morning's fish to him." He squints up at me, holding up his hand against the sun. He winces as he pokes at his damaged eye. "That son of a bitch tells my pa that I've been doing nasty things with *the white whore*." His voice is harsh and fills the air. Every bit of his kindness has disappeared.

I never heard him swear before.

"The what?" I say.

"You heard me." Drops of spit burst out of his mouth. *"The white whore."*

Both my fists are on my hips as I stare down at him. "What in damnation are you talking about?"

"You!"

"Me?" I back off and stumble over a rock, landing on my behind. "Me?" I ask again, my breath stuck in my chest.

"Yeah. That shit Elwood tells my pa that he seen us go off into the woods two days ago, kissing each other. And...."

"What? Kissing and what? What did that shit-faced son of a bitch say to your pa?" I holler as I scramble to my feet.

"He said...." Booker looks up at me then drops his head into his hands and moans.

"Tell me."

"That," Booker whispers. "That I put my hand up your... dress."

Words scramble out of my brain, gathering, but stay stuck in my mouth. I want to tell him about Elwood touching me and threatening me. I want to say to Booker that I know he would never do that to me. I want to say that Elwood is evil and he was in these woods with a gun. But my fear for Booker clogs up my throat like sour vomit. So I just stand there, my mouth hanging open.

"Then Pa punched me," he points to his eye, "in front of Elwood and said that Elwood could rest assured that he'd kill me himself if I ever did that again."

My stomach lurches and I gag on his father's words.

Booker holds his head in his hands, his body slowly rocking back and forth. Fury and pain rise from him like heat waves off a tar road. I know I shouldn't, but it's only right. I sit down beside him and wrap my arm around his shoulders.

"Oh, Booker," I murmur. "Oh, Booker."

He lets me hold him, his body sinking into mine.

CHAPTER 12

Sweat dribbles down my face. Lugging this bucket of water from the river, through the vines and briars is as bad as scrubbing Granny's floor on a hot day. But I just couldn't drink that water in my bucket. Not after Booker washed his bloody face in it. I didn't have the heart to tell Booker about Elwood and Hog being here last night. Or that I'm scared they'll come back tonight. Now I don't know when I'll see him or Promise.

I'm grateful to know my way to the river but I wish I could figure my way to town. My pants and dress are still damp from my dip in the river but I'm sweating from carrying water back to the boxcar. My armpits smell like they never even had a bath.

I swing the full bucket of water into the shade under the boxcar. My fingers sting from that rope handle grinding into my hand. I look up at the sun and guess it's about three or four in the afternoon. My stomach growls seeing as how it's been empty since that pitiful breakfast.

Using my new stairs, I get me the last chunk of bread and a small piece of salted fish. I grab the detective stories magazine and back out of the boxcar, my toes reach for the piled up rocks. So far my day after Booker left has been my trip to the river, moving all my possessions around on my splintery shelf and rearranging the branches and rocks so they don't look like stairs but a pile of junk. I am so bored I could poke my eyes out for fun.

I got to get myself into town but I couldn't ask Booker to show me right after his pa punched him in the eye. He don't really understand that I don't know my way in these woods. So, instead, I settle in the shade and lean up against the bark of a tree and flip through the magazine to see which story I'll read again. I try to make my eyes focus on the words but all I can think about is Elwood and if he's coming back here tonight and what he will do if he finds me.

I try to read but I practically have the body in the cellar story memorized, so it's not a surprise to me that the killer was the nephew. I turn to the bank robbery story and the ending pops into my head, almost word for word. I fling the magazine, watch it fly, pages flapping, into the blueberry bush. As I lean back against the tree, my sock full of money shifts on my chest, the coins tinkle against each other. I take it off my neck and untie the top of the little bag and dump the money into my lap. Out of pure boredom I stack all the dimes and nickels, quarters and pennies, each with their kind. Then stack by stack I count the coins. Yep. Still got $11.10. I got to buy me some food pretty soon or I'll starve to death. Almost everything's gone. Wish there was a path I could follow. Surely I'm stuck here same as a mule in the mud.

* * *

The sun is almost down to the horizon and yellow light reflects across the sky. The crows squawk at each other as they fight about whose branch is whose for the night. I try to decide if I'm going to eat the last of the salted fish now or save it. I'd eat the hash, even cold, but I need Booker's knife to open the can. I'm jittery and trying not to be afraid.

I pick up a stone and throw it at the trunk of a tree.

My heart leaps at the tromping in the bushes thinking it's Elwood and I'm sitting out here plain as day, but then Booker and Promise break through into my little clearing. I jump to my feet.

"Look what we brung you," Booker smiles holding up a rag with grease staining the bottom half. The purple bruise fades into his dark skin, but his eye is partly closed. "Promise made fried fish and we saved some for you."

"Great!" I throw my arms around her and squeeze real tight before I realize what I'm doing. Her body goes stiff then slowly softens a tiny bit. I don't want to let go, but I do.

"Thank you. Heavens. I can't wait. I was hoping you two would come. " Her eyes smile and the corner of her mouth twitches as I reach for the fish and unwrap the cloth around it.

"Look at you in them pants," she laughs.

"Them dang prickers scratch up my legs something awful."

She holds out one slender leg, hardly a scratch to be seen and cocks her head.

"You got to know how. You can't just be tramping through the woods every which way."

Booker laughs as Promise imitates me walking through the woods as they each choose a rock to sit on. I claim my very own rock and gobble up that fish, sucking every drop of grease off each one of my fingers.

"My stomach says thank you," I mumble through the last mouthful. I take a breath. "I have to tell you something."

Booker's eyes narrow and his face clouds up like a storm coming. Promise don't blink an eye.

"Last night Elwood and Hog came by here hunting for deer." My voice cracks.

"What?" Booker jumps to his feet, pacing and his eyes darting in every direction.

"Did they see you?" Promise asks.

"No. I took the curtain down and they were way over there." I stand and point.

"I told you mans come hunting in these woods," Promise says. "But Elwood...."

64

I am about to jump out of my skin thinking about Elwood being that close to me.

"What if he comes tonight?" I ask. "What if they look in the box car?"

Promise leaps up.

"You can't stay here," she says grabbing my arm. She let's go quickly and her hand flops at her side. "But what's he doing hunting out here? He's got plenty of woods."

"It don't make sense," Booker says, "Every idiot know these woods been hunted out of deer. Anything bigger than a possum been shot and butchered."

"Well." I say. "Elwood is an idiot."

Booker is quiet, biting his lip.

"I don't think he'll come here again," Booker says. "I mean he's stupid, but not stupid enough to walk this far when all the deer are gone."

He looks at me.

"Was he holding any dead animals?"

I think for a minute, picturing Elwood and Hog, then shake my head no.

"Did they have a special interest in the box car?" he asks.

"No. Elwood told Hog about it, but they kept on walking."

"What time they come?"

"Light dusk, but they had a torch for dark."

"And they didn't have Beau for coon hunting?"

Promise interrupts. "You can't stay here. You can't."

Booker reaches out and squeezes her shoulder.

"Don't worry. He ain't coming back." He sets his shoulders like he's real certain. "I'm sure."

"But—" Promise sputters.

"Do you know this or are you just guessing?" I say, my stomach skittering.

"Well, I cain't read Elwood's mind," he says all blustery. "But I'd bet my knife on it."

Promise and me glance at each other.

"Promise and me can stay until after dark tonight to be sure," Booker says, his voice softening. "But I know he ain't going to be hunting for deer in these woods when there ain't none. He's mean, but like I said, not that stupid."

Promise shivers even though the sun is still above the horizon.

"I don't trust that Elwood," she says.

"It will be fine." Booker's voice ends all discussion.

Promise turns her back to Booker. She stands for a moment, then wanders over to the blueberry bush and plucks the magazine from its branches.

She squats onto a rock, studying the front of the magazine.

"How come you're both here?" I say changing the subject. "Thought your pa was watching, especially you Booker."

"Pa was already crazy drunk, hollering and just looking for someone to smack," Promise says. "And you know that would be Booker." She thumbs through the pages of the detective magazine. "You read this?"

"About twenty times."

Promise looks up at the sky. "There's still light to see by. Would you read some to Booker and me?" I can tell Promise, like me, doesn't quite believe Booker about Elwood. But there's nothing more to be done.

"Sure," I reach out for the magazine. "Sit closer so you can see the pictures. Aren't as many like in comic books, but there are some."

They sit on either side of me.

I leaf through looking for the body in the cellar story. Booker's finger pokes at the front cover.

"What's that five on the front for?" he asks. I close the magazine and look for myself.

"That means five cents. That's how much it cost. Though Miss Charlotte gave it to me for free."

"Five cents?" Booker touches the cover again. "What's that little thing next to the five?" His finger rests on the red circle.

"It means 'cents'."

"You spell five cents like that?"

"Not really spell. It's the symbol for cents."

"So if I make a sign for my fish, I could write a five and that little squiggle?"

"Yep."

The tension slips away as Booker grins like he just won a prize. Promise leans into me, her shoulder lightly brushes mine, as she studies the cover. I hope she settles in against me.

"Teach me one of them letters," she says. Excitement rises in her voice and her finger points at the word DETECTIVE.

"You didn't go to school?" I ask, wondering how that can be.

Both Promise and Booker are silent. Then Booker squints at me with angry eyes.

"We ain't white."

"But,"

"There ain't no buts. If you're colored way up in these hills there ain't no school."

I don't know what to say. I never really knew. Or thought about it. I only knew no coloreds were allowed in my school. But no school?

"How'd you know the number five?" I ask Booker.

"I know a lot of numbers. Customers write down the price or how many pounds sometimes."

My school's closed because of the depression going on. There's no money for our teacher now but until I was almost thirteen I always went to school.

Promise touches my arm. "Teach me, Maisy. Teach me my name."

I look at her face. Something swells inside me, a warm feeling that keeps getting bigger. I take a deep breath.

"See that one?" I point at an E. "It's in your name."

"My name? My name is in that book?"

"No. Not your name. But the letters of your name."

Promise squints her eyes. "Tell me that one you pointed to."

"E. It's an E. It's the last letter of your name."

Promise picks up a twig and copies the letter E into the dirt beside her. "Like that?"

Booker grins and Promise laughs out loud. "E," she says. "Show me another."

I hold the twig and write PROMISE in the dirt.

"That's your name." I take Promise's hand and point her finger at each letter. "P-R-O-M-I-S-E." Holding her hand makes my whole body flood with warmth. I don't want to let go.

"That says Promise?" she says, disbelief and wonder float in her voice. Booker hoots for joy. She slips her hand out of mine.

"I'll point to a letter and you tell me what it's called. Remember. P-R-O-M-I-S-E." I lightly touch each letter.

After only two tries, Promise remembers every letter and grins like she's queen of the alphabet and Booker's clutches one of his hands with the other. Probably to stop himself from hugging me for making Promise so happy. I lean toward him smiling and our foreheads touch. Just for a second but long enough for me to notice his black eye.

I pull back thinking what Elwood accused Booker of doing to me.

* * *

The last streak of orange fades from the sky as the darkness gobbles up the clearing. Booker collects two handfuls of twigs and, with only one of my matches, gets a fire started.

"I'm keeping it real small." Booker sits near me on the ground and pulls the bucket of water closer. "We hear anything and we'll splash it out, but I know Elwood won't be coming."

He must have seen the doubt on my face.

"He's mean, but way too lazy to walk out this far again unless there's something for him to kill."

Promise is giddy with learning her name and keeps saying the letters out loud as she dances around the clearing. Booker seems happy for Promise and I think he wants to ask me to teach him his name but probably he's too proud to say it out loud. Maybe tomorrow I'll think of a way to write it in the dirt.

"Listen Booker," I say. "I got to get into town. I'm desperate for food and I got to see if Miss Charlotte will give me a job. I got to get money to get to Detroit. I got to get there. Will you show me how to get to town tomorrow?"

"You don't want to be in town."

"I do. I need a job."

Booker scuffs his toes into the dirt and a sizzle from damp wood pops an ember next to his foot.

"Your granny's still bad-mouthing you all over the town telling everybody that you stole from her and left the cabin on fire with her in it."

"What? Still?" I leap to my feet. My body's shaking. "I blew that lamp out." Now I'm maybe wishing I hadn't.

He looks up at me, the orange from the fire flickers across his face. I sit down beside him.

"I don't believe her," he says.

"*Nobody's* going to believe her."

"Elwood does."

"Elwood." I spit into the fire. "But nobody else."

He studies the fire like it's the most interesting thing he ever saw.

Promise flops down beside me. "What? What are you talking about?"

"*Other* people is saying bad things 'bout you too." He looks at me with sorrowful eyes.

"What?" Promise shakes Booker's arm.

"But it's not true," I screech. "What about Miss Charlotte?"

"Not that I'm hearing. Mostly them folks that eat at Elwood's." He looks at Promise. "People are bad-mouthing Maisy in town. 'Specially Elwood and her granny."

I didn't think for a second that old Granny or Elwood or anyone would miss me, let alone gossip about me, or even notice that I was gone.

I want to hurt Granny for making up lies. Punch her. Rip her hair out of her head. Kick her in the knee and pour her hooch all over her. Even when I'm gone she ruins everything for me. Now it will be harder to get a job in town. My body sags against Promise. She rubs my back, her hand as warm as a summer day.

"Booker. Please. Tomorrow will you show me the way to town from this god awful place? I have to talk to Miss Charlotte. I know she'll give me a job. Otherwise I'm going to starve to death. I don't know my way out of your woods. Every tree just looks like the other."

"I tole you it's them colored woods. All us coloreds look all the same."

"Booker. Please."

"Course you can follow the river. Only take you two or so hours each way. You ain't got nothing else to do." He smirks at me, anger flickers across his face.

I stare at him.

"How 'bout looking for a job in another town?"

"The nearest town is twenty-five miles away. That's the stupidest idea."

Booker sits real quiet poking the dirt with a twig.

The fire crackles softly. A crow caws once.

"When are you going to learn? You know I can't take you to town. Look at this eye." His fingers gently touch the side of his head. "I show up with you after you been gone two days. What do you think they'd do to me?"

My body shakes so hard my brains might fall out. I'm ashamed that he had to remind me.

"I'm sorry. I do know. I'm sorry."

70

"Elwood won't come here because he don't know you're here. But in town, he'll do whatever he wants to you or to me," Booker says in a harsh whisper. "And get away with it."

We sit staring at the embers. Two crows argue high above our heads.

"I can't stay here. Stuck in this boxcar. I got to get a job to get to Detroit." I poke at the glowing coals with a stick. We all sit quiet, not looking at each other.

"All's left is to go back to Granny's," I say. "Least I can find my way around there."

"No!" Promise shouts. "Are you crazy? She'll beat the living be-jeezus out of you."

We stare some more. The embers flicker, getting ready to burn out. A mocking bird sings its good night song.

"I'll take you," says Promise. "Just stay away from Elwood. Him and your granny are the ones causing all the trouble. You don't want Elwood to know that you're around. Other peoples won't hurt you. Sneak in and see Miss Charlotte."

"Really?"

Her braids jiggle as she nods her head.

"Miss Charlotte might give me a job. Then I'd have enough money for a ticket to Detroit. There's sure nothing around here for me."

Booker studies his fingers in his lap and Promise leans her head on my shoulder.

"What about us?" he says, sharpness slicing the air. "You got us."

"That's true. Surely true." I look at their solemn faces. "But I got to follow my ma's dream."

CHAPTER 13

ood to her word, the next day Promise shows me the way through her woods. We walk a long time, following some path that only Promise seems to know. My breath hitches as I practice my speech to Miss Charlotte in my head.

"It was hard leaving you last night," she says.

"I was scared, for sure. But no Elwood or Hog or anybody."

"Booker was right," she says. "I'm glad, but in town you see Elwood, you run like crazy. Right?" Promise nudges my arm.

"He's always in his café this time of morning. He never goes out before lunch. Don't worry." I hold back a branch of leaves to let her pass. Something sweet and sweaty lingers as she passes by me.

"And you know I'm only taking you to the tracks behind town, right?"

I'm surprised. "You're not coming into town with me? What about Miss Charlotte? I thought for sure you'd come see her."

A vine with thorns grabs at my pants. Stooping down, I free my leg.

"You know you got to step around them vines not tramp through them."

"Come into town with me," I say as I watch her long legs step around every vine and bramble. I get snagged again on some kind of bush that grabs at me. She waits while I untangle myself still not answering me.

I beg her with my eyes.

"You know why I can't," she finally says.

In fact I do. But I just don't want to believe that it would make things worse for Booker. I mean Elwood's surely making lies and everybody knows me since I was born. I always been cheerful and helpful. They won't believe him.

The path is free of brambles making it easy to walk and the sun shines warm on us. The hem of her dress ripples from side to side as she strides ahead of me. It sort of caresses her behind. What is the matter with me? That's just plain sick, me thinking of her behind. The rude voices of the men sitting in Elwood's café echo in my ears. *Homos. Pansies. Fairies.* You don't ever want to act like them.

Against God's will and the laws of nature.

My breath must be running out from all the walking. I realize that Promise is talking to me and pointing.

"Look," she squats and picks at something on the ground. "Strawberries. Wild strawberries." She plucks four tiny red berries from a leafy plant tucked up against a rock sitting in the sun.

Standing, she smiles at me, kind of shy like, and holds a strawberry up to my lips. I open my mouth and a burst of sweet and sour rolls across my tongue.

"You like it?" She holds up another, almost teasing me, then pops it into my mouth.

Truthfully I can hardly taste it for all the electric feelings running up and down between my mouth and my toes.

"I do," I say studying her face for a clue about what's happening.

She pops the two other berries into her mouth, smiles, tosses her head and motions for us to walk, her in front of me.

"…and I miss my ma," Promise says over her shoulder.

"Me too." I'm glad for something to distract me. "Sometimes I can hardly remember my ma," I say raising my eyes up to the trees and the blue sky. I don't really believe she's dead. I'm still waiting for her to show up.

"With my ma gone, there's nobody to talk girl talk with." She pushes through a patch of undergrowth, holding it for me to pass by. She smiles and sunlight fills her face.

"But now I got you," she says.

That jiggly feeling leaps through my chest.

Then we're walking in tall grass. The ground's bumpy but I'm thankful nothing grabs at my legs. She slows until I'm walking beside her

"So." She stops, turning to face me. "We're almost to the tracks. You can find your way from here."

"But how will I know where to get back into the woods? All them bushes look alike." I really want her to come with me. I suppose that's selfish. The sun light reflects off her cheek and lips. There goes that jiggle again.

Promise touches my hand for a second. "Follow me."

We walk toward the tracks but stop just short of them where the rocky bank begins. Promise searches the ground until she finds a reddish rock the size of a tomato.

"See this here rock? I'm putting it right along the edge of the grass. That's where you go into the grass then just keep heading straight with your back to the sun. You'll hit the river by the mill and you know your way from there. Right?"

I beg her with my eyes but she turns her back and steps up onto the tracks.

I follow her and we're both standing smack dab in the middle of the tracks, facing each other. Some weird force feels like it's pulling us together. Promise bites her lip and a wave of excitement lurches into my chest.

"So," she says moving a piece of gravel with her bare toe.

"So."

Clouds move across the sky hiding the sun and leave us standing in the shadow. Then it passes. The rags tying her three braids are red with white dots. The leftovers from someone's dress? Hers? I want to know more about her. I want to know everything.

"So. Will I see you tonight?" I hate the begging in my voice. She smiles ever so slightly.

"I gotta work for Miss Lizzie this afternoon. She's having company for dinner. So I don't know."

My shoulders slump.

"But I'll figure a way to come tomorrow." Her breath stutters softly in her chest. "To hear about if Miss Charlotte gives you a job," she adds quickly, turns and disappears into the underbrush.

In my mind I see her strong legs striding in front of me and her dress.... I shouldn't think of her that way. I'm surprised when I miss her already. A big grin grows across my face. Even though I try to stop it.

* * *

I can see the back of Elwood's café through the bushes standing here on the tracks. Gives me the willies thinking about what he done to me, touching me and all. I head away from Elwood's and follow the tracks behind the town until I'm at the back of Mr. Carter's Market. The buildings look all ramshackle from the back, some of them almost falling down. I take the path worn by people coming the back way into town. Then I walk through the little alley way between the market and Jimmy's shoe repair shop. The paint is peeling off the outside walls of the market and the doorknob jiggles like it's going to fall off in my hand as I push the door open. Mr. Carter's got one of them dang bells on his door. Just like Elwood. Makes my skin crawl as it ding-a-lings. I touch my sock with my money in it really hating that I have to spend some of it for food. But I know Miss Charlotte will give me a job.

"Maisy," Mr. Carter says to me, looking over his little round glasses, his voice sharp. Then turns his back to me and fiddles with his cash register. Every time I'd come in for Granny he'd talk my ear off. Now he acts like I smell real bad. Probably from listening to all that

75

jabber at Elwood's, and now he's probably wondering if he should sell me something. But, for sure he needs my dimes and nickels. These are real bad times for making money. I wave to him and wander down the main aisle of his little store listening to the latest Lone Ranger episode blasting on his radio.

First thing I look for is a can opener. He's only got one kind and it costs ten cents. That's outrageous, but I need it. I load three cans of beans into my arms, each of them nine cents, but I can make them last for a couple of days each. Potatoes are only one penny a pound so I get me seven of them thinking I'll boil them over a fire in an empty bean can. I can't resist grabbing three apples for four cents. My arms are bulging with food but I squeeze a jar of Skippy peanut butter on top of the potatoes. It's twenty-three cents, but will last me a long time and I seen it in an advertisement in *Good Housekeeping* when I worked at El-wood's. Mr. Carter eyes me suspiciously as I lay the food on his counter by the cash register. The light from the window shines off his bald head.

"I got to get a few more things. Can I leave these here?"

He gives me a squinty-eyed look and I know he's been listening to Elwood. He weighs the potatoes as I turn my back on him. I can't pass up the magazine rack. Not that I can buy me a new magazine, but I open the latest *Modern Screen* and flip through the pages. Bette Davis with them eyes and Clark Gable. Picture of John Wayne on a horse. Horse is better looking than him. Don't know why Lucymay used to swoon over him so much. I slide the Modern Screen magazine back in the rack and touch the front of the new *Life*. Someday I'll be buying myself whatever magazines I want. I see there's a story about Amelia Earhart in the newspaper. I can't resist even though it's five cents. I have to know about her. Besides, then I can read the comic section to Booker and Promise. A smile pushes its way onto my face as I imagine leaning up against Promise, reading the paper.

Mr. Carter carefully loads my items into a brown paper bag. He still don't say anything to me. Then I notice the rack of candy and gum. Wrigley's spearmint gum. My mouth waters, spit pooling around my tongue, just looking at it. Three cents though. But what a surprise for

Booker and Promise. I can just see the three of us sitting on our rocks chewing our gum happy as pigs. I hand him a pack.

"That'll be seventy-four cents all together," Mr. Carter says, his eyes barely meeting mine.

I dig the right change out of my sock, mumbling in my head about how expensive these few things are. What a gyp. I place two quarters, two dimes and four pennies on the counter. That's more than I used to end up with from Elwood for the whole week. Mr. Carter's still not talking to me. Meanness creeps into my heart about him ignoring me and believing them lies. Just to be spiteful, I'll make him talk to me.

"So," I say in my fake friendly voice. "How is Mrs. Carter? Heard last week she had a bad cold. Hope that's gone."

"Yes," he stammers. "Much better." He pushes the paper bag toward me, but I let it sit on the counter between us.

"And Margaret. Isn't she getting married soon?" I hope my smirk is not showing on my face.

"Yep. Next month." The words barely squeak through his thin lips pressed tight together. He gives the bag another push towards me. It's going to be falling off the counter before he knows it.

"And Sunny. She's still in high school."

"Well yes. But the high school closed. You know that. No money for a teacher." He lifts the bag and holds it out to me.

"My granny took me out of school almost four years ago. But that's a real shame about the school closing. So what's Sunny doing instead of going to school?" His arms make little movements toward me practically begging me to take the bag.

"She helps her mother at home," his arms quiver from holding them out.

"Well. You give them all my hello and tell them I was asking after them."

The paper bag crinkles as I take it and hold it in my arms. I wing the door open, letting it bang against the wall, that little bell ringing like crazy as I head toward Miss Charlotte's store.

* * *

The bag is heavy in my arms as I stay in the shadows of the store fronts up Main Street, looking over my shoulder from time to time, even though I know this is still Elwood's busy time. I stop in front of The Angel, Mrs. Setter's homemade candy store. I lean my nose closer to the window pretending I'm choosing between the pulled taffy and the hand-dipped chocolates to take back to Promise and Booker. Mrs. Setter sees me pressing close to her window and waves me in. I check down the street for Elwood as I step through the door. Waves of warm sugar and rich chocolate make me dizzy.

"Maisy. How's your Granny? Rumor has it she's been feeling poorly. She any better?" She tilts her head, dark hair pulled back in a bun and her gray eyes kind.

I didn't know Granny was feeling anything but ornery. Seems as if Mrs. Setter hasn't heard the new set of rumors. Besides mostly my mouth waters looking at all this candy in one place.

"She's better. Thank you for asking," I say.

"You need anything?"

I open my mouth to say yes, strawberry taffy, and chocolate covered caramels, and those little chocolate drops with the pointy tops. She's waits and I don't say anything.

"Must be hard on you when your Granny's sickly. Anything I can do to help out?"

Oh that. "I'm doing fine, Mrs. Setter. Thank you." I breathe in the rich, soothing smell of chocolate. "I have to get going." I hitch my bag of groceries up, getting a better grip on them. "You know. Granny and all."

"Wait. Why don't you choose a candy to take with you."

Tears sting my eyes and my heart beats an extra thump. Nobody is hardly ever nice to me. I choose a chocolate covered caramel with a little curly on top.

"Thank you." I say over my shoulder as I swing open the door and step into the street carefully closing the door behind me. I head toward Miss Charlotte's store, walking a few steps down the street then I stop. I bite half the candy and hold it in my mouth to melt. The pleasure of the chocolate washes through my body like warm water. I stand there enjoying it, my eyes closed and the rich taste of chocolate on my tongue. I open my eyes to take a second bite and there staring me in the face is a poster stuck on the rickety fence that stretches between the candy store and the barber shop with its red and white pole. I read it and then I read it again.

EVERYBODY WELCOME

Fun Games Food
Pony Rides and Pie Eating Contest

Wren's Park---Sunday 1 to 8 pm

Knights of Ku Klux Klan

Those people are wicked. Who'd even go to their picnic? How dare they have a picnic in our town. I wonder who nailed it up. Nobody in our town would belong. Would they?

Hefting my bag onto my hip, I cross the street toward Miss Charlotte's store when I am practically knocked down by Elwood who charges me out of nowhere. He grabs hold of my arm real tight.

"Well, well. Here's sweet little Maisy, our town tramp walking the streets again." I back away hugging my groceries close to me. I try to make a run for it, but he's got hold of my arm. Real tight. Out of the corner of my eye I see Sam and his daughter slow their steps. They look our way. They'll tell Elwood to shut up. Sam's known me since I was baby. Like most folks around here.

They stand still, looking at us. Not moving a muscle.

Elwood drops his grip on me but stands right up close in front of me. The smell of stale whiskey and rotten teeth make me choke.

"You almost killed your Granny, stealing from her then leavin' that lamp aburnin'."

"I didn't—"

"Liar. You're a liar, liar, liar." His voice rises.

I swivel on my heel and march toward Miss Charlotte's with my groceries clutched in my arms. Now Evie and Doc Samuels stand beside Sam. They've known me all my life too, but they stand there gawking. Sam's red hair stands on end like always. Elwood's hand squeezes my neck from behind stopping me. Then he steps in front of me bending close to my face, that finger with the ugly blue nail shakes an inch from my nose.

"You bring shame and damnation upon this town, Maisy Wharton."

My stomach lurches, bubbling up into my chest. What is he talking about? Surely this isn't all about Granny. He can't know what I feel about Promise. *I* don't even know.

I back away. His nasty old hand clenches onto my shoulder, shaking me. My grocery bag rips and everything I spent my money on scatters onto the dirt street. Mrs. Setter peeks over the curtain in her window and out of the corner of my eye I kind of see Charley with his porkpie hat pulled down over his forehead step towards us. But then he stands there and watches like the rest of them. What's the matter with everyone?

"Leave me alone, you dirty old man," I scream. I look from side to side hoping someone will stop him. He grabs my dress front, all wadded into his fist, and pulls my face up real close to his. I gag on his breath.

"Fornicating with that…that…colored boy will bring Almighty God's wrath on you." I try to yank away from him.

That colored boy? Booker?

"I never did nothing like that. You are lying," I scream, struggling to get out of his grip.

"Nobody believes you, Maisy Wharton. No one."

I look frantically at the crowd that's gotten even bigger for help. I point at Elwood. I'm going to tell the truth about him.

"He's the one. He…..he put his…." The words are leeches in my throat.

"No one believes you." A slow, ugly smirk spreads across his face, his lips twitching. "It was *you* that broke the law of this state and broke the heart of our precious Jesus Christ Our Lord. Fornicating with that boy. God had no intention for the races to mix. Not ever." He shakes me hard.

I got to say what he done to me, speaking of God's law. I got to tell these people so they know Elwood is lying.

"Him. He…" I point my finger at Elwood. "He done what….what he shouldn't…" I can't spit the words out of my mouth.

An evil glare slowly crawls into Elwood's eyes. Then he laughs. He laughs because he knows I can't say those words. My throat is clogged with shame.

His grip on my dress tightens and he pulls me up nose to nose with him. "You're a white girl. Trash but white. For your own good, stay away from that colored boy. You understand?" His spit sprays in my face. "It's against God's will."

The store fronts spin making me so dizzy I almost fall to the ground. Nausea lurches in my chest and the odor of vomit lies on my tongue.

A door opens and slams shut. Joe strides toward us from his barber shop.

Elwood tightens his grip as Joe comes up behind him. Mrs. Setter opens her door but hesitates. The bitter taste of bile creeps into my throat.

"Hey Elwood. Let go of Maisy." Joe, still in his barber's apron, tugs at Elwood's arm but Elwood wrenches it free from Joe and sticks his dirty finger in my face again still holding me up close by my dress.

"You hear me. You stay off our streets. I see you in town and I'll beat you 'til you wish you were dead. Like a daddy would if you had one." Spit from his filthy mouth sprays on my face again. Bile gurgles in my throat and before I know it, I vomit all over Elwood's chest. If I weren't so scared and ashamed, I'd of laughed when I see the bits of my chocolate covered caramel and a fleck of strawberry stuck on the pocket of his blue plaid shirt.

"Look what you done, you stupid whore." Elwood looks hard at me then lets loose of my dress and pushes me backwards. He turns and kicks one of my apples. One of my precious apples. It smashes into the fence, the skin splits open then rolls back into the street, covered with dirt. Something snaps in me and before I know it, I'm kicking Elwood's leg and trying to rip that shirt off his back screaming for all I'm worth.

"You god damn lying stupid son of a bitch." I yell it over and over pounding at his back. Mrs. Setter steps forward and pulls me away from Elwood as Joe leads him away from me and further down the street.

"Hush," she says. "Hush, now. Let's pick up your groceries. Hush now."

I finally hear her and calm myself down. By now Elwood is walking past Miss Charlotte's store and is three blocks from his café. My neighbors turn their backs on me and go about their business. No one offers to help pick up my things besides Mrs. Setter.

"Here's your other two apples, Maisy. Oh, and here's your newspaper." She gathers every item except my splattered apple. I pull up the hem of my dress, which I'm wearing over my denims, to make a basket to carry my things.

"Thank you," I manage to mutter to Mrs. Setter before I run down the street, shame loping behind me like a hound dog. I cut through the first alley and head for that reddish rock in the grass. And home.

Disappointment yaps at my heels. I just know Miss Charlotte would've given me a job. I know she would.

CHAPTER 14

P romise and me sit on my flour sacks stuffed with leaves that we dragged outside, our backs resting against a tree trunk. Sun light through the trees speckles our legs. Promise stares so hard at my *Modern Screen* magazine it might burst into flames. Her finger pokes at the letter H again and again.

I think on how to tell her about Elwood, but anything I say will rile her up and probably make her afraid for me. Besides, sitting side by side, leaning into each other is heaven. I'll tell her later.

"I knowed that letter yesterday. It's not in my name but you told me just before we went to town. What's the matter with me?" She flops the magazine into my lap and looks at me with pitiful eyes.

"You look like some poor hungry dog, begging for a bite of food," I laugh, not meaning to hurt her feelings, but those serious eyes make me want to take care of her.

She gives me a shove with her elbow and I wait for two seconds thinking she's mad, until the corners of her mouth twitch into a grin.

"If only learning to read was as easy as a dog begging." She stretches. "So you didn't talk to Miss Charlotte. Thought that was the point of you going into town." She waits for an answer. I can't tell her what happened. I'm ashamed to tell her the truth. I could fib but there's something about her that keeps lies from rolling off my tongue. So I say nothing.

"Maisy?"

"I'm going to see her in a day or two."

She scrunches up her eyes and studies my face.

"That don't make sense."

I hitch one shoulder.

She grabs the magazine off my lap and finds the H pointing her finger at it. "So what is that letter?"

"H. Like hog. Or house. Or ….." I look at her waiting for her to say the next word

"Home? Wait. I know," she says. "Hammer." She grins like one of them movie stars in the magazine, her eyes clear and one side of her smile a tiny bit higher than the other. Little delicate spots of sweat ride across her nose. "Horse!"

Her shoulder leans into mine. Warmth gathers where we touch. I never sat with anyone like this since my ma got herself shot. I like it but my stomach's got the jitters. I'm starting to think I might like Promise. That certain way. But surely, it would be wrong.

"Now tell me that H word," her finger points at the magazine page.

"It's Harlow. Jean Harlow. She's an actress in this place called Hollywood." I find the word *Hollywood* and point at the H. "They make moving pictures there and she's a movie star."

"Whyn't you go to Hollywood instead of Detroit? Especially because you love them movies so much."

"My ma was going to take me to Detroit because you can get anything and be anyone you want to be there. Like in these magazines. That's what Detroit is like. Easy." I bite the inside of my cheek. "It's not as hard as life is here."

"Can I go with you?"

Somehow that question makes my toes curl up with pleasure. I examine her face but that don't tell me nothing.

"Who'd take care of Booker and your pa, then?"

She looks into her lap, her long fingers twisted together.

"Yeh."

A dragonfly flits around our heads and lights on Promise's chest. She absently brushes it away.

"How come your ma died?" I ask.

"If anybody knowed, nobody told me," she says into her lap.

I wait, watching her chest breathe in and out.

"When my baby sister was borned there was blood all over. More than I ever seen. Then my sister was sickly and died before she was a few weeks old."

An ache reaches from my chest to my toes as she talks. But at least she knows where her ma is.

"My ma just never got out of bed." Her eyes search the trees like maybe she could find the answer there. "We buried her beside my sister a few weeks later."

She reaches for the magazine and flips a few pages.

"I wish you were going to Hollywood instead of Detroit." Then she starts at the beginning and turns each page one by one. When she's looking at the Phillip Morris ad on the back cover she lays it gently in my lap.

"I couldn't go anyways." Her dark eyes look straight into mine. "There ain't no colored people in Hollywood. They prob'ly wouldn't let me in."

I never thought about a colored person not being able to go someplace.

That's real terrible. Not to be welcome where you want to be.

* * *

Promise and me are stretched out on my flour sack mattresses, the sun bakes our skin and a soft breeze whispers across us. Her breathing is even except for a little snore now and then. I lie here thinking about what happened with Elwood in town yesterday and I wonder how I'll get to Miss Charlotte without Elwood beating on me. Promise shifts in her sleep curling into my side and pressing herself up against me. The strangest, most exciting feeling I ever felt, sweeter even than that chocolate on my tongue, rolls through every inch of my body. The hairs on my arms stand up as if I been struck by lightning and the nipples on my breasts stick out like on a chilly morning.

Promise's behind walking in front of me on the path flashes in my mind and I am ashamed. The shame sinks deeper and deeper crowding out all the other feelings. What I feel about her is wrong. I scoot away from her napping body. Her arm flings across my stomach. I want to roll into her, to hold her. But everybody says it's wrong.

Leaves thrash and twigs snap. Booker hollers. I jump to my feet, straighten my dress over my stomach with both hands and hitch up my denims. Promise stirs. Booker's in the clearing and I just know he can see shame crawling all over my face.

"I heard what happened in town with Elwood," he blurts out heading straight toward me. He throws his arms around me tight, his strong body pressed against mine. He lets me go right away and steps back. "Are you all right?"

Promise stretches, waking from her nap. "What? What happened in town?"

Booker cocks his head and I know he's asking why I haven't told Promise.

"What?" she says. "You didn't tell me something?"

She jumps to her feet and puts her face up close to mine. "You been keeping things from me Maisy Wharton?" Her black eyes are steel.

I step back, the strength of her anger knocks me off balance.

"Don't you ever lie to me. You and me. We got a special friendship. Lies will tear it apart." She steps away from me swinging those eyes to Booker.

"What'd you hear in town?"

Booker stands, his feet fidget.

Now her face, like stone, swivels toward me, her teeth peek through her snarled lips.

"Sit down," I say. "I'll tell you both what Elwood done yesterday."

I pause.

"And I'll tell you everything he done to me before when I worked for him."

CHAPTER 15

Booker paces back and forth across the clearing, kicking pebbles, dirt flying. Promise and I both duck as a rock whizzes past our heads.

"That son of a bitch. Damnation. That son of a bitch Elwood touched you *both*?" He glares at me and then at Promise. Stopping, his fists clenched at his side and his eyes fierce, he squats, picking up a hand full of rocks and one by one wings them at tree trunks. "I can't believe it. Both of you? I'll kill him, that son of a bitch. He had no right putting his dirty hands on you." He points at me and then looks at Promise. "Or you."

He stops and stabs his finger at Promise. "I understand Maisy not telling me, but why didn't you? You're my *sister*."

Promise hangs her head, shame crawling out her pores. "I couldn't tell no one."

I'm as shocked as Booker that Elwood touched Promise too.

"Stop, Booker," I say. "You're making it out like Elwood touching both of us is our fault and it surely is not. It was the shame that kept us quiet." He don't understand that we were ashamed to say anything. Who would believe us?

"But you was with Pa. He had to been there," Booker snarls at Promise. "What'd *he* do?"

Promise wrings her hands in her lap. "It was just once. That's all."

"What. Did. Pa. Do?"

Promise bolts up straight. "I'm sorry I told you Booker because what in damnation *could* he do?" She waits, her nostrils flared. "You want to know? He stood watching while Elwood's grimy hands run all over my nine year old body. Prob'ly his heart was breaking. Then he grabbed my hand and took me out of there. He never let me go back with him."

Promise sniffs in the brittle silence. I reach for her hand, but words explode out of her.

"Pa did what he could without getting himself killed. You know that." She breathes hard. "So stop."

Booker collapses onto a sitting rock, his body sags, empty as a dirty shirt thrown on the floor. Holding his head in his hands, he moans.

Promise's eyes skitter between Booker and me. I hold my hand out. Her fingers touch mine and we wait.

We sit like that for a long time. I try to think of what to say to make it better. But there's nothing to be said. Then I remember the chewing gum in my pocket. That might cheer us up. I reach into my pants pocket and wrap my fingers around the Wrigley's spearmint chewing gum. I pull my hand out and uncurl my fingers. That little pack of gum lies in the palm of my hand.

"Who wants a piece?" I say. Booker looks up and a tiny flicker of light comes into his eyes. Promise smiles, looks at me and smiles even more. I hold the pack and open the end, being careful so I can fold it closed again. Handing each of them a stick I keep one for myself. The thin white paper wrapped around it crinkles as I unwrap the gum, fold it over and pop it in my mouth. The sweetness soaks into my tongue before I chew.

"One for today and one for tomorrow," I say sliding the half empty pack back in my pocket.

Booker stands up and paces again. He's still all steamed up.

"Sit down Booker. It's all said and done." He glares at me.

"There ain't nothing you can do," Promise says.

"Wait a minute. I got another surprise." I jump to my feet and climb into my boxcar. I wave the newspaper out the door.

"I got this in town yesterday." I sit on my favorite rock and point to a story at the bottom of page one. "Look. Booker. Amelia Earhart. Like you brought me."

"I don't give a damn," he snarls.

It's quiet. None of us speak. A jay squawks and a bumble bee wobbles past my shoulder. Booker looks up and must have seen my face. Them crows fly over screeching at each other.

He doesn't smile but nods at the paper. "You read it to me?"

"I will. And," I open the paper to the last page. "Comics. These'll make us feel a whole lot better."

They both squeeze up close to me. Booker's shoulder leans up against me as he holds one edge of the paper while I hold the other.

"Read Dick Tracy," Booker says. "I ain't seen what's going on with him in a while."

As soon as I finish Dick Tracy, Promise wiggles the paper, her finger pointing at Popeye.

"I love Popeye and skinny Olive Oyl." She laughs. Her eyebrows flick up as she looks at Booker leaning up against me.

We read every strip on the page ending with Smitty who I think is kind of silly, but Booker likes him a lot.

"Look," Promise points at a little box with words in it. "What's that say?"

"It says," I read the whole thing to myself. "Okay. You have to guess this." I look at them to be sure they're listening. "What was discovered in space in 1930 that has something in common with the comics?"

"A shooting star?" Booker guesses. "No, a comet strip." His head leans against mine for half a second. "Get it?"

Promise play punches him in the arm. "A new star named Hollywood?"

"You'll never guess," I say. "A tiny planet that's the farthest out in space. Guess what its name is?"

They look at each other, shaking their heads.

"What?" says Promise.

"Pluto!"

"Like the dog in the comic book Pluto?" laughs Booker.

"Nobody'd name a planet that," says Promise.

"Yep. Pluto." I say. It feels real good to laugh together again.

* * *

"I got to go set my nets and traps," Booker says still chewing on his gum. "You stay away from that Elwood." He points his finger at me.

"I surely will." I stand and stretch, my behind tingles from sitting on that rock so long. "Wait. I got something I forgot to show you."

I squat on the ground and pick up a twig. "Come here for a minute."

He stands over me, casting a shadow on the ground. His fingers lightly touch my hair. With my twig I write some letters-- BOOKER-- then look up at him. Two crows squabble in the tree above us.

"You know what that says?" I ask.

He shrugs and scuffles one foot in the dust.

"That's your name."

"I knowed that," he says.

"I know you do."

"Just say them letters so I be sure to remember them." He kneels down, his knee pressing against mine, and places a finger on the B.

"B-O-O-K-E-R." I say.

"That's a funny looking letter," he points to the K. "I seen the others around a lot, but not that one much." The Ku Klux Klan poster flashes through my mind.

"That's what makes your name so special," I say. A grin starts at one corner of his mouth and travels across his face. He gently tousles my hair, jiggling one of my curls.

90

"Thanks," he says. "Maisy with the Amelia Earhart hair." He puts his hand on Promise's shoulder.

"You be careful, you hear me?" He turns toward the woods.

"Booker," I say. He stops and looks at me, his eyes curious and a tiny bit scared. I been meaning to say this to him every day. It's time I did it.

"For sure, Booker, I know you'd never do what Elwood said you did. Never."

His black eyes look straight at me and his head makes a tiny nod. Then he's gone.

* * *

"I got to get home pretty soon. 'Fore it gets dark," Promise says squirming in that uncomfortable way as if her shoes are too tight. But she's got bare feet, so that's not it. I hope it's because she's not wanting to leave but afraid to say so.

"I'm starving." I say. "I know the sun's still up, but I could use some supper." Sounds like there's a café right across the street. "I was thinking about one of them cans of beans. I got a can opener now. We could share them."

"Sure," she says right away. "I'm always hungry. I'll get us some twigs for a fire."

As she gathers wood, I climb into the boxcar for a can of beans, my brand new, shiny can opener and a match. I grab one of my leaf mattresses too because there aren't no rocks to sit on near the fire. By the time I get back, Promise has a pile of twigs and a couple larger sticks lying in the fire pit.

"We better use a piece of the paper to start the fire," I say. "Only Booker can start a fire with one match."

I toss the mattress on the ground and rip a half page of the want ads since I won't be getting what I want from them anyway. There's nothing listed in the Help Wanted column. Not one single job. I crumble up the paper and push it under the pile of twigs and light the match. The flame flares then dies down and looks like it's going to die out. Promise leans in close to the fire and puffs with long, slow breaths. It glows. It fades. It catches and the twigs start to burn.

"Yay!" we both holler at the same time and hug each other. Her breasts are soft against me. Heat rises in my face and I let go of her real fast. She leans back and looks up at the sky like a flock of the most amazing birds were flapping over our heads. Finally our eyes meet. She bites her lip, and I work real hard to get that can of beans open with my new can opener. I want to say something, but I don't have the right words inside me to ask what's happening between us. But surely something is.

We got the beans heated up pretty good except we burned the very bottom ones. But we don't care. We sprawl out on the mattress, sticking our fingers in the bean can, and enjoy the molasses taste. Every once in a while, Promise scoots a tiny bit closer to me.

"I can't get these beans in the very bottom," I say stretching my fingers into the can.

"Hold on." Promise leans over and sits up with a sturdy twig in her hand. She holds it out to me. That lop-sided smile makes my stomach jiggle.

"Here," I balance a clump of beans on the twig and hold it up for her.

Our eyes catch each other and my hand shakes. I'm afraid I'm going to drop them beans right down the front of her dress. But she opens her mouth, wraps her lips around the beans and swallows them.

"You finish them up," she says licking her fingers and wiping them on her dress. She stands up and gathers more twigs to keep the fire going then sits down even closer to me on the mattress.

"So when you gonna go see Miss Charlotte?" Her arm presses against my shoulder.

"How do *you* know her?" I ask.

"You're not the only one that knows her." An edge of sass floats in her voice. "I knowed her since I was little."

"I knowed her since I was little," I tease her in a singsong voice. She pushes me and I roll clear off the leaf mattress.

Standing up, I wipe the dirt off the knees of my pants. "Now look what you done. You ruined my best outfit. Miss Lizzie will cancel my invitation for dinner."

She pulls at my hand and I stumble onto the mattress right next to her. "You're crazy." She laughs.

"So how did you know Miss Charlotte *since you was little*?"

She picks up the empty bean can. "You should rinse this out 'fore it gets caked on. You'll need this to boil water."

"Yes ma'am."

She gives me a warning look.

"Sorry. But how did you know Miss Charlotte? Really."

"My ma." Her eyes get a far distant look.

I wait.

"My ma sewed for peoples. Like mending clothes and fixing up rips and tears."

I wait some more thinking her heart must hurt talking about her ma.

"So Miss Charlotte was always real nice to my ma. And sometimes she'd give Booker and me some clothes she got or give an extra spool of thread to my ma."

"Like she gave me them denims."

We lean into each other, touching from shoulder clear down to our hands, thinking of Miss Charlotte's kindness. The sky turns a pale blue as the sun reaches toward the horizon. Promise leans forward and pokes the little fire with a stick. Sparks fly for a second then disappear. That smoky smell fills the air. She leans back solidly against me with her face only inches from mine. My skin feels like it's going to jump off my body.

"After ma died, Miss Charlotte come to visit me and said if I ever need something, to ask her."

"She's real nice," I say.

"That's why I know she'll help you." She raises her eyes to meet mine. My breath leaves my body and I want to put my lips on hers and kiss her. I try to push away but there's some magnet pulling me toward her. Her eyes hold me as if she wrapped her arms tight around me.

I sit up real straight, looking close into the fire. My insides are jiggling and jumping all over.

"I think we're both missing our mas," I say.

"Maybe." She lays her hand lightly on my back. "And maybe not." My back warms under her hand and before I know it my whole body wants hers.

"I better be going," she whispers and runs her hand all the way down my back.

Disappointment pools in my chest and fire skitters down my spine.

"Probably a good idea," I murmur.

CHAPTER 16

The next morning, after sneaking along the tracks behind town and cutting up to Main Street way south of Elwood's café, my hand is on the doorknob of Miss Charlotte's shop. My armpits sweat and I'm practically biting my lip all the way through. Wish I had some of that fancy stuff I seen in my movie magazines that keeps your armpits from smelling.

I open the door and peek my head in. Miss Charlotte is standing at her cutting table and there's nobody else there. Her head turns and she smiles, so I walk on in. The smell of all that clean material comforts me. It's so familiar.

"Maisy. I've been wondering where you are." She comes out from behind her table and gives me one of them shoulder hugs like men do with each other. But leastwise she don't seem to hate me.

"I am so glad to see you Miss Charlotte. You always been such a help and I'm—"

"I heard you left your granny. She's been looking for you."

I don't say anything because whatever came out of my mouth right now might shock Miss Charlotte.

"She needs you, Maisy. She's real old. You can't leave an old woman out in the woods by herself. She's real upset."

"Where did you hear about me not being at Granny's?"

"Everybody heard about that. Aren't too many secrets in this town."

Now I wonder what she thinks of me. Does she think everything is all my fault? Should I tell her the truth? Granny prob'ly already got to her and told her a pack of lies. I take a deep breath.

"Miss Charlotte. I really need a job."

"You had a job at Elwood's. Why'd you quit?"

I want to tell her everything. Everything he said and done. I'm pretty sure she'd understand. But something holds me back.

"He fired me, ma'am." Her eyebrows crawl up her forehead. "Me and him had a little falling out. But I'm a good worker. You know that about me. I was just hoping…"

"Did you go back and try to make it up to him?"

Shadows move real fast in front of my eyes. I grip the counter with my hand. The room whirls and my knees turn to jelly.

"I can't work there. But I'd be real good help for you."

"Elwood's telling folks that you and Booker…. Well, he's telling folks all the nasty things that you and Booker are doing. That you're hiding down by the shanty town part of the river to be with him." She looks real hard at me, her eyes squint and her mouth puckers into a tiny bunch of wrinkles. She totally believes Elwood.

My fingers turn white gripping that counter. All them colors of material fade together and swirl close around my head.

"That's a lie, Miss Charlotte. Booker and me, we never even touched each other. We're just friends. He's a good person. He'd never do any of that stuff Elwood's telling around town."

Miss Charlotte's real quiet. One of her eyebrows comes down, but the other is still perched up high on her forehead.

"Why would Elwood ever say such awful things if they weren't true?" Suspicion and something else, maybe righteousness, worms itself into her voice.

I pick the threads on the end of my cloth belt. The truth about Elwood is gathering in my mouth and pushing against my lips. I press them together tighter.

"Why would he, Maisy? If you did nothing wrong?" Her question dangles in the air.

"Maybe because I yelled at him?"

I can see from her face she don't believe me. I hate her thinking those things about Booker and I can't stand that she believes stinking old Elwood. All the words of truth keep pressing harder against my lips then finally burst out of my mouth.

"He kept touching me, Miss Charlotte. He touched me… in them places he had no right touching." I look her straight in the eye. "You know what I mean?"

"Booker?" Miss Charlotte says shaking her head in kind of a sad and kind of a satisfied way. "So it's true."

"No! I'm not talking about Booker. I'm saying about Elwood. It's Elwood that done that awful touching."

Her eyes widen, disbelief filling them.

"He wouldn't stop." The words pour out. "Every day he'd put his hands on me. He just wouldn't stop so I hit him with a frying pan and then he fired me."

The silence between us stretches the same as pulling Double Bubble gum out of my mouth until it finally breaks.

"Maisy," she says in an extra patient voice. "You must have misunderstood."

"No ma'am. I know what I know. He tried to touch me almost every day."

She coughs daintily into her curled up hand and leaves her finger right under her nose, looking at me.

"Sometimes. Sometimes girls your age are real persnickety about an accidental touch and make it out to be more than—"

I pace back and forth across her wooden floor. "It's true what I said. It wasn't accidental. You got to believe me, Miss Charlotte." I'm practically yelling. "Of all the people I thought you would believe me."

"Maisy," she looks at me pitifully. "Elwood has been helping folks in dire straits for a long time, including your Granny." Her lips press tight. "Besides he's a deacon in his church. And president of the Chamber of Commerce."

97

Her words echo in my ears, clanging like that big iron bell in the steeple of Elwood's church every Sunday morning.

"He does a lot of good in this town," she says like that's that.

We stand looking at each other, goose bumps crawling up my arms. It's real quiet except Seth's Model T rumbles and chugs up the street. I got to ask her, beg if necessary. It's my only hope.

"So. Miss Charlotte. There any chance I can have a job here? I really need one. I don't have a thing to eat and I'd work real hard." Her clock ticks. "I'm starving, Miss Charlotte."

She looks like she's thinking. Maybe she is and maybe she's not.

"I'm afraid not Maisy. It's just not a good time."

I don't know what in the damnation a good time would be. I'm living in a boxcar, starving to death and I'll never get to Detroit. I pivot on my bare toes and walk straight for the door.

"Wait," she says. I stand with my back to her as she fusses with something. I know by her footsteps she's coming up beside me. Maybe she's changed her mind. My heart lifts and I am hopeful.

"Here," she says as she hands me a pair of worn overalls and a flannel shirt. "You might need these."

I take them into my arms but I can't quite get myself to thank her. "So what did my granny say about me?"

"Said if she saw you, she'd shoot you dead."

My head busts open. This isn't the Miss Charlotte I know. The one who held me and told me everything would be all right. Who gave me a red satin square.

Clenching my teeth together tight, I open the door, walk through it and leave it hanging wide open.

I guess it's easy to be a good person until something hard to do comes along.

* * *

I pass Joe's barber shop and wonder if I should ask Mrs. Setter for a job but my heart just can't take no more pain if she refuses me. My eyes fall on the poster about the Ku Klux Klan picnic this Sunday stuck up on the rickety fence. I stop in front of it, my body shaking and my teeth gritted real tight. I read it one more time.

Placing my overalls and shirt carefully on the ground, I grab that poster with both my hands and rip it right off the fence. Without even looking around, I tear it in half, then in half again and keep going until it's in tiny pieces. I turn around, walk into the middle of the street and let them pieces flutter to the dirt not caring who is looking. Brushing one of them pieces off my front, I pick up my clothes. Something in my chest feels lighter as I head on home.

CHAPTER 17

As I make my way back to my boxcar, I realize I called it *home* in my head. That's pathetic. I break into the clearing and stand in the shade and, at first, I think I'm going to be all right. Then something like hot oil boils out of me. I might explode and blow myself to smithereens. I pick up one of them gray rocks with both hands, lift it over my head and slam it down. It smashes against one of my sitting rocks and pieces fly in every direction. A sharp splinter stings my leg.

"Take that you stupid son of a bitch Elwood." I smash another one.

"Wish this was your head, Granny. Shoot me? Right, you shriveled up, hooch drinking, broom swinging son of a bitch." Then I howl from the bottoms of my feet, the rage turning into a growl. I grab me a good size branch and whack the nearest tree trunk, screaming so loud it hurts my ears. The bark bites into my palms, hurting me. But it feels good as I whack it again and again and again. And again.

"You traitor. You dirty traitor, Miss Charlotte. How could you?" I smack another tree my arms aching with every jolt. "How could you. You're as lily-livered as the rest of them." And I slam and slam that branch against another tree, hollering my heart out 'til I run out of steam, dropping that branch on the ground. "I was a fool to trust you."

I kick the dirt.

"You damn, damn, damn stupid sons of a bitches. Every one of you go to hell."

I kick the dirt again and again, dust flying all around me until I can't even breathe, and my eyes and nostrils are full of dirt. I finally stop. I am a rag doll, my arms dangling at my sides.

I'm never getting to Detroit or anywhere.

The dust settles and I look around. *This* is what I call home? In the goddamned son of a bitch woods? In a goddamned son of a bitch broken down boxcar? Turning slowly, I spit at anything in front of me, specks of saliva hitting me in the face. I clench my fist and throw a punch into the air, swinging my body clear around and there's Promise, leaning against the poplar tree. Her arms are folded over her chest and her eyes hold me, one eyebrow slightly cocked.

"Seems like Miss Charlotte broke your trust," she says in a raspy whisper.

First all I hear is silence. Then my body collapses, right into the dirt, my bones are rubber and a hole burns where my heart's supposed to be. Ugly gags choke out of my throat. I can't stop.

Promise is right. I was trusting her, thinking she would help me. Them retches keep choking and choking out of me along with every bit of trust I ever had in me. A long, low moan crawls out of my belly.

Without my hardly knowing it, Promise's arms are around me, holding me tight. She's whispering to me. I can't understand the words, but they're speaking right to my broken heart. She rocks me and hums what sounds like a lullaby my ma used to sing me. *Hush little baby, don't say a word....* Finally I can breathe but I don't ever want her to let go of me. I never been held in quite this way since my mother left, and I sure don't want it to end.

"Think we can wash up your face?" she whispers. "Come on. Lean on me." We stand together and she leads me over to my bucket.

"Sit on that rock," she says as she pulls the bucket closer to me. "Just you sit. I'll take care of your face. You got soap?"

I shake my head no.

"It don't matter." She stands in front of me and leans down dipping her hands into the water. Then she holds that water in the palms of her hands for me to place my face into. I do and her callused hands gently rub my face. She takes the hem of her dress and wipes around my eyes, then dips for more water. Her fingers follow the contours of my face, around my cheeks, my mouth and chin. After the third time she holds my chin in her hand and, bending down, looks at me.

"There now. You're looking much better."

"I am." I start to pull away but her hand moves to my cheek, the flat of her palm lightly holding me there. I look down at the ground, all the while my heart's leaping out of my chest, and my skin's dancing all over my whole body.

"Maisy," she says. I look up. Her face is so close to mine our noses almost touch. Her eyes are real scared, but at the same time they're asking. I nod, my head barely moving. Then slowly, ever so slowly our lips touch. My breath wings out of my body. I lean into the softness of her lips. Both her hands cradle my face and I can't breathe.

She sits down next to me and we grin at each other. We just sit there grinning. Grinning with the sun shining on our faces.

"We're in big trouble," she says, laughing.

"How can something as sweet as your kiss be trouble?" I ask, knowing for sure we are.

CHAPTER 18

I hold the overalls Miss Charlotte gave me out in front of me, her voice echoing in my head. But I need some pants to wear since mine are covered with dirt. I still hate her as I slip my feet in the legs, put on my old work shirt, rolling the sleeves up above my elbows, and pull up the bib, latching the clips over the little buttons. While I'm changing, Promise has been poking around my things, picking up the tiny picture lying on my table.

"That your pa?" she says squinting then looking back and forth from the picture to my face.

"Yeah. I never knew him, but I like to think he remembers me somehow."

"He's dead, ain't he?"

"Don't you think the dead can remember?" I ask.

"Never thought about it."

"I bet your ma remembers you."

She looks at me for a second then gently puts the picture down. Her long, slender finger lightly skims across the gold surface of my mother's compact.

"What's this?" She sets it in the palm of her hand.

"It's all I got left in the world of my ma," I say as I hold her hand with one hand and with the other unsnap the clasp, lifting the top. I turn the mirror toward her face.

"Lordamercy." Her mouth falls open. "That's me?" She touches the mirror with her finger. "I ain't seen a mirror since I was, maybe, ten years old. I only seen myself passing by the storefront windows. And once

I snuck into Miss Lizzie's bedroom and peeked in her dresser mirror." She caresses her cheeks and lips then runs her finger along each eyebrow, moving her eyes up real close to the mirror.

"That's what I look like now?"

"You're beautiful," I say, my mouth hanging open a tiny bit.

She takes the compact out of my hand and holds it close to her face, moving it around, looking at herself from side to side.

"Look at my hair, though. Real scrabbly looking." She tugs at her braids. "Gotta do something about that." She holds the mirror up close to her eyes again. "Um. Not too bad." She smiles real wide at herself in the mirror.

I notice how one front tooth crosses over the other one ever so slightly. It seems like a little treasure she just gave me.

"Maisy? Promise?" That's Booker hollering for us.

"Be right there," I yell back.

"I got fish for dinner."

Promise closes the compact, laying it on my table. She reaches for my hand and gives it a squeeze then climbs out of the boxcar. I gather up my dirty clothes, put them in a pile to wash in the river and follow her.

Booker's holding up a string of three fish already gutted. My mouth waters.

"I brought these for dinner. Get a fire going." He looks mighty proud of himself.

Promise and I gather twigs then light the fire while Booker finds sticks sturdy enough to hold the fish over the flames. He slips each stick into a fish's mouth, pushing it into the tail so's it don't slip around.

Sitting on rocks, we hold our fish over the fire, the skin crackling and juices sizzling into the embers. The smoky smell fills the air and makes my stomach growl. Booker's smile wraps around me like they were his arms, pulling me close. My breath stutters and my stomach flip flops as I look down, studying on the fire like my life depended on it. I have to talk to him. Especially because of Promise and me. Because of whatever's happening between us.

"So Maisy," Booker says, leaning up close to me. His arm grazes mine. He lets it rest against me, his skin pressing against my arm. "I been thinking I want to know my whole name. You can teach me that, right?"

"Sure." I hand Promise my fish, shifting my body a little away from Booker. I write FREEMAN in the dirt with a twig. "Which of them letters you know already?"

Booker points to the R and E. "And I know the A, too." I am captured by the warmth of his smile. I shift and point at the F. Promise makes a tiny cough.

"That's an F," I say. Then one by one, I teach him the other letters until he picks up a twig with his hand not holding his fish and writes in the dirt, saying each letter out loud. B-O-OK-E-R F-R-E-E-M-A-N. He beams like he won a million dollars, the fire reflecting in his proud eyes.

"Now I can sign my whole name." He points to his last name. "My great granddaddy picked that name when he got freed from slavery. He was a couple of years older than me."

I try to imagine what it's like to come from a slave, but I can't. I have no idea.

He stares into the woods, biting on his bottom lip. He taps the twig against the letters of his name.

"Now I don't have to mark no X like my great granddaddy and granddaddy did and our Pa still does." His eyes hold Promise and both sit absolutely still. "Now I can write our name."

Promise hands me both our sticks with fish. She stands then squats by Booker's name. She runs her fingers along the lines of each letter in Freeman, whispering the letter names to herself. After she done it four times, she looks at Booker.

"Freeman," she says. "Promise Freeman."

Something real important passes between them that I don't think I could ever begin to understand.

CHAPTER 19

n my dream Promise is dancing with my ma who's singing, her voice floating in my ears, when someone calls my name. I jump so hard my hand bangs against my table, pain shooting up my arm. I can hardly take a breath.

"Maisy. Are you awake?" Hazy light seeps through the door of the boxcar.

I fling myself out of bed, clutching my quilt in front of me.

"It's me. Promise. I'm coming in." The curtain we finally put back up last night for privacy moves sideways and I see her fingers holding it. She grins up at me.

"I couldn't wait 'til tonight to see you."

The shadows in the boxcar are still deep and the clearing behind Promise is a hazy gray. The sun's not even over the horizon. It's practically the middle of the night.

My toes tingle and a ripple of electricity zings down my body seeing her face with that crooked smile.

She stands on the top of the piled rocks, leaning through the doorway.

"Maybe I shouldn't of come," she says. "But I brought you some soap."

I stand, dropping my quilt, and reach for her with both hands pulling her all the way inside the boxcar.

"I was dreaming and then you came true," I say as I hold her close to me, my arms tight around her waist.

"I hurried with my chores 'cuz I just had to see you before I went to Miss Lizzie's. I couldn't go all day without...." She studies my face and I know what she was going to say.

"Without touching me." I pull her closer. "Me too."

Her arms slide around my neck, our cheeks soft against each other and we hold each other, swaying ever so slightly. It seems a long time that we hold each other but it's still not enough to soak in the feeling of her against me. Our arms loosen and we back up to look at each other.

"I can't believe this," I say sliding my hand along her cheek. She takes my face into her hands and, I don't know who started it and it sure don't matter, but we're kissing each other. Soft kisses. Long kisses. Kisses on our eyelids. Kisses with tongues. Kisses on our necks. Kisses. Kisses. Kisses. Exploring our bodies. Shivering with joy.

Gently, I push her to arm's length. "You know Miss Charlotte would be telling us this is wrong."

"And old Elwood would be preaching at us and beating on us at the same time." Anger snakes into Promise's voice. "I know they'd say we're sinners."

She pulls me closer, her eyes reaching clear into my heart. "But when I'm kissing you, it feels more right than anything I ever done." Her voice is stronger than I ever heard it.

"Me too." I whisper. "I can't keep my mind on anything but you. Not a job. Not Elwood. Not even Detroit." I pull her tight up against me.

"I feel like I just woke up from the dead," she says, her finger tracing the contours of my face. She laughs. "Maisy Wharton you still got dirt all over your neck and in your ears from all that kicking and hollering. You need a bath."

"But what about us being white and colored?" I ask. "That's what's making everybody in town so crazy about Booker and me. And it's not even true." I touch her cheek. "But it is true about you and me."

"You're right. It would make them lose their minds. But with both of us being girls I bet they'd never even guess. They're so stupid." She pulls me up close and I wrap my arms around her. I can feel her heart beating against mine.

Then she pushes me out to arm's length.

"We can't let Booker know. Not yet, anyway." Promise says. "I wouldn't hurt him for the world."

"We can't tell nobody." I say. "Not a single soul."

* * *

After Promise left, the day went right down hill. I ate one of my apples for breakfast, rearranged my stuff—again—and finally decided to take the soap Promise brought me and go to the river to wash my dirty clothes and me. She says there's dirt all over my neck and in my ears.

At first I get goose bumps from the water being cold but it feels good once I get used to it. I bathe in my dress because I don't know who might be coming along in them woods. They're surely big woods, but every once in a while, someone comes hunting or just poking around. But even with the dress, I manage to get that soap up into my armpits, around my neck and all those other places that get smelly. I dip my head way back into the water and decide to use the soap on my hair as well. My Amelia Earhart hair as Booker says. My breath stutters. How will I ever tell him we don't feel the same ways about each other? I can't think of any words that wouldn't hurt him.

I float on my back and wonder what Booker would think about me and Promise. Probably jealous. Definitely sinners. Not because he's mean like Elwood but it's what anybody would say. Even part of me feels that way. Only when I'm with Promise, it don't make any sense that our loving is a sin. It's more like a blessing.

Putting my feet down, I stumble to the shore, slipping on the rocks. I shake the water off me as best I can then pick up that flannel shirt Miss Charlotte gave me and use it for a towel.

"Good a use as any except maybe for wiping my behind," I mutter, my teeth clenched. Ever since Miss Charlotte carried me away from my mother's body, I believed that maybe she'd be like a ma and we would have a home together. She said I could always count on her. Heat spreads across my face. But no use getting mad all over again so I grab my dirty clothes, the soap and stand up to my knees in the river and scrub the dirt out of them. I rub the rough denim against itself then rinse it. My wet dress clings to me reminding me of Promise's hands sliding along my skin.

No point going back to the clearing to sit there, doing nothing. I spread my wet clothes out on a couple big boulders in the sun and spread that flannel shirt on the ground. I stretch out. The sunshine warms my skin and dries my dress while I think on Promise and me. Prickles creep through my body as her face rises in my mind.

"How can what we feel be wrong?" I laugh looking around. I must be crazy talking to myself. Picking up a stone, I toss it and it skitters along the rocky shore.

"I don't want trouble for Promise if anybody finds out. And I surely don't want to hurt Booker." I say, almost like I'm praying.

But.... But. I don't even have the right words. All's I can say is I'm different now. Somehow I finally know who I am. Every speck of me tells me that this is right. Even if people say it's wrong. A huge wave of heat crashes through my body, pressing at my ribs and filling me up to the edges of my skin.

This is who I am.

What I don't know is how me and Promise — and maybe Booker, too — are going to get out of these woods and find our way to Detroit.

Something swishes and it sounds like someone's tramping in the woods. I sit up real fast and pull the flannel shirt over my dress. Tugging my wet denims on, I stand up and look around. Why didn't I bring my pointy scissors or something for protection. I don't see nothing, but I still hear footsteps tramping not too far away. All I can think of is that it's Elwood. With his gun.

I lean down and grab two river stones. Each one fitting snuggly into my hands. Maybe I should get me a good solid branch instead. I look around and don't see nothing that would be of use. I'll go with the stones. The rustling stops.

"Howdy," a man's voice says from somewhere behind me. I whirl around ready to smash him in the head. Nobody's in back of me. My eyes dart every which way until I see two colored men standing on top the river bank far enough away for me to run if I need to. They're real shabby looking and one's got a bundle slung over his back. They've got to be hoboes and I know they are out looking for trouble. That's what they do. Especially colored hoboes. I lick my lips and squeeze the rocks real hard. I know nobody else's around and I'm a good mile from the boxcar. It's just me and them. With me being white I hope they're not like those boys in Scottsboro.

"Nice day," one of them says. I keep my eyes stuck right on them as I inch my way down river, stumbling on a good size rock.

"Don't mean to scare ya'," the other one hollers. "Just passing through."

Nausea fills my nose the same as when Elwood touches me. My knees get wobbly, but I keep moving slowly. I watch every step they take, ready to run.

"Just on our way to the train track to catch us a train," the one with the bundle yells.

I shouldn't of come here by myself. Stupid. Stupid.

"Mighty nice day to be walking through these woods." The other one shouts.

Right. I know about them hoboes.

The one with the bundle waves and they disappear into the woods towards the tracks. The sound of their tramping finally fades and I drop each rock to the ground.

One at a time.

I always thought hoboes were just plain bad. Seems it not always easy knowing what's true of another person.

But seeing them reminds me I don't want to be no hobo living in a boxcar. I got to get myself out of here and on to Detroit. And Promise, too.

CHAPTER 20

P romise brought me corn bread that looked mighty good, but when she heard about my day at the river, she grabbed my hand, pulling me through the woods and back to the water.

"I been sweating like a pig working at Miss Lizzie's all day," she says splashing into the water. "I need to be in this river to wash off all them complaints of hers." Slipping under the surface she springs up, sputtering and shaking water off the end of her braids. Then she dunks herself again.

I watch her and feel sunshine gleaming out of my eyes like I just discovered America. She pops up next to me and splashes a big handful of water all over me.

"You," I act mad and chase her, grabbing her shoulder and pushing her under the surface. She stands up and we both laugh, clutching at each other, trying to push the other one under the water. She stops and looks at me real innocent like.

"Come and give me a hug, I ain't had my hug yet."

I know she's fooling me, but I just can't stop myself from going close to her. Course she wraps her arms around me and pulls us both under the water. Sputtering to the surface, we giggle because we both look like water rats. Before I know it though, her hands are holding my face and pulling my lips against hers. Then. Then our wet bodies are pressed together and the world tilts from the pleasure of feeling her up against me.

I could have stayed like that all night and all day, but we both got goose bumps from the breeze. We make little ripples as we walk through the water, holding hands, until we get to the rocky shore. I wrap the flannel shirt around her because it's still warm from sitting in the sun, and I put on my work shirt with the long sleeves.

"I can't wait for your corn bread," I say. "How about we open a can of hash to go with it?"

Promise slings her arm over my shoulder. "You know, we could live here like this."

My heart jitters at that possibility. We could build ourselves a little shack out of the box car. Except we'd still be poor and hungry and on the lookout for Elwood and his kind. I got to keep to my plan of heading for Detroit.

But how can I have Promise and Detroit?

* * *

"Is Booker coming?" I ask cranking my can opener around the top of the can of hash.

Promise looks over her shoulder from where she squats lighting the fire. Her lips press together and her eyes harden.

"What's wrong?"

"My pa. That's what." She strikes a match against a rock. "He got crazy drunk last night like always, yelling at Booker 'bout what everybody saying."

"What?"

She bites her lip and leans toward the fire with her match. I wait.

"Pa tole Booker he ain't going nowheres unless it's fishing or delivering with him." The match burns out so she tries another one. "Because of you and him. Those lies. He don't want to get smacked again so he's lying low for a bit." The fire lights and she tosses the match into the flames. She studies on that fire real fierce.

"He figures a coupla days and Pa will forget." She blows gently on the fire then looks at me sheepishly. "I was so happy to see you, I forgot to say all that to you."

That familiar jiggle ripples through my stomach.

We both freeze at the faint baying of a coon hound that floats through the woods. Listening, our bodies rigid, we wait for what seems a million years. Finally there's another bay, but we can barely hear it. We collapse into each other knowing they are moving away from us.

Promise blows the fire to life again. When the hash is warmed, we lean against each other and I hand her the can for her turn to dig out a finger full of hash.

"This cornbread is the best I ever ate," I say.

She grins and breaks off a piece of hers and puts it into my mouth. I nibble her finger. She nudges me with her shoulder and hands me the hash.

"You know, Maisy Wharton, I might be falling for you." She ducks her head and bites her lip.

"I know the feeling, Promise Freeman."

Before I know what's happening, we leave that can of hash sitting right by the burned out fire and we climb up them rocks, push that curtain aside and tumble into the boxcar, landing on my leaf mattress holding each other so tight I don't think we'll ever let go.

We don't even talk, but somehow our low moans guide us. My fingers are on fire as I trace the curves of her hips, and belly and breasts.

Then we are lost in each other's magic.

CHAPTER 21

The early morning sky is dark as coal and threatening to rain. Every once in a while, thunder rumbles in the distance. But me and Promise don't care. We're together. Last night I begged her to stay, but she said her pa'd beat her bloody if she didn't come home. Unless he was passed out cold. But we couldn't take a chance. So she left. Then this morning she came almost skipping through the woods as the sun was barely rising.

"I can't stay too long," she says sitting on my table which we cleared off and I'm kneeling behind her, braiding her hair. "I got away cuz I don't got Miss Lizzie today but I got to get home before Pa do or he'll have my hide."

"Hold your head still. It's hard enough to braid your hair anyway."

She holds up my mother's compact aiming the mirror at the new hairstyle I'm making for her. I put my hand over the mirror.

"I want to surprise you."

She leans her head way back, looking at me with them eyes. I bend and kiss her lips.

"Oh, don't start that or I'll never get my hair fixed up."

I'm making two braids and figuring out how to tie them close to her head. Maybe on top. Or maybe along the nape of her neck. I stand up and try each one, holding the braids and leaning in front to see how it looks.

"I been thinking to talk to Mrs. Setter," I say smiling at them big eyes staring at me. I kiss her mouth and cheeks and forehead. She leans forward and her arms reach for me.

"Wait. I got to finish your hair." I tuck in a loose clump of hair. "So I think I could work in her candy store. She helped me out when Elwood...." I decide I like the braids on top and grab one of them red polka dotted ties and work it through the braids to get them to stay on top her head.

"What are you doing?" Her fingers creep across her head.

"Just wait." I laugh. "So if she gives me a job, I can get enough money to get us to Detroit."

"Us?"

"Yep. Us. You're stuck with me now, Promise Freeman." Her eyes go soft and her smile spreads across her face in the compact mirror she holds up.

"Booker too?"

"If he wants," I say. "I'm sneaking into town tomorrow. I'm hopeful she'll say yes."

"She'll just blab to Elwood that you're there," she says.

"I don't think so. I saw the look on her face the other day. And she helped me pick up my groceries with everybody looking on and doing nothing."

I tug at the braids on top of her head to be sure they'll stay stuck there for a while.

"Now look," I say. My hands rest on her shoulders.

She holds the compact up close then straightens her arm, still looking in that little mirror.

"I look like I just growed up five years older." Wonder fills her voice.

"You're beautiful," my hand skims along her arm and she carefully sets the compact on the table. She stands and pulls me against her body and then we're on the mattress again, kissing and holding each other's faces gentle like precious treasures.

115

When her hand reaches under my raggedy dress, my heart flings my body into pure pleasure. It's like we're on one of them carousels I seen in *Life* magazine spinning and whirling, lights flashing and feelings swirling. And then, I don't know how much later, here we are, holding each other tight. Every part of our bodies touches, head to toe. She whispers in my ear.

"I don't ever want to stop doing this with you. I ain't loved nobody, except Booker, since my ma died. But Maisy Wharton, I think I love you."

I pull her tighter against me. "Promise. Loving you like this is coming home. I never had a real one since my ma, but you are my home now."

She snuggles tight against me.

"I wish Booker had someone to love like I love you," she whispers into my shoulder. "Pa's so hard on him and he deserves to be loved like this."

She lifts her head, a glint in her eye. "But he can't have you. You're taken."

Booker touching my Amelia Earhart hair and wanting to hold my hand in the movies flits through my mind. That's too hard to think about so I burrow my face into Promise's warm neck.

CHAPTER 22

I t rained all day, only clearing late in the afternoon. Mrs. Setter'd be closing her shop by the time it took me to get to town, so instead, I gather twigs and branches and spread them on the ground to dry them out. I'm hoping tonight's fire won't smoke. The clouds are moving north and the sun's setting in the west making a double rainbow spread clear across the sky. Must be for me and Promise. I never thought I'd be so crazy about a girl. At Elwood's the men laugh and say bad things about two girls. I don't know if there's a name for us since I only heard the nasty ones. But our loving don't feel nasty. I sure hope she comes, but it's late, so probably not. The sun's down below the tree tops.

Just as I decide she won't come, she bursts through the bushes. That sunshine on her face makes it glow. We grab each other, holding and holding each other tight, just swaying and hugging, feeling our bodies pressed together head to toe.

"Look," I point at the rainbows. "For us."

"I couldn't run fast enough to get here," she kisses me on the mouth, long and lingering. Finally we got to breathe. "And Booker's gonna sneak out tonight to see you after Pa's drunk himself into the ground. So you get me until after dark because then Booker and me can walk home together."

"I really miss him," I say. "I can't wait." I squirm a little inside about me being with Promise when he's liking me.

"Do you and Booker ever talk about, you know, him liking me?"

Her arms fall away from me and, for a second, I am bereft.

"I ain't ever said anything. I'm afraid he'll ask what difference does it make to me and then I'll tell him about us." She bites her lip. "Then he'll go crazy."

"Me too. Except it don't feel right not making it clear about liking him as a friend but not a *boyfriend*." I hold her hand, playing with her fingers. "Most probably though, don't you think he's over that by now?"

"I wouldn't be so sure." She presses her lips together. "He talks about you all the time. I think you got to tell him. He'd hate that you were tricking him somehow."

"You're right. He gets that hurt look every time he makes a hint and I ignore him."

Squeezing her hand, I lead her toward the boxcar. She climbs the stones and limbs to the boxcar ahead of me. I can already imagine her soft skin under the palms of my hands.

"I'll tell him tonight," I say. "When he comes."

* * *

Darkness settles around us. We crouch over the fire pit and touch each other's hand or face, our bodies still sing as we try to get the damp wood lit. Finally with enough paper, the fire lights, casting shadows, though it smokes like crazy.

"I brought some bread I baked yesterday," Promise holds up a big chunk wrapped in newspaper.

"I got another can of hash. How's that sound?"

I lean against her, our shoulders soaking into each other where we touch. We share the hash and rip off pieces of fresh bread. I don't think I could be more happy. Even in Detroit. Not that I'm not still going. But right this moment it's pretty much paradise making me wonder if living here could be our lives. No. We got to get to Detroit. Eventually.

I pat Promise's hair up on top her head. "You like it this way?"

"I do. My braids ain't flopping in my face all the time."

118

"What'd Booker say?"

"Said I look mighty fancy." She wiggles her shoulders all la-ti-da. The crows squawk, arguing over a branch for the night.

Something crashes in the woods. Could be an animal, but it makes too much noise shuffling through the dried leaves.

"Must be Booker," Promise says. She presses against me for a moment. "This is 'bout the time Pa'd fall asleep with his head in his dinner plate."

The footsteps get closer and I'm sure Booker can't see us through the woods yet so I pull Promise up against me for one last quick kiss before he gets here. As I'm giving her a squeeze I hear Elwood's voice stab through the air.

"Look at them two fornicators. Right there by the fire."

The fire? I forgot about the fire and people being able to see us.

But Elwood? That's impossible. Booker promised Elwood wouldn't come again.

We let each other go and stand up searching for the direction where he's coming from. Beau barks, then bays, meaning he's spotted a raccoon.

"Look," Promise points. Elwood's got a torch. The light from the fire waving in the air glints off the barrel of a shotgun that dangles from someone's arms.

"You think they're coming to kill us?" Fear crawls out of her throat.

"No! They must be rabbit or raccoon hunting because they got Beau."

"Booker said…" she stutters.

They tromp closer and closer.

Elwood yells. "Lookee over there. Ain't no 'coon but we caught them two varmits in the act." Hog laughs a real nasty laugh. They head toward the clearing. The torch flickers through the trees and Beau trots toward us, his tail wagging.

"What are we gonna do?" Promise's voice rises. I stand and grab the bucket, dowsing the fire. Steam sizzles around us.

"Quick. Get in the boxcar," I say. "You got to hide."

"Not without you."

They're almost to the clearing now. Fear rattles in my bones.

"Now, please. You remember the hole in the floor? Pull back that rug and climb under the boxcar and don't move."

"But."

"Elwood won't actually shoot me. My granny's his cousin. He's trying to scare me. But you. Go. Now."

Elwood and Hog tramp through the underbrush into the clearing. Beau lopes toward me, his tail wagging like crazy and his ears flapping. Looks like a smile on his face.

"We gonna teach them a lesson. Once and for all." Elwood's voice slices through the night as they approach the clearing. The torch lurches in the dark.

Promise climbs inside the boxcar and I stand at the top of my stairs in front of the curtain as the men crash into the clearing. Hog is holding the torch and he's meaner than Elwood, if that's possible. Out of the corner of my eye I see Promise pull back the rug and toss the tar paper aside.

"Climb down there," I whisper desperate for her to be safe. She stands there holding the rug, jaw set, waiting for me.

Elwood swaggers across the clearing and kicks at our fire. Wet ashes scatter. He turns and walks toward the boxcar. Stopping, he stands, rocking on his heels, at the bottom of my steps. He knows there's nobody around to stop him this time.

"I was right. Caught you two in the act of fornicating." Elwood waves the gun at me. Hooch reeks from his mouth and seeps out of his pores. "Come outta there boy!" he yells. "Stop hiding behind a girl's skirt."

I realize Elwood mistook Promise for Booker.

"He's gone," I say. "Ran when he seen you." I wave my hand in the direction of the river.

"He ain't gone," says Hog. "He's hiding like a lily-livered chicken in that there boxcar."

Elwood leans in even closer to me. I slip under the curtain then peek over the top in the space where the sun shines through in the mornings. Not that the curtain will stop any bullets but it's harder for Elwood

120

to know what we're doing and I can keep my eye on him. I hiss over my shoulder to Promise.

"Get them bottles and cans and anything hard. We got to get them idiots out of here." I turn quickly and tip my table top up, dumping all my things onto the quilt and gather the four rocks holding up my table and pile them by the door.

She brings an arm full of them bottles, handing one to me. I fling it out the door aiming straight for Elwood's head. It misses and shatters against a boulder. Promise puts the bottles by our feet except for one which she wings at Hog. It hits him in the shoulder. He yelps.

"Stay behind the wood. Don't stand in the door. Elwood's got a gun," I whisper. "I don't think he'll use it. But just in case."

I throw one of them rocks at Elwood. This time it hits him in the leg. Promise hands me something hard and bumpy. I look down and it's a potato. I aim at Elwood's head, hitting him in the ear.

"You fornicating son of a bitch," he yells. "I'm gonna give you both what you deserve." He lunges toward the boxcar, rifle raised to his shoulder. Promise and I both throw bottles and rocks, not waiting to see if they make their mark. Elwood grunts then swears.

Then he fires. The curtain between us rips right up the middle.

I'm so shocked I can't move. He *is* meaning to kill us.

But he knows me. I'm related to him.

Evidently it don't matter that he's Granny's cousin.

"Promise," I whisper. "You got to get out. Now. Please."

"No."

Elwood lowers his rifle, standing real still for a minute. I'm thinking he'll leave now having given us a good scare and all.

"No use wasting bullets, Hog. Light that car on fire. We'll burn 'em both up."

"No bodies, huh?" Hog chuckles and steps toward us. "No one will ever know."

"They're going to the sulfur fires of Hell anyway." Elwood's face wobbles with the reflections of the torch.

121

I look around frantically for something heavier to throw. My eyes light on the can of beans. I grab the can and wing it at Hog's head hoping he drops the torch.

Hog grunts as the can whacks his chest, but he still throws himself toward us, waving his torch. He reaches out and my curtain bursts into flames.

"Promise. Get down that hole and run into the woods. I'm coming right behind you. Go."

She looks at me.

"Go."

She throws her last bottle out the door and heads through the hole. I only have one bottle and one potato left. I throw the bottle through the flames, not knowing if I hit anybody. Seeing my stuff scattered on my quilt, I bundle it up as best I can. My money sock bangs against my chest. Sweat drips off the end of my nose. I stand and, with all my might, I throw that potato hoping it cracks Elwood smack in the head breaking his skull wide open.

I'm scooting my legs through the hole when I hear a voice.

"Promise! Maisy! Where are you? What's happening?"

"There you are." Elwood sneers. "You white tramp fornicator."

"How in the hell you get out of that boxcar?" Hog hollers, the screeching of crows drowning out his voice.

Promise grabs my leg, pulling hard on me making whimpering sounds.

"It's Booker," she whispers hysteria rises in her voice as I settle next to her. I can hardly see through the tangles of bushes, but it sure is Booker.

"Hold that torch up close to his face, Hog. I want to get me a good look at this bastard's face. A real good look before somebody *accidently* shoots him." His voice drips with slime.

"Run Booker," I scream. "Run."

Elwood looks toward the burning curtain. "Neither one you sinners running nowhere, missy. You ain't getting away this time." He laughs. He must think I'm still in the boxcar.

Promise gasps for breath. Terror radiates off her body.

"Booker," I yell with all my might. "Run. Get in the woods."

Hog lurches for Booker and grabs him by the neck of his shirt. It rips as Booker struggles.

"We don't go for trash like you around here. Fornicating with our white girls, even if they're tramps." Elwood raises his rifle, resting the butt against his shoulder. He aims straight at Booker.

Deacon of his church and president of the Chamber of Commerce pounds through my mind.

Promise and I watch Booker struggle loose from Hog and dash for the woods, her hand squeezes my arm so hard it hurts.

Elwood pulls the trigger and there's a single shot.

Then another.

Promise and I freeze, our bodies rigid. Flash. I'm in Elwood's café. Flash. My mother's blue eyes fly wide open. Flash. Sheriff Judd's lip sneers under his black mustache. Flash. My mother's mouth makes a perfect O.

Promise buries her face against my shoulder.

We can't see Booker. Prob'ly Elwood missed and Booker's hiding in the woods.

"Throw that torch in the boxcar Hog. We can't have that tramp yapping her mouth all over town. It'll burn like dry tinder," says Elwood. "And let's get ourselves out of here before someone discovers the *accident*."

Their harsh laughter follows them into the darkness. Seems like Sheriff Judd is traipsing beside them.

* * *

Promise and I claw our way out of the briars to get to Booker. We can't see him from here, but there hasn't been a sound. That don't mean a thing. Booker will probably be sitting there with a big old grin across his face, laughing to himself for faking dead and tricking Elwood.

"I knowed he got himself into the woods. I just knowed it," Promise chants under her breath.

She is a wild person flailing through the underbrush. I'm right behind her as she clears the brush and stands up. Raging flames from the boxcar light up the woods. Shadows jump all over. Them dried leaves in my mattresses must of caught fire real fast. Flames lick their way up the trunk of a couple of trees. Sap sizzles in the night. I sure hope Elwood and Hog are truly gone.

"I see him," Promise breaks into a run then falls to her knees next to Booker, who lies flat, face down, on the ground. The flames flicker and jump. His eyes are closed. I squat beside him and put my hand on his back, feeling for a heartbeat. Nothing. Except my hand is wet. Confused I hold it up and something real dark covers my hand, a single line of blood crawls down my wrist. My stomach lurches, bile climbs up my throat.

"Turn him over," Promise screams.

We tug him onto his back, the reflection of the flames jump across his face and his eyes are open in surprise. He don't move one tiny bit. His arms lay limp by his sides. I put my ear to his chest no longer caring if his blood covers me. I deserve it. No heartbeat. Promise lays her cheek up close to his nose, her face stricken so I know she don't feel his breath.

She shakes him. "Booker. Booker. Wake up." She shakes him some more, screaming his name over and over.

"He's dead," I say.

Promise slaps my face, howling then pounds on my chest with her fists. "No he ain't. He ain't." She shakes him again. "Booker. Please Booker."

Next I know she's lying on the ground, her arms cradle his head and her body squeezes up against his. Then a high-pitched, ear-splitting wail that sounds like it comes from the middle of the earth fills the night, but it's coming out of Promise. She's rocks him and her keening slices through the eerie darkness.

I want to lie on the ground and wrap my arms around her, but I'm crouched like an animal on all fours. I can't stop vomiting, one heave after another, bitter bile, vomit and spit dribble off my chin.

The brown splotch on Elwood's floor sits in my head.
I can't cry.

* * *

"We're not just leaving him lying here." Promise's voice rises hysterically. "Even for a minute."

"We can't carry him all the way to your Pa's. Through the woods. In the dark."

She growls at me, her eyes flicker in the dying flames of the boxcar. I know there's no reasoning with her. She's gone someplace else right now.

I stand, shoulders slumped, thinking. I know I got to figure this out. Promise surely can barely breathe right now.

"Here's what we're gonna do," I say, my voice steady and low. "You put one of his arms over your shoulder and I'll do the same. Then only his feet'll be dragging. How's that?"

We hang him between us on our shoulders. I got my bundle in the hand not holding Booker's arm. Both of his feet drag behind us, him being taller than both of us, as we stagger through the dark woods. His head bobs from the joggling and every time it moves I think he's about to say something, 'specially with them eyes being wide open. Once we get away from the burning boxcar, the only light is the quarter moon. Not much light, almost pitch black, but Promise can lead us through these woods sleepwalking.

Somehow we stumble along the trails. We stop to lift Booker up higher on our shoulders when he slips down.

"Maisy," Promise's wail ricochets through the darkness. "I can't carry him no more."

"You can. I know you can," I gasp. "I'll hold you both up."

I don't know how I'll do that. I can barely hold myself up.

We struggle through the dark woods. Once we have to lay him down. Our backs are breaking, but Promise won't have no resting. We

125

don't say a word to each other as we're stumbling, step after step, carrying Booker. That's it. The only sounds in the dark night are Booker's feet dragging on the ground, us grunting and panting, some varmint in the underbrush. And Promise's soft keening.

I know I should wail and fall on the ground, tears rolling out my eyes. But I am numb. Like everything inside me froze. Just like with my ma. Only difference is that Elwood pulled that trigger this time. I still got Booker's blood dried between my fingers. Sour bile lurches into my throat every once in awhile.

Finally we see the bunch of shacks where Promise lives. A few windows got some light shining like someone's still burning a candle, but most are dark. Promise silently points at her house and we carry Booker home.

CHAPTER 23

I t's dark as pitch as we struggle through the doorway holding Booker tight so as not to drop him. Promise leads the way, me stumbling over my feet. Her pa snores real loud so for now, he's asleep. We get through a tiny room that maybe is the main room and haul Booker through a doorway. I can't see a thing, but Promise bends down and so I do too. Seems she lays Booker onto something.

"That's his bed," she says. "I'll get the lamp." She fades into the darkness. The smell of kerosene fills the air mixed with sulfur from the match being struck. Dim light falls through the doorway of the room where we laid Booker down and I see another narrow bed squeezed into this room. Then my eyes fall on the dark stains all up and down my clothes. For half a second I could be a crazy person writhing on the floor, screaming. But I can't. I won't. *Oh Booker.*

My whole body's numb, but I got to help Promise.

"Pa." I hear Promise and I walk toward her. "Pa, wake up." She's shakes him but he's not moving all sprawled out on a wooden bed barely big enough for two.

"Pa," she yells still shaking and shaking him. I stand beside her and see that her clothes and arms are stained with Booker's blood. That same stink that comes off Elwood's breath floats in the air around her pa.

"Wha..," he finally groans.

"Wake up. Booker's dead. You got to wake up," she screams in his face.

He rolls onto his back his eyes not really focused anywhere, and he don't say anything. Promise grabs the front of his shirt and shakes him.

"Booker's dead. Do you hear me?" She puts her face up real close to her Pa's. "He's dead," she screams so loud and shrill you could of heard it clear in town.

His eyes open, looking at Promise. Then they wander and land on me. He sits up rubbing his face in his hands then looks back at Promise.

"Booker's dead?"

"Elwood kilt him," Promise hisses. "He shot him in the back."

"Where's Booker now?" he asks, the slur gone from his voice.

Promise motions toward what must be their bedroom. For the first time she sees Booker's blood covering her arm and down her dress. That keening comes from deep inside her and she falls into her Pa's arms. He holds her, both of them rock and cry.

I don't know what to do with myself so I back away and stand by the wood stove looking down at my cut-out shoes.

* * *

I wait for Promise and her pa in the main room. I want, with all my heart, to help Promise, but I am frozen. Inside my head, wails bounce against my skull and my chest hurts so bad with tears that won't come out. If I did cry, I know I'd fly into a million tiny bits and never come back.

Pa charges out of Booker's bedroom jabbing his finger at me, hollering at the top of his lungs.

"You did this." He swoops closer, his finger poked at my face. "You kilt him. I heard what them peoples say."

"Booker and me, we never—"

"All over town I hear 'bout you and Booker. You knowed better. You knowed what would happen." He grabs the front of my dress, shaking me back and forth, my head snapping. "*You* kilt him."

Promise pulls at his arms. "Pa. That ain't true. Let her go."

He bats her backward and keeps shaking me. "You kilt him. You might as well of pulled the trigger."

"It's not true," I shout struggling to get out of his grip. Promise yanks at his shirt.

"Pa. Let her go. It ain't her fault."

He pulls me up real close, my dress chokes me so I can hardly breathe. The callused fingers from his other hand curl around my throat, the hard skin bites into my neck.

"You kilt him," he screams in his crazy voice. "You gonna pay. You kilt him." His fingers tighten and I gasp for breath, my lungs burn.

"Pa. Stop." She tugs and yanks on his arm.

His fingers squeeze even harder and little stars flash in my eyes and everything starts to go dark. I can't hear Promise. Where did she go?

"Please," I whisper with the last little bit of breath I have. And then his fingers loosen. He tumbles to the floor, lying there, still as a stick.

I breathe and breathe sucking in air as fast as I can keeping my eye on him in case he reaches for me again. But he don't. He lies there, not even a twitch.

I look up and there's Promise, a split log dangling from her finger tips, looking real sad at her Pa.

"You kilt him?"

She drops the log. It thunks against the rough wooden floor.

"Nah, just knocked him out. But he'll kill you when he wakes up."

I grab my bundle and pull the latch on the door.

"Where you going?" Promise demands.

"I'm getting out before he wakes up." I look deep into her dark eyes. They're changed now, holding more sadness than one person should have to carry. "I 'spose I'll be heading for Detroit."

"Can't you stay someplace 'round here. So we can be....." Her voice fades and tears jiggle at the bottom edges of her eyes.

"I can't stay here. If your Pa don't kill me, Elwood will. He's sure not gonna let me blab about what he done. He knows I know."

Promise is silent, chewing on her bottom lip.

"Besides, Detroit is where I belong. It's where I'll find a home. I got to go there," I say. "That's what my ma said."

We stand and hold each other with our eyes, her Pa lying between us on the floor. Her knees jitter and something changes in her face.

"Take me with you to Detroit."

"But, your Pa."

"He tried to kill you." Tears tumble over her lower eye lid, making silvery streaks down her cheeks.

"Besides. My staying here won't bring Booker back."

* * *

After washing Booker's blood off ourselves as best we can in Pa's water barrel, Promise grabs two empty flour sacks, handing one to me.

"Put your stuff in that. Be easier to carry."

I drop my quilt in the sack not knowing what's really in it since I grabbed it in the dark. I consider putting my money sock in it too, but it's better around my neck.

Promise rolls a bunch of dried fish in a piece of newspaper and shoves it in her sack along with two loaves of bread she must have made.

"Here," she hands me four potatoes. "We can eat these raw if we need to."

"Or throw them at Elwood," I say. She doesn't smile. Her shoulders are slumped as she stands at the door of her bedroom.

"I got to get me some clothes." Maybe two minutes tick by and she's still standing in the door, frozen.

"Want me to get your stuff?" I ask gently, barely touching her shoulder.

She jumps. "No. I got to say goodbye to Booker. But I don't know how."

Tears travel down her face. I wait.

Finally she walks, back straight, to a shelf and shoves some clothes into her sack. Dropping her sack on the floor, she kneels beside Booker. She wraps her arms around him and lays her face close to his, humming softly. *Hush little baby, don't…..*

I can't watch. Shrieks and screams and curses push against my ribs, so I tiptoe back into the other room and wait, my chest hurting something awful. Her Pa still hasn't stirred.

"Let's go." She's got Booker's fishing knife in its sheath in one hand and her bundle in the other.

"Here," she hands me the knife. "Tie that to your pants like Booker did."

"You're really going to do this?"

She puts her hand on my shoulder and pushes me toward the door. She don't even look back at her pa sprawled on the floor.

"Well, it don't seem possible," I say as she pulls the door shut behind her. "Now we're like them hoboes with no kind of home at all."

CHAPTER 24

"I'm not going to Miss Charlotte for nothing," I say grinding my teeth together.

"Maisy Wharton, you're stubborn as a mule. And just about as smart right now."

We walk on the dirt road toward town in the light of the quarter moon because there's no road going the other way. But truthfully, I don't know which way to go to Detroit. Or anywheres. But going to Miss Charlotte's sticks in my craw.

"She can tell us where to go for the nearest train yard or even a side track to get a freight train."

"We just go north. That's what my ma told me."

"So smarty. Show me which way is north."

My eyes scan the sky, looking for the North Star. My ma used to point it out to me, holding me on her lap, her arms around me and talking about Detroit. But now them stars all look the same. North could be anywhere.

"All right so I'm a tiny bit not sure."

Promise doesn't even make a remark. We trudge along the road and I can feel her getting sadder and sadder. Booker being dead must be weighing on her something bad. I take her sack and sling it over my shoulder, carrying it for her until we stand outside the white picket fence in front of Miss Charlotte's house.

"It's pitch dark in her house," I say. "We can't wake her up in the middle of the night."

Promise stares at me, her eyes empty as an old tin can. Her mouth hangs a tiny bit open. She's beyond making any decisions. I open the gate and hold it for her to walk into the yard.

"See that big rhododendron bush? We'll sleep under that until morning," I say as I walk toward it. Promise follows as if she were a sleep walker. She stands in a trance while I spread out our flour sacks as best I can, using our stuff for pillows. I tug her hand and help her settle herself, then I spread my quilt over both of us. I wrap my arm around her and press myself against her back. I kiss her shoulder.

She lies real still. Like nobody's there.

* * *

We stand on Miss Charlotte's back step, the sun still low on the horizon and frying bacon fat sits in the air. I knock and Miss Charlotte opens the door. The bacon mixed with the sweet smell of cinnamon rolls engulfs us and I realize how starving I am.

"What are you two doing? You look like hoboes." She says her hand on her hip. "And look at your clothes. Covered with.....what *is* that nasty looking stuff?"

"Booker's blood," Promise whispers.

"What? Did you say Booker's blood?" We both nod while Miss Charlotte purses her bright red lips real tight and squints her eyes at us.

"You better come on in and tell me what happened." She stands back waving her hand at the kitchen table. "Sit."

We drop our sacks onto the linoleum floor by the back door and each take a chair at her table. Her plate, with little red roses around the rim, sits there with fried eggs, cinnamon rolls and bacon. It's all I can do not to grab the plate and run.

"You might as well have something to eat while we talk," she reaches for the frying pan and cracks two eggs into it. Then with a plate exactly like hers in front of each of us, we eat, not being able to talk until both our plates look like they never been used.

She offers each of us another roll. I take mine, my thumb sinking into the soft, warm dough.

"Now tell me," she says. I wait for Promise to tell the story her way, but she don't look like she can even talk.

"Booker's been kilt," I say.

"What!" Miss Charlotte's hand shoots across the table and covers Promise's balled up fist.

"Is this true?" she demands.

Promise nods, her chin drops to her chest.

"Elwood shot him," I say.

"Elwood? Maisy, you're always blaming Elwood and after he gave you that job and helped your granny so much."

"Miss Charlotte. I am not lying. Promise and me were there. We seen Elwood raise his gun and shoot Booker in the back."

She pulls her hand away and crosses her arms over her chest real tight. Her lipstick-red mouth puckers.

"And then he tried to kill me," I say.

"Maisy Wharton. That's enough. Why would Elwood even want to kill Booker and you?" She slaps her hands flat onto the table. "I know that you and Booker done...." her eyes travel across the ceiling, "but, Elwood. He'd never kill you."

I'm sinking into a hole, getting sucked further and further into the darkness. Into the lies flying around about me.

"It's true. Maisy's right," Promise says, her voice breaking up same's as that static on the radio as big old tears roll down her cheek. "I seen it. With my own eyes."

"Something should happen to Elwood. Like hanging him," I say.

Miss Charlotte looks down at her lap, picking lint and putting it in the palm of her other hand.

"You know nothing will happen," whispers Promise. "Not now. Not ever."

Like Sheriff Judd I think to myself. He killed my ma and walked away.

"What are you two going to do?" Miss Charlotte asks.

A real long minute hangs in the air. Promise's face is blank, as if she moved out of her body.

"We're going to Detroit," I say.

We all sit real quiet as the sunlight creeps across our empty plates. Miss Charlotte finally gets up from the table and goes into another room. Me and Promise stay sat. I hope she's not coming back with a gun. She struggles through the kitchen door, her arms full of clothes.

"You can't be running around in bloody clothes. Look through these." She lays some overalls, pants, shirts, dresses and shoes on a couple of chairs. "You two change into something you can wear. These are from our women's auxiliary for helping the poor." She looks at us and shakes her head. "And you two are the poorest looking folks I've seen for a while."

While we change, both of us, into overalls and shirts, Miss Charlotte clears the table and fusses with something at the kitchen counter.

"We look like boys," Promise almost smiles. "That'll be better for us."

"That's true." I hand her a pair of shoes to try on.

"'Cept for your hair. That golden hair ain't ever gonna look like a boy."

"Wait," says Miss Charlotte. She comes back with a cap, handing it to me.

I tuck my hair under it. "What do you think?"

"That's better," says Promise.

Miss Charlotte hands a cap to Promise too. "Boys don't wear red ribbons in their hair." She smiles.

"What about our bloody clothes?" I ask.

"Dump them in a heap on the back step. I'll burn them in the barrel tonight with my trash."

I gather up all our old clothing, bundling it so you can't see much blood and put it out on the stoop. Promise meets me at the door and hands me my sack. She turns to Miss Charlotte.

"Thank you for your kindness. We just got one more question." She looks at me, meaning I should ask.

"As I said, we're trying to get to Detroit but don't know what direction to go," I say. "Do you know the closest train yard so we can catch a freight train, seeing as how we don't have enough money for tickets."

"I fixed you some food to take." Miss Charlotte sighs real long. "But now I don't know how long it will last, you travelling so far." She hands me the bundle of food. Turning back to the counter, she grabs a tall glass Mason jar with gold lid. She gives it to Promise.

"Fill this with water from my rain barrel on the way out. You'll need it for such a long trip."

I look at her face, her eyebrows furrowed together, and wonder how I ever dreamed she could make me a home and be like a ma to me.

"Thank you, ma'am." I take a breath and say again. "Do you know what direction we should be heading?"

She taps her foot like I asked her a real hard question.

"You have to follow the river north to Ashland. There are trains there. If you stay close to the tracks, you might get lucky. Sometimes the trains slow down for one reason or another and you could catch it on to Ashland. Then take one east to Cincinnati then another due north to Detroit."

She takes Promise by the shoulders.

"You sure you want to do this? It's a long dangerous trip, especially for girls. And what about your Pa?"

"I'm sure. There ain't no reason to stay no more."

"Wait a minute," Miss Charlotte says and disappears into some other room in her house. Promise and me peek into the food bundle. More cinnamon rolls, cheese, apples and two cold pork sandwiches.

"I told you she ain't bad," says Promise.

"But she still believes that talk about Booker and me."

136

"That's sadly true. But nobody's perfect."

Miss Charlotte comes back into the kitchen with an envelope in her hand.

"Here," she hands it to me. "It's a note to my sister who lives in Dayton, Ohio in case you get to there. It's asking her to help you two out." I peek inside the envelope and two one dollar bills are lying in there with the note.

"Those are for you two. A little bit of help."

"Thank you Miss Charlotte," I say trying to smile, but sadness fills me up instead. The front door closes behind us as we tromp down the stairs and out the path to the road.

"Told you," Promise says taking the envelope and stuffing it in her pocket.

"Maybe so," I say. "But I can't settle for tiny specks of goodness here and there anymore."

CHAPTER 25

"I can't walk much more," Promise groans. "My feet are killing me in these shoes."

We been following the river and the railroad tracks for two days. Last night we slept in the woods, holding on to each other all night being scared to death what with all the rummaging and creeping going on. I thought it was Elwood with each sound even though I knew that was crazy. But pictures of Booker getting shot in the back, his arms flying out to the side and then falling face down onto the ground kept flashing in my head. Just thinking about it now makes me sweat.

"I got to stop. I got to sit down," Promise pitches sideways, her body leaning hard against mine.

"The river ain't but down this hill," I say.

"I can't walk another step. I got to stop." She drops her bundle to the ground.

"I'm sweaty as a hog," I say trying to be cheerful. We are in the middle of nowhere and our food's running out. I can't let her collapse. We'll be dinner for the coyotes.

"How about we wash up, eat something, fill our water jar and rest for a time?" I look up at the sun and it's in the afternoon sky but we got plenty of time before dark.

I pick up her bundle and hold her arm as we slip slide down the bank, then I steady her as we pick our way across the rocky shore until we find a patch of sand big enough to spread out on. We drop our sacks and Promise kicks her shoes off, letting them fly over the rocky ground.

"I'm going barefoot. I ain't wearing them shoes no more."

"Be hard walking on them tracks," I say pulling her close to me. Her body collapses into mine, her shoulder leans into my chest and her head on my shoulder. She stays that way maybe three seconds, then she yanks herself loose, sitting bolt upright.

"I'm going to bathe in the river. You watch for peoples then you can wash." She stands, tossing her cap on the ground. She slips out of her overalls, unbuttons her shirt, and drops them onto the sand. I watch her strong back, long legs and round bottom make their way into the water until only her head shows. I miss her something awful. I know she's real broken up about Booker, and I don't blame her, but she gets real stiff every time I touch her or try to comfort her. I'm thinking she might blame me.

I do. I blame myself for thinking Booker and me could be friends. I should have known better. Especially the way he looked at me. I never believed anything bad would happen to him.

She dunks her head, sputtering as she comes up. Standing, she washes herself all over with her hand, then walks toward me on the shore. She looks so beautiful, like something magical rising out of the water. I stand and step toward her, wrapping my arms around her, kissing her neck and searching for her lips. She turns her head away from me and lays it on my shoulder. Little droplets of water run down her brown skin. Promise lets go of me and fills our water jar then puts her clothes back on while I bathe, the cool water as refreshing as a bowl of ice cream. When I come out of the water, dripping wet and stark naked, she's looking in her bundle like she might find a treasure. I wait, goose bumps pop up all over me while I hope she'll look up and smile. She don't. I grab my shirt to dry myself off. I have to stop being disappointed and let her grieve for Booker. I know her heart is broken.

I get dressed, tucking Booker's knife with its sheath into my deep side pocket then pull my money sock back around my neck. Promise holds out the two dollar bills.

"You should put this with your money so it don't get lost." Her voice sounds stronger.

I tuck them in my sock and reach for my bundle, dumping it upside-down. My quilt tumbles out first.

"I don't even know what's in my sack," I say. "I just grabbed whatever was on my quilt and now everything's at the bottom." Out roll two potatoes, a chunk of cheese with our teeth marks on it, two apples, four cinnamon rolls, and one cold pork sandwich. I reach in and pull out my scissors and some needles and thread, one match and my *Modern Screen* and *Life* magazines. All the rest of my magazines are ashes. Burned up. I shake my *Modern Screen* and my father's picture falls out onto the sand. I hold it against my cheek and put it back in the magazine. Then I reach to the very bottom of my sack, my fingers searching. I find my comb but not what I'm looking for. Turning my sack inside out, I give it a good shake. Nothing. It's gone.

It's gone. Feels like someone punched me in the stomach.

My mother's compact. Burned up in that old boxcar. The last piece I had of her is gone. Lost. Burned up. Now I've got nothing of her. Nothing at all. The ground shimmies under me and everything gets hazy for a minute. I held that compact every day, like cradling my ma in my hand.

I turn to tell Promise, but seeing her mournful eyes makes me remember that Booker's dead. That's what matters. Not my compact. Least I still got my ma's dream of Detroit.

Finally I comb my hair and pull my cap on, tucking stray hair up into it.

"How about some bites of cheese and we split one of them cinnamon rolls for lunch?" I say stuffing everything else back into the sack. "And we need to drink some of that water or we'll be parched."

Promise scoots closer to me, almost touching. A flicker of a smile crosses her face even though her eyes are deeply sad.

"I'm sorry we had to run," she says. "But since we did, I'm glad I'm doing this with you, Maisy Wharton." She reaches for the chunk of cheese. "But it ain't easy."

Something like joy jumps in my heart and I reach to touch her. My hand stops.

Booker lying flat on the ground flames reflecting off his skin flashes through my mind.

No. It ain't easy.

* * *

We fling our bundles over our shoulders and we're back to walking along the tracks. Promise got her shoes tied together and slung around her neck. I don't know how she walks on them pointy rocks between the tracks, but she does.

"You got real tough feet," I laugh.

"Been walking barefoot since I took my first step." I can hear some pride in her voice. She stops. "What's that?"

I listen, then bend and lay my hand on the metal rail. Sure enough, the vibrations shimmy up my arm. Walking and talking with Booker on the railroad tracks floods my head. Him showing me Amelia Earhart's picture and reaching to almost touch my hair. Telling me about his pa. My chest tightens and, for a minute, I can't breathe.

"A train's coming. Not too fast and not too far away." Finally I take a breath. "This is our chance," I say. "Let's step into the bushes so's we can see how fast the train's going and so's them engineers don't think we're hoboes hitching a ride."

"Which we are," she laughs, but I can tell she's nervous. Truth be told, so am I.

The big old black engine comes poking around the curve, tooting and huffing. It's going real slow so I think we can do it.

"See them little handles on the sides of the cars?"

"We got to grab them?" Her voice tells me this is stupid.

"Let the engine pass us then run toward the back of the train until we see a car coming with the door open. Then turn around and trot alongside, waiting for the car to catch up to us." She looks at me like I'm speaking a different language.

141

"I can barely stand up. How am I going to do that?"

"You got to. Listen to me. I'll grab the handle and throw my bundle in. You grab my free hand and jump as hard as you can and I'll pull you up. You get in and reach for me if I'm still hanging from that handle."

"And if you're not. If you're lying on the ground?" Her eyes are round circles of fear.

"That won't happen. I'll hold on real tight."

"This is crazy. We should just walk."

"We'll be dead before we get anywhere." My voice is harsh, but she's got to know the truth.

The engine of the train slowly rumbles by us. The whistle blows and steam comes out of it like it's on fire. The train is barely moving. I'm sure this will work. Real sure. Sort of.

"Go," I say pushing her in front of me. "Wait. I see an open door about six cars down," I holler. "Turn around and run right in front of me. Run with the train."

It seems like forever for that car to reach us. The clacking of the wheels against the rails rattles my brain. We got to do this right.

"Here it comes. Remember to grab my hand as I go past you." Fear stomps through my chest and pounds in my head.

I don't know how, but I grab that handle pulling myself onto the step to the boxcar and fling my bundle inside. Promise clutches my hand, practically crushing my bones, and I pull her up as hard as I can.

"Jump," I yell. "Jump hard." She tugs my arm as she leaps forward and I yank her as hard as I can.

"What the hell..." shouts a deep voice over my head.

"It's some of them young boys," another voice hollers. I'm so startled I loosen my grip on Promise and she falls backwards onto the ground.

"Promise," I scream. She stands up and starts running like crazy her bundle whacking her back. She's catching up, but the train goes a little faster. "Can you make it? Run."

She runs faster, but she's losing ground and gasping for breath.

One of them men wraps his hand around my arm and pulls me into the boxcar, the sharp edge of the doorway scrapes my side. The other man jumps off the train and runs toward Promise, throwing her over his shoulder. He runs back to the box car, tosses her through the open door like a sack of potatoes and swings himself back into the grayness of the car.

"Must be the first time you boys rode the rails," a young scruffy looking white man with a ragged beard says.

The older man, also white with tired eyes and a porkpie hat shakes his head.

"Bad enough we have to do this. Not right you young'uns aren't in school."

By now, Promise and me have scooted into one of the corners as far as we can get from these men. She clutches my arm and her body shivers next to me. I can't say anything because the only thing in my mouth is my heart beat.

I know Promise is thinking the same as me. I pray they keep on believing that we're boys.

CHAPTER 26

"W here you from?" the younger man asks. "Round here?"

"The hills above Paine Hollow," I say, scooting closer to Promise. She leans her shivering body into me, the skin of her arm chilly against mine.

"Never heard of it," he says. Me and Promise never been out of Paine Hollow except me once with my ma and now we're leaving it. Fear leaps in my ribs. I push the fear away as best I can. When you think about it, what we're really leaving behind is all that meanness. I'm thankful my granny took me in and raised me, but in the end, she was only mean.

"I'm Alton, by the way." The older one kind of leans forward and I'm afraid he's going to want to shake hands. But he sinks back against the wooden wall.

"I'm Luke," says the younger one. "Where you boys heading?"

"Detroit," I say. Promise sits against me shivering. Somehow saying 'Detroit' when we're bumping along in a freight train smacks me in the face. I realize I only know my ma's dream. Me and Promise have no idea what we're doing, or what's ahead, or how to get there.

"You know the way?" I ask.

"At Ashland you got to catch a freight to Cincinnati, clear into Ohio." That's the same as what Miss Charlotte told us, so maybe they're not tricking us.

"How do we know which one of them trains is going to Cincinnati? They all look the same," I ask.

"It'll be the middle of the night," Luke says, "when we pull into the train yard. Alton and I will show you."

I clutch Promise's arm. Can we trust them? But if we don't, we could end up on a train to California.

But they're hoboes. Everyone knows you can't trust hoboes.

"It's a shame so many schools are closed," Alton says.

"Alton was a school teacher in California. We've been half way round this dang country looking for any kind of work."

"What did you do?" I ask.

"I'm a brick layer but nobody's building nothing, nowhere," he laughs one of them sad sounding laughs.

"How long you been looking?" Promise's voice squeaks.

Both men laugh. "Your voices sure haven't changed yet."

My heart pounds against my chest and Promise's fingers dig into my arm. The train's going real fast and if they find out we're girls we'll have to jump out. But neither of them move. In fact, Alton's shuffles some newspaper.

"Got some pieces of salami left," he says. "Would you like some?"

Seems neither Promise nor me knows what to say. I can't figure if this is a trick. I mean they *are* hoboes. But I know I'm starving.

"That'd be real nice," I say. "We got some bread we can share to make sandwiches."

I look at Promise thinking she'll reach into her bundle. But she leans against me her eyes real glassy so I stretch over her and rummage in her sack, pulling out the loaf. I tear off two good sized chunks and hold them out. Luke stands and wobbles across the car, trading me two chunks of salami for the bread. I keep my other hand on Booker's knife. Just in case. Promise tenses beside me.

"How is it that you two hitched up travelling? Kind of unusual, you know, you being white and..." Luke flops down next to Alton. "Got any family?"

Everything in my head goes blank. What can I say that don't give away that we're girls?

145

Luke twists the bread around his salami, looking at me. He waits.

Is everything going to be this scary?

"Yep. We..." I look at Promise but she's studying her lap like she's counting her million dollars. "We know each other from..."

Now both Luke and Alton stare at me. I can't even hear the train wheels beat against the rails because my heart's banging so loud in my ears. I got to think of something.

"Truth be told, his ma was my granny's help. But then, his ma died."

"So you do have some family—"

"Both my ma and pa are dead. And. My granny died shortly after his ma died. So. No family. We stuck together, being orphans and all."

Promise's body sinks against me, letting out the longest breath I ever heard.

"Pretty sad story," says Alton.

I take a giant bite of my salami and bread. Promise hands me the water jar and I take a sip.

Nobody talks for a while, just them metal wheels clanking against the rails.

"Should get some sleep," Alton says. "You're going to be tuckered out otherwise."

Promise and me whisper to each other 'bout who'll sleep first and who will keep watch.

"You sleep first," I say and she don't fight me. She lays down beside me with her head on my thigh, her arms squeezing her bundle. I take Booker's knife out of its sheath in my pocket and hold it in my right hand, leaning it against the splintery floor. I sit up as straight as I can, hoping I look like an almost man.

Luke and Alton whisper something to each other and I grip that knife real tight.

"You boys don't trust us," Alton says. "That's good. Help keep you safe."

Luke nods. "Most of the men on the road are like us, but every once in a while you'll come up against a real mean one."

"Or a drinker," Alton says. "Best not to trust anyone. It's real dangerous out there."

Promise's body tenses. I rub my hand lightly across her back hoping that helps a little.

I'm thinking we're going to have to trust them some if we're going to get in the right boxcar to Cincinnati. Even if they are hoboes. Then I think of Miss Charlotte and those two dollar bills. You never really know about a person, I guess.

When it comes down to it, though, me and Promise really only got each other to trust.

* * *

We've been rocking back and forth for a long time. Luke and Alton seem to be asleep and Promise snores lightly with her head in my lap. I keep my eyes wide open and have been seeing lights every once in awhile. I wonder if we're close to Ashland.

Suddenly the train lurches and a terrible squeal fills the night. A red light flashes into the boxcar as we pass it. Luke and Alton jump to their feet.

"Grab your stuff. We got to jump out soon as the train stops so we don't get caught."

Promise sits up straight, groggy but grabs at me and our stuff. The train slows and I see trains all every which way and them lights on poles like I seen in the picture of Detroit. My breath fills my chest and chills tingle all up and down my body.

"See them lights? They got electricity." I squeeze Promises' hand. "Just like Detroit. That's a real good sign."

She nods but her big eyes got more fear in them than excitement. The car pitches from side to side and another eerie squeal lasts a long time.

"Get ready. Be sure you got your stuff because you can't go back once we're out," warns Alton. Luke's practically hanging out the side door. I slip Booker's knife back into the sheath in my deep side pocket.

Promise whispers to me. "Should we go with them?"

"What else we going to do?" I squeeze her hand which is freezing cold. I'm hoping we made the right choice.

The train slows and the whistle pierces the night air as the brakes screech and the train lurches to a stop.

Luke jumps and Alton follows. Part of me is glad they are helping us and the other part hopes they run off without us.

They both reach back into the boxcar toward us.

Promise and I look at each other, fear buzzes between us. Her head does a quick nod.

"Hold your stuff, take my hand and jump," Luke says. Promise and me each take a hand and fling ourselves out of that car, landing on the dirt, dust fluttering around our feet. My brain jiggles in my head, jumping from so high.

"Come on," Luke whispers over his shoulder. "Don't talk and follow me." I sure hope we made the right choice.

We run after him, our bundles joggling over our shoulders. Alton runs behind us.

"Sh! Stop," Luke hisses. He presses himself against the closest boxcar and we do the same. Footsteps crunch on the gravel on the other side of this boxcar. I could pee my pants from being afraid. Promise stares real blank, her mouth slightly open, holding onto the back of my overalls. We wait.

"Let's go," Luke says and we all follow him, darting between boxcars and stepping over tracks that seem to go every which way. Luke stops and looks back at Alton. "This it?"

"Yep."

We creep along the string of boxcars in the dim light, barely enough to see anything. Luke stops at a car with the door open about a foot. He sticks his head in, and although it's pitch black inside the car, he proclaims it's empty. No cargo. No people.

He and Alton pull the door open about another foot and reach for our bundles. They toss them inside.

"Now don't trust anyone," Alton says.

"That's not a problem for me," I say. "I don't trust anybody." Except Promise.

He grins at me. "Keep that fishing knife handy." Guess he don't miss much. "And make your voices deeper when you speak so people will believe you're boys." He's not grinning, just looking real serious. He knew the whole time.

He and Luke grasp each others wrists and make a step up for us. Promise goes first and tumbles into the darkness.

"Thanks," I say as I step on their arms. "You made it possible that we can get to Detroit."

(HAPTER 27

Promise and I crawl across the wood floor of the boxcar. A splinter stabs my thumb. It's pitch dark except for a streak of dim light that slashes across the floor then shoots up the wall from them electrical lights on poles. Seeing the lights makes me so happy that I almost don't feel the fear pound against my ribs or Promise clutch my arm so hard I'm sure the blood can't get to my brain. We stop for a minute, both of us on our hands and knees, then we both crawl for that tiny splash of light on the back wall like them pigeons that know their way home. We hold our sacks to our chests and lean against the wall, its roughness bites into our backs. I listen for anyone else breathing. Nothing. My shoulders drop back where they're supposed to be.

"What if this ain't the right train," Promise whispers, fear falling out of her mouth. "What if someone's hiding in here, waiting to —"

"Promise," I slip my arm loose out of her grip and wrap it around her shoulders pulling her close up to me. "We don't know what else to do. Might's as well do this. Besides, we don't have any other choices. Right?"

She doesn't answer, but she's sniffling softly. I know she's crying. And I don't blame her but I sure don't know how to fix anything, at this moment, since we both know we can't go back.

I do know we're both thinking of Booker and him lying dead on his bed. All's I can do is fold her into my arms and rock her. That's all. Her body stiffens as I slip my arms around her. I hold her even though it's like trying to comfort a rock.

My biggest wish is that Booker hadn't mistook the way I liked him. I could tell that he liked me in that special way, but I never said a word to him. If I had, he'd never have been there that night because he would have said no to coming to the woods so late. There would have been no reason.

His body, flat on the ground, in the flickering light of the flames flashes through my mind. *Run Booker. Run.*

The train jerks forward and rocks from side to side shaking everything out of my head. The whistle blows over and over and the iron wheels clackety-clack against the rails. We must be heading out for Cincinnati. I can't help but be excited even though I know this isn't what Promise ever imagined. But it has been *my* dream since my ma got shot. The first time Granny Wharton beat me with that broomstick, I knew somehow I'd get out and that Detroit was going to be my home. I tighten my arms around Promise and hum softly in her ear. Her body relaxes some and melts into me, soft and warm. I kiss the top of her head. She starts to say something but lays her head in the crook of my neck instead.

"How long?" She mumbles into my shoulder.

"Real long."

"I'm scared being here. It don't feel right."

"I'm scared too, but we'll be fine."

"How will we know when we get there?"

"We'll know. Hush now and go back to sleep."

She straightens herself up, sitting bolt upright. "I wish with all my heart Booker was with us."

"Me too." I can still feel the stickiness of his blood on my hands even though I washed them real good. Twice.

We sink back into each other, the boxcar rocking back and forth. The wheels clack and a star slips through the slice of open door.

"I can't sleep. I'm starving," Promise says.

Now it's really darker than pitch. The train moves real fast and we must be out of Ashland because there's only a window with a light every now and then. Not even any moonlight to speak of.

151

One of the bundles leans on my leg. I squeeze it with my fingers. Must be Promise's because I feel the bread. Reaching in, I break off two pieces. I hand one to her and keep one for myself. I can't help thinking of Detroit even though I should only be thinking of Booker. And I am, but still, excitement ripples through me and I smile. My dream is coming true. Me and Promise will get our own place. There won't be beatings, crying or cussing. Just us together, loving each other and making a real home. Not a pretend one in a boxcar.

"Can you find the water jar?" she asks.

Groping around with my hand, I find it and twist the top open then hand it to her after taking a long sip myself. There's a tiny rustle.

"Shh." I whisper, leaning up close to her ear. "Sit real still."

I slide Booker's knife out of my pocket, gripping the handle.

We both sit like statues for the longest time with the boxcar rocking and lurching. The wheels clank their rhythm against the tracks and the wooden walls creak and groan. Nothing else, not even the slightest whisper. I let my breath out.

Promise sips from the water jar again, making little swallow sounds.

"I know you're real sad right now. And me too. But in Detroit, we'll have a good life." I touch her cheek. "Booker would want that for us."

"Besides them tall buildings, paved streets and feathered hats, what's so great about Detroit? It ain't worth Booker getting killed."

"Nothing's worth Booker being dead. But Detroit didn't kill him. Elwood and his hate kilt him."

"People don't hate in Detroit?" Promise takes a third long drink of water. I know she needs it but I worry about us running out. I keep my mouth shut, though.

"Probably everywhere people hate. But in Detroit there's lots more people to choose from. And now thousands of them are marching in the streets for what's right."

"What good will that do? Booker's still dead." Promise hands me the water jar.

152

"I surely wish Booker was with us," I say snuggling her close to me, my arm around her shoulders. "But he's not." Her breathing stutters. "He'd want you to have a better life."

"A better life? Them big buildings don't give you a better life."

"Detroit's not just them fancy dresses and that fox stole that bites its own tail." Promise laughs a tiny bit. "We can have a refrigerator so our food won't go bad. And a washing machine with a wringer. And electricity in our house. And running water inside that comes right to our sink and maybe one of them flushing toilets."

Promise shifts and lies her head in my lap. My fingers gently follow the edges of her shell-like ear.

"But mostly, in Detroit, we can be free and choose what kind of life we want. You can go to school and learn whatever you want. I can get a job that pays more than that stingy Elwood paid me. And we can sleep together in a real bed, holding each other all night long if we want."

She buries her face in my lap and curls her knees up to her chest. A soft moan rises in the darkness.

"I can't think of nothing but Booker," she says, sadness lacing her voice. "Not Detroit. Not how we'll find our way out of here. Not even about you and me. Nothing matters anymore. Booker being dead fills up every bit of me."

All my happiness about Detroit sinks, settling in my lap with Promise. Not even her and me? How can we not matter? A little bit anyways. She wanted to never stop loving me. She's all I got left.

"Promise," I have to ask her if she still loves me but tears clog my throat and push all the words away. I unscrew the water jar for a sip of water.

A ragged cough vibrates through the dark.

Promise sits up real fast. The water sloshes on my arm and drips off my elbow. I screw the lid on, hand the jar to Promise and clutch Booker's knife, slipping it out of my pocket. Promise has pushed herself tight behind me. Maybe we just imagined the cough. Maybe we're too nervous and made it up. But I have to find out.

"Somebody there?" I say remembering to keep my voice real deep.

Another cough bounces around the walls of the boxcar.

"Who are you?" I demand in my deepest voice.

"Name's Joe. Sorry to scare you all." He sounds like a white southern man. I heard plenty of them eating at Elwood's restaurant every now and then. Certainly doesn't sound like a colored or like a northerner.

"Why didn't you say something when we stuck our heads in here?" I sound like we own this boxcar.

"I, well, I was asleep and you surprised me. Decided to see what was going on before I showed myself to you all." His voice is silky. Sounds friendly, but there's something slithering under the words that makes me squirm.

"Where are you going?" I ask. Promise is still wedged between my back and the wall, her breathing ragged in my ear.

"Headed for Cincinnati. Got a brother there who might have work for me." He coughs again. "What about you two girls?"

"We ain't girls," I snap. Promise's fingers claw into me. Something like danger smells real sour.

"Heard you talking." He draws out 'talking' like it was a nasty thing to be doing.

"We're getting off at the next stop anyways so we won't be bothering you." I try to snarl from deep inside my chest.

"You girls won't be any trouble." There's that slithering in his voice again.

"I don't like this," Promise whispers in my ear. "I don't like this one bit." I squeeze her arm to let her know I feel the same. The trouble is that neither of us know how far the next stop is.

I grip Booker's knife real tight.

"We have to stay awake listening for him," I whisper back.

* * *

Promise's piercing scream wakes me up. The morning sky has lightened making it so's I can see, barely, what's happening. I was dreaming Promise and me were walking down a paved street in Detroit, our stomachs full and silky skirts swirling against our legs.

Damnation!

I fell asleep if I was dreaming.

I was supposed to stay awake. I told her I would.

Her arms flail and one of her legs kicks in every direction while she's screaming bloody murder. Her body slowly moves across the floor toward Joe. He's pulling on her leg.

He grunts as one of her kicks hits him.

I jump to my feet, my body rocking back and forth with the train, and grab one of Promise's arms. She flings it around so fast it's hard to catch. But I do and then I pull, but she still keeps moving toward Joe. That son of a bitch. Realizing my other hand is empty, I let go of Promise and feel around the floor for Booker's knife. Finally my fingers fold around the handle.

"Let her go," I scream waving the knife. "I'll cut your eyeballs out."

He stops for a second, then throws his head back and laughs.

"You think I'm worried about a girl using a knife. Come near me and I'll take it away from you and cut your precious friend here."

I grab Promise's arm again. Icy cold starts in my finger tips and travels up my arms and chills me through and through until my heart freezes with fear. Promise fights like a wild cat, but her body keeps traveling closer and closer to Joe. The boxcar rolls from side to side, the trees flicking past the open door in the weak light of dawn. I don't know how, but a plan spreads itself out in my head.

Letting go of Promise, I rummage through our stuff until I find the water jar. My fingertips can almost read the raised writing on the Mason jar as I grip it.

Promise's high-pitched screams are frantic and Joe's filthy hands struggle with the straps of her overalls. I step close as I dare and take careful aim, slinging the jar of water straight at his head. It hits him sounding like a watermelon busting on the ground. Glass tinkles against the wall. Both his hands fly to his head and he yelps, startled by the blood on his fingers.

"Promise," I holler. "Get up, grab our stuff and jump out. Now. Just do it."

She looks at me for just a moment like I'm a crazy person. Then she scrambles barely out of Joe's reach and I step closer, slashing Booker's knife across his arms and face. I stab his leg, the knife slipping in and out of his flesh. He screams and pitches toward me, but I'm already by the door. Promise, holding both our bundles, is frozen watching the ground whip by. I take one from her and place my hand in the middle of her back.

"Just jump. Now. Jump, Promise. He's coming after us," I yell looking back at Joe. He wipes blood from his face with one hand and grips his leg with the other, but I know we don't have but a minute.

"Hold onto your bundle and roll when you hit the ground. Promise. You can do it." Joe moves in the shadows. I push Promise and clutching my bundle to my chest, I leap into the flickering shadows of the unknown.

I hit the ground. Sharp rocks rip my skin and a white-hot pain stabs up my leg and something in my wrist snaps. I see Promise wobble to her feet and the wheels of the train crash past just as everything goes black.

HOPE

CHAPTER 28

I wish I had stayed knocked out. I never hurt so much before, ever. Even when Granny beat me real bad, making bruises on my back and blood spurting from my nose. Somehow Promise got me down from the raised rocky track bed and into the woods, tucking us under another rhododendron bush. These rhododendron bushes were not part of my plan to get to Detroit.

My cheek presses against the coolness of packed dirt while Promise cuts up one of them flour sacks with my scissors. I slowly move my eyes and see my stuff scattered on the ground. Must be my sack she's ripping up. I grip my wrist real tight with my other hand. Blood seeps through my fingers and red-hot poker pain shoots through my arm and a moan rolls out of my mouth without me even knowing it.

"Hush," Promise croons. "I'm going to fix you up. Just keep breathing and don't move that arm."

Next thing I know, she leans over me, packing moss around my wrist and wrapping it real tight with strips of sack. For an instant I relax into the cool of the moss, then she moves my wrist and I scream and scream and scream. Reaching for Promise with my good hand, I swirl down and down into the dark.

The darkness fades and I hear the ripple of a river flowing nearby and chickadees chirping at each other in the branches above me. My shirt is all bunched up around me and my dungarees are twisted. I'm afraid to open my eyes even though I can hear Promise breathe. No telling what she'll do to me this time. I crack my eyes half open and she looks back at me, her face full of sorrow.

"Shush. Don't move. You're hurt real bad," she says. She wipes my face with a cool, wet cloth. First around my eyes, then across my cheeks and finally my chin and neck. Shadows flit across her face in the afternoon light.

"Our water jar broke," I mumble touching the dampness on my face with my good hand.

"I found an old can some hobo left in the bushes and washed it out in the river while you was sleeping."

I push with my good arm to sit up but pain screams through me. Even my teeth throb.

"Take a sip of water." She lifts my head to help me swallow. Tastes like rain after a dry spell. "I think you broke your wrist. A bone is sticking out through your skin." I gag and the water I just swallowed starts up my throat.

"Breathe. Just keep taking breaths." Her cool hand caresses my forehead and rests on my cheek. The water stays down. She offers me more but I press my lips tight. She laughs. "Wish I had some of Pa's hooch to give you for that pain." I try to smile but can't.

"Your ankle's maybe twisted, but I don't think it's broke. Maybe tomorrow I'll make you a crutch and we can try walking." She points at my arm. "I wrapped your wrist with a piece I tore off the bottom of my shirt and made that sling for your arm to keep it close to your body."

I know she's hoping for a thank you and gratitude, but I hurt too much to say any extra words. Her finger travels across my eyebrows.

"You need to sleep."

Even though the sun's still in the afternoon sky, she lies down beside me and wraps us in my quilt. The last thing I hear before I fall asleep is her breathing close beside my face. And little whimpers in her sleep.

* * *

I wake to footsteps near my head.

"Take a sip," Promise says offering the can's jagged rim against my lips. She waits. My stomach lurches. "You need to drink something."

"I can't."

"It don't matter that you can't. You got to. Don't be so dang stubborn."

I press my lips tighter knowing I'm being an idiot. She holds it up to my lips again and I try a tiny sip. My stomach doesn't roll over so I try another sip. Then a swallow.

"Eat some bread," she holds a bite close to my mouth. I press my lips. She squints, her eyes becoming little slits. I can't fight that look. I open my mouth. She feeds me four good bites, waiting while I chew and swallow each one.

She helps me sit and lean against a tree ignoring my moans and hollers then puts a chunk of bread in my good hand. She cuts an apple into quarters with Booker's knife. There's no blood on the blade. She must have washed it. I remember the feel of the knife cutting into that man and the bread and water start back up my throat. I breathe. And breathe again, willing the bread to stay in my stomach.

"Here, take these pieces of apple and eat. I'm almost finished with your crutch."

"I'd rather have a kiss than a crutch," I say almost whining.

"You'll have to settle for a crutch."

"A kiss would help all this hurting in my arm."

"A kiss would just make you want more kisses and we ain't doing that. We can't sit here all day."

I sort of know she's kidding with me, probably to make me laugh but I can't help feeling that she's serious. That somehow she's changed. Oh I know she's grieving Booker, but I wonder if her father's words to me *you kilt him you might as well of pulled the trigger* buzz in her head. They do in mine. Maybe I did kill Booker. Surely if it weren't for me, he'd be alive. No wonder she's beginning to hate me. She probably will leave.

161

I take a bite of apple, the bitter juices trickle down my throat. I could hardly blame her. For leaving me, that is. Fear oozes through my body, and for a minute, that's all I can feel. Not my arm, not my leg, not my banged up body. Just my veins clogged with fear. It's not even about being scared that she'll leave me sitting against this tree in these woods. It's that my heart hurts more than my arm if I think of her walking away.

She works on a good size branch with Booker's knife, cutting off the tiny sprouts. The top has a V to put under my armpit where she's wrapped some cloth around it to make it softer. Without looking at me or talking to me, she packs up our things, drinks the water and puts the can in the bag then slips Booker's knife into her overalls pocket. With my good hand I fumble for the sheath in my pocket, but it's gone. I know it's right that she have Booker's knife, but somehow it feels wrong. That was always my job.

I'm not sure how we manage, between me screaming for the pain and her pushing me up the steep slope up to the tracks with them sharp rocks biting into my knees, but we make it. Back on the railroad tracks we stand, catching our balance, then we stumble along, our one bundle over her shoulder and me leaning on a crutch complaining every step of the way. I don't mean to but it hurts like hell.

Something doesn't feel right. I look at the sun to verify our direction.

"We're heading in the wrong direction."

"This is the way to Ashland. That's where we're going."

"I'm not going back to Ashland." I stop and clumsily turn myself around.

"Don't be a twit," she says. "Cincinnati could be five hundred miles for all we know. At least we know where Ashland is."

"It's over a hundred miles away," I shout.

"You need a doctor you stubborn mule," she shouts back. "We know there's doctors in Ashland."

"I'm not going backwards." The inside of my head is all swirly and a moan escapes from my throat. I hold onto the crutch so's not to

162

fall on my face. The trees wobble and the ground rises up close then falls away. The apple rumbles in my stomach.

"From the looks of it, you ain't going nowhere. Sit down before you fall."

I point at her, my finger shaking. I'm afraid she'll leave me standing here weak and broken.

"Go ahead. You go anywhere you want." My legs fold under me and before I know it I'm sitting on the metal rail of the track. "Go. Go do what you want."

You might as well of pulled the trigger.

"And leave you sitting on the tracks? What's the matter with you Maisy Wharton?"

"You might as well leave me now. I know you want to." I clutch my throbbing arm to my chest. I hate needing her. "You act like you hate me." Her father's words pound through my head....*pulled the trigger.*

"You're an ass." She stomps down the track toward Ashland. She stops and turns. "My brother just got kilt and I'm trying to help you." She shakes her finger at me. "What do you want?"

"Just say it." I hear myself snarl.

"I don't know what in God's name you're talking about."

I truly can't help myself. Maybe it's the pain. Maybe it's the guilt. Maybe I'm scared she really will go to Ashland and not Detroit. Maybe I am just an ass.

"I know you're not loving me anymore," I holler.

She huffs and marches down the tracks toward Ashland, our bundle jiggling against her back. Her body flies around and she drops the sack, planting both hands on her hips.

"You. It's always you." Her arms flop at her side. "My brother's dead and I helped kill him."

"Not you Promise. Not you."

"He wouldn't be dead if I'd been home with him."

My heart's bursting apart. I can't even open my mouth. Or maybe I'm scared she really believes it's her fault. I never been this

163

scared. Only angry. Never scared like my body might fly into a thousand pieces.

She stands looking at me, her eyes hard as marbles.

"You know I love you," she says.

"Then how come you won't kiss me? Or hold me."

"Is that what this is about? That I won't *kiss* you?" Her voice rises to a pitch.

I look at my feet in the old leather shoes with the cut out toes then let my eyes wander along the silver rail glinting in the sun until I see her bare feet. I raise my eyes to her face.

"Or just hold me."

"I'll tell you why I don't kiss you, Maisy Wharton. I'll tell you why."

I wait, hardly able to take a breath.

"Every time I kiss you or think about kissing you, I see Booker's big dark eyes staring at me. Staring at me, you hear?"

Grasping the crutch, I pull myself to my feet and pain shifts through my body like lightning. I cram the crutch under my good arm and take a step toward Promise.

"You didn't kill him," I shout to be sure she hears me. "That goddamned son of a bitch Elwood killed him."

She backs up as I slowly stumble toward her.

"It's surely my fault. If I hadn't—" Promise stammers.

"It wasn't you loving me that killed Booker." Rage engulfs me like a firestorm. "Is that what you're saying?"

Her arms dangle at her sides.

"It was me," I whisper. "Thinking Booker and me could be friends even with all them people talking." I gasp, air refusing to fill my lungs. "It was me thinking we could be friends when he liked me the way I love you. It was not you."

She don't say nothing. But even from here I can see tears run down her face.

"You go on home, Promise Freeman. I don't deserve you."

We stand looking at each other across the distance between us. A cloud throws its shadow over both of us.

"You go home. I'll go to Detroit by myself." They say you can't actually feel a heart break, but I do.

Her chin thumps against her chest then she raises her head and looks up at me.

"We all kilt Booker," she says taking a step toward me and then another. "You got to know, no matter what, I can't stop loving you."

Her legs collapse and she falls to her knees as if she's praying.

"I can't bear that he's dead," she wails. "And we're alive."

With every part of my body hurting, I inch toward her, step by step. My stomach lurches and little sparks flash in the darkness moving through my eyes. My good knee wobbles and I lean against the crutch to keep from falling down. The trees wobble and them little stars flutter behind my eyelids.

She looks straight at me. "He was too good to die. To be killed by hatefulness."

We face each other, defeated, with the tracks running between us. Both my knees give out and my body lurches forward as I realize the stillness of the woods is the only witness to our pain.

(HAPTER 29

"**W**ake up. Wake up."

Something shakes me and yells in my face. My arm screams with pain and my foot aches something terrible. All I want to do is sleep. My shoulder wobbles back and forth. Fingers dig into my flesh. Last I remember we climbed up the hill of rocks to the tracks, yelling at each other. Then everything went black.

"Maisy. Wake up. Please. You got to wake up. Now."

"Go away," I mumble. "Just let me sleep." The sharp scent of pine makes me want to snuggle closer to Promise.

"You got to get up. Now. We're going to get killed." Something tugs at my pant leg.

"Don't matter," I mutter. "I must be dead already."

"You're lying on the train track and a train's coming. It's coming now. Get up. Get up."

Her voice screeches, tearing at the air, but I don't know what the words mean.

"We're sleeping under the pine tree," I mumble.

"A train, Maisy. Get up. Get up. You ain't under nothing. You fell like a rag doll. Get up."

Something yanks my leg and pulls at me, sharpness scrapes at my skin as my body moves a tiny bit making my arm hurt so bad stars and lightning flash behind my eyes. I holler at the top of my lungs. A faint whistle of a train flits into my head. I love that sound.

My leg drops and someone is crying and crying. I hope it's not Promise. I hate it when she cries. Hurts my heart something awful.

Finally. There's quiet except for some sniffling and I can sleep now.

Footsteps crunch close to my head but I don't care. I let myself float into the darkness.

"Maisy." My good hand jerks away from my body like it has a life of its own. My arm stretches and my face scrapes across what feels like razors. With all my strength, I pull my arm back toward me, but it keeps tugging in the other direction.

"Stop pulling at me," I scream, but my arm keeps stretching and stretching. There's that far off whistle.

"Shut up. Feel this, Maisy Wharton. Just feel this with your hand."

My palm presses against something cold and hard. I try to pull my hand back to my body so I can sleep, but it won't budge. Something grips my wrist real tight. I'm about to scream again, but vibrations purr against my palm. I know that feeling. I've known that feeling since I was three years old when my ma, smelling like warm vanilla, held my hand against the iron railroad tracks. Her face lit up. 'What's that?' she asked, her eyes sparkling with mischief.

"A train," I mumble. "It's a train."

"We got to run now," my ma says, her voice filled with laughter. I open my eyes to smile up into her face. Only it's not my ma. It's Promise staring down at me, her eyes brimming with fear and tears making tracks down her brown cheeks.

"You got to get up, Maisy. Now. It's coming fast."

For a long time, I stare at Promise. Her mouth opens real wide and words shoot at me like bullets. The high pitched screams stab my ears, but I don't understand what she's saying. Then she moves behind my head, shoving her hands under my shoulders. She grunts as she sets me up. All I can hear is my groaning, but she keeps lifting me until she slings my good arm over her shoulder. For half a second I stop crying and I hear it coming. The train. The clackety-clack of the metal wheels against the iron tracks. The soulful whistle. The rhythm of the steam engine.

I make my feet move, all the time leaning against Promise as she stands me up. I stumble, and she yanks at me. I want to sit down but Promise pulls me again.

"Faster, Maisy. You got to move faster."

The deafening screech of the brakes makes my body shake. Promise and I look at each other, her eyes wide with terror. Then she pushes me, flinging me into the air off the edge of the tracks. I am in the air for a long time, my toes barely skimming the ground. Promise leaps beside me, like we're dancing, floating. The train roars by, its whistle frantic and the giant iron wheels fling rocks that hit me like bullets as I fall, landing on the ground at the bottom of the track bed, my head in a pricker bush and Promise flung across my body.

* * *

After the train roars by, we sit in the bushes for a long time, neither of us saying one word. Promise holds onto my good hand real tight and her body shivers something fierce as the morning sun travels across the sky. I find my voice first which is not surprising, I suppose, but she isn't ready to listen so we sit leaning against each other. After maybe a hundred days, I speak. "I'm parched," I say sounding like an old bull frog. By pure good luck, we jumped onto the river side.

"Me too," Promise says rummaging through our sack for the tin can. She hands it to me as she climbs the rocky slope to the tracks and rescues my crutch which got wedged between the tracks without so much as a broken splinter.

"Look at this," she hollers holding up the crutch. I can tell she's relieved not to have to make another one. Stumbling down the rocky slope, she drops the crutch beside me and takes the can down to the river. She gulps two cans of water herself and brings one back to me careful not to slosh a drop. Sitting back down in the weeds with me, she doesn't touch me. Not even our toes touching.

"You still mad?" I say.

"I don't know what I feel, Maisy." She leans forward so she can look me straight in the face. "We got to get you help."

"I'm thinking there's got to be a small town somewhere around here."

"We know Ashland is just a day away. We need to go back."

"A half day by train. That could be five days by foot. I know there's got to be a settlement of folks closer than that. People live tucked away in these woods."

"Maisy, you don't know nothing of the sorts." Promise stands, both hands on her hips staring down at me. "You are the most stubborn mule I ever met."

It's true. I am a stubborn mule and, even though we don't say so, I know we decided to continue heading north. Toward Cincinnati. And, of course, Detroit. What I know is that once we're there, Promise will be as happy as me.

She grabs the can from me, slamming it on the ground. Then she rustles in our sack pulling out a dried up cinnamon roll. She rips it in half and drops one piece in my lap without so much as a glance, picks up the can and stomps back down to the river.

After maybe ten minutes, she walks toward me, her steps deter-mined and her face grim. She hands me the can of water and stands over me with them dark eyes burning holes in me.

"First," she says, "we will not walk on the tracks long as you're stumbling and flopping around." I nod.

"We'll walk in the woods, following the river and the tracks until they separate." She looks hard at me. "I ain't losing sight of them tracks so when they go their separate ways, we'll decide what to do." She pauses, her lips pursed tight and her nostrils flared. "Only at that point, I'll do most of the deciding." Promise gathers our sack and drags me to my feet.

"Goddam. Son of a bitch," I holler at the pain going every which way through my body.

"Just keep walking," Promise says as she steps in front of me, her back rigid. Part of me understands that Promise can barely hold herself up. But the other part of me needs her to hold me and help me. I hate being weak.

"He's not ever going to get better," I shout. "He's dead." *Run Booker. Run.*

She looks back at me and a tear dribbles down her cheek.

"I'm sorry," I say. "I'm just being a big old crank."

She ignores me and we walk in silence for a while, me hobbling over a bed of rounded river stones with my crutch and my bum arm tied to my body. Promise, in front of me, carries our sack of sorry belongings which snags on a stray sticker every once in a while. She stops and untangles the sack each time, never once looking back at me.

About five minutes go by and she stops dead.

"I don't see how we'll know where we're going or if we're getting lost in the woods. Or where one of them goddam so-called settlements are." Her voice stings the air, letting me know I'm the stupidest person she knows. But as sure as I ever knew anything, I know that we have to keep heading toward Detroit. It's not like I'm not scared same as her, but something in me knows to keep going forward. Like them ducks that fly back to the same lake every year. They just know. And what I know for sure is that going backward holds nothing but pain for both of us.

She walks ahead of me again, her eyes to the ground.

I stumble, crashing into a tree trunk. I *oomph* and *ouch, ouch, ouch* but Promise don't even glance back to see if I'm lying on the ground or not.

The sun dips behind the hills taking the light out of the sky. We have not seen one person all day. I was hoping we'd see a hobo or another traveler like us who could tell us how far the next town is. I have to admit that my arm is hurting badly and sometimes I'm so woozy I'm sure I'm going to fall down. Not that I'll tell Promise. She'd give me that 'I told you so' look. Besides, she's got enough pain thinking about Booker. I wiggle my fingers to touch my money sack around my neck so's I can remember what this is all about. It's not about all them modern conveniences and paved streets anymore. It's about getting us a better life together and making a home. A real home.

"I don't like this tramping through the woods when we don't know where we are," Promise whines, shifting our sack of stuff to her other hand. "Besides, it's getting to be darker than pitch."

"Just a little farther. There's got to be something or someone who can help us." I stop for a minute, practically falling on my face. "Besides, we can still hear the river, so we aren't lost." A freight train lumbers by behind the trees and bushes as if to prove my point.

"My shoulder hurts carrying all our stuff," she whines for the third time.

"I'm the one hurting every step of the way and you don't hear me complaining."

"That was surely rude," she squints at me, slows and walks a few steps behind me. For half a second I think I hear a voice, but when I stop, there's nothing but the leaves in the breeze and the squirrels squawking at each other. I shuffle on, Promise behind me.

I know it's real hard for her missing Booker and all. I miss him too, but her whining is getting on my nerves. Besides, she's in such a state I can't be sure she won't turn around and march the other way, leaving me stuck alone in these woods.

The sun's setting and shadows creep beside us, making it darker and darker. Behind me, Promise drops the sack on the ground and stops in her tracks.

"I ain't going no further." She steps next to me and looks me in the face, her arm accidently smacking my slung up arm. Fire shoots through me.

"You got to—" I growl.

Laughter and the loud voices of men bounce through the woods.

"See? I tole you so," I whisper looking at Promise with satisfaction pasted across my face. "I knew we'd find someone who can tell us some directions."

"But Maisy. What if it's hoboes camping in the woods? We're in this mess because of that hobo on the train that...." Her voice rises hysterically then fades.

She's right. I stop, ready to turn back, but there's banging and clanking. What would hoboes be doing to make that noise? That's farmer noise. I know it is.

"That's farmer noise," I crow tugging her forward. "Sounds like somebody putting tools away in their barn, probably at the edge of a town. Maybe a family who might be happy to help us."

"Help you. But not me," she mutters. "They ain't helping no colored."

She could have slapped me smack in the face. There's a long silence as we listen to the sounds while the evening breeze brings the sweetness of honeysuckle close. I know what she says is true.

"Let's creep up and take a look," I say. "Then we'll know for sure."

Her chin juts out, but she creeps with me as quietly as we can through the underbrush for maybe five or ten minutes. Using the crutch, I inch forward with Promise behind me. The racket gets louder, the closer we get. Prickers snag my shirt and grab at my pants leg as we creep through the vines toward the voices. Darkness has settled so we step carefully.

"Here," whispers Promise. "This is close enough and I can see through the bushes."

I squint through the trees and thicket. A bunch of men are laughing and shoving at each other maybe fifty or sixty feet away. Other men are around a fire pit that's made of piled up stones. The fire throws orange flickering light across the clearing and maybe a dozen wooden barrels stand by each other in clumps around the open space. A metal contraption, almost the shape of a turnip with a long spout, sits in the middle of the clearing. Hickory smoke settles around us like a soft blanket and the air is full of talking and laughing. Something bangs and my eyes follow the sound. Two men lift one of them wooden barrels into the back of a truck that looks like Seth's model T with a box on the back.

"Wish we had some coloreds to do this lifting," one man grunts.

"Couldn't trust 'em not to drink everything in sight." Rude laughter reaches through the bushes and smacks us. Promise shrinks into herself.

172

"Bootleggers," I whisper to Promise. She leans up close to my ear.

"We got to get out of here." Fear threads through her whispery voice. "We ain't safe here." She grabs my arm with clammy fingers.

I know she's right, but my desperation to get directions to Detroit swells in my chest and fills my head, leaving no more space to think. I got to do something. Maybe if I went — only me — into their camp. I could hobble into the clearing and ask. Being hurt and all, maybe they'd tell me where we are. Maybe even give me a bite of food. They wouldn't do anything, not with me being white... The memory of Elwood's hand sliding down my back and resting on my behind rises as real as if it were happening right this minute. Bile stings my throat.

"You're right," I say.

Promise tugs at my good arm.

"You got to come," she says. The softness in her voice lets me know she read my thoughts.

I can't make myself turn away. Yet. I stare at these men not ready to give up a chance for directions to Detroit. To where we can live without all this pain.

Twigs snap and bushes rustle behind us.

"One of them mans is coming." Promise chokes. Her eyes are frantic.

I listen. Something tramps through the underbrush.

"Hide behind that," I say pointing to a wall of prickers hanging from the tree next to us. "Crawl inside and don't move."

"You can't do that with your arm and leg. You'll be screaming like a hurt cat."

Fear sits between us, heavy and solid. Neither of us can breathe.

"Go," I say as the thrashing gets closer. "I'll lean against this tree and try to hide behind these vines. It's dark. Go." I squint at the clearing to make sure no one heard our whispers.

"Go," I hiss again.

Promise stands totally still, the flickering light from the bootlegger's camp jumping across her face, jaw clenched and eyes wide open.

"Go."

Footsteps stomp through the undergrowth and Promise turns to run. She hits smack dab into a man who bursts through the bushes. Her hands fly across her mouth to silence her shriek and I'm thinking this is it. We're dead.

"Omph! What the—" he yells. "What the hell?"

"Shh. Shush." I whisper.

A tall, skinny dark-skinned man has his arms wrapped tight around Promise and I know in one half second she's going to start scream-ing. And I don't blame her.

"Who are you?" he says loudly.

"Those men are bootleggers and they're not going to be real friendly about you or us hiding in the woods spying on them. So don't say a word and let go of her." I can hardly see him, but his shirt and pants are raggedy and he's barefoot like Promise.

He looks down at Promise like he's surprised he's holding onto someone. His arms drop and Promise backs away, stumbling over a rock and clutching our pitiful sack of belongings to her chest. She catches her balance and steps next to me, her shoulder pressing against mine.

He scratches his head. "What's going—"

The banging and clanging stops and a broken beam of light flits across the leaves and tree trunks.

"Sh-h-h," I hiss.

All three of us crouch, burrowing into the vines, thorns biting our skin. The beam from the flashlight flickers through the woods again, stop-ping now and then. The men are quiet and I'm sure they can hear my heart pounding.

"Must have been a deer or 'coon," one of the men says.

"Sure sounded like talking," a raspy voice growls.

"You got your rifle?"

I will myself to be invisible.

"Probably just an owl or possums squabbling over territory," someone says. Promise sniffs softly like she's trying not to cry.

"I ain't so sure about that. We can't afford no spies," the raspy voice speaks.

"Well, you can tramp through them briars if you want. I ain't that crazy."

All the spit is gone from my mouth and sweat's running down my ribs.

"I ain't tramping through no woods. Besides that fancy flashlight of yours is flickering. Almost out of battery."

"Yeah," a couple of voices grumble. "Let's get this hooch loaded."

The weak beam of light disappears, leaving us in darkness with only an occasional flicker from the fire. Promise's hand snakes through the jumble of vines, searching for me. I grab it and we squeeze until my fingers hurt.

Gradually the banging and talking and laughing gets as loud as before. Promise creeps out of the brambles and sits beside me, her breath still coming in tiny gasps.

The raggedy man slowly stands and carefully makes his way over to us.

"You got to whisper," I say.

"Well, that surely ain't no settlement," he says. "I seen the fire through the bushes and heard the voices. Hoped it was a town or some-thing."

"No. They're bootleggers. Hooch makers. And there's not one of us standing here they would be happy to see," I say.

He squints through the bushes toward the camp and watches the men load more barrels into the back of the truck and others stir something that's in a big pot on the fire.

"Holy shit," he whispers. "We need to get out of here. They catch us….." His hand caresses his neck but his gaze is far away. He slowly walks back the way he came from, his head turned and his eyes glued on the camp. Promise follows him and then me, knowing I got to give up my idea of asking them for directions to Detroit.

When we get a distance from the bootleggers, I reach for Promise and feel for Booker's knife stuck deep in her pocket. Booker's face, eyes staring empty up at the sky, flashes in my head. I carefully move the knife to my pocket. Just in case. It makes me weary being suspicious of everyone. But, truth be told, Promise and I are the only ones we can trust.

"Promise. I got to stop and rest. I can't walk another step." I lean myself against the rough bark of a tree trunk, my shirt stuck to my back with sweat. Besides, it's dark except for the light from the slice of the moon, so I'm stumbling on every rock and branch and sticker bush there is in this woods.

Promise helps lower me to the ground with my back against a tree. She whispers in my ear as she settles me, then sits down herself.

"We got to get rid of this man." Fear hangs heavy between us. "I don't trust anyone, anymore."

I squeeze her shoulder then reach into my pocket with my good hand and pull Booker's knife out and lie it close to my leg, my fingers wrapped around the handle.

"I'm thinking we're just fine now," I say in my strongest voice, struggling to keep the waver out of it. "You might as well be heading on."

The slight moonlight reflects off his face and he nods. His hair is cropped short against his head and his teeth flash white as he talks.

"'Fore I go, I got a question." He pauses, waiting for permission, I guess. "My name is Zekial, by the way."

"What's your question?" Promise asks her voice flat with impatience.

"In your wanderings, I'm thinking you might have seen a settlement... maybe even a town. Of colored folks." His eyes flick toward Promise.

It takes me a minute to understand what he said. I can't even picture what he's talking about.

"There's surely no such thing," I say, astounded that he would even imagine that was possible.

Promise leans forward.

"My pa talked about rumors of some of them towns, but further west," she answers. "He never believed it was true, though." I hear the interest in her voice. But surely colored folks don't know how to make a town.

"When I was young, I heard talk there was a settlement like that 'round here in this neck of the woods," Zekial says. "But I guess not."

Even though I want him to leave, I got to ask him.

"You know about Detroit?" I ask.

"Somewhere up North, I hear."

"Can you give us directions so's we can get on our way to Detroit? That's where we're headed."

He laughs, the sound jagged in the night air.

I wait for instructions on how to get to Detroit. I know we're going to be on our way now.

"Detroit?" he says. "You ain't going to make it. It's farther than you could even imagine. You got to know that you two getting to Detroit is surely an empty dream."

He turns and disappears into the night, his foot falls getting dimmer and dimmer. Still I clutch Booker's knife as Promise leans on my shoulder, soft whispery snores coming out her mouth.

An empty dream?

I don't believe him. More than that, I hate him.

I believe my mother's dream.

CHAPTER 30

After Zekial left last night, his footsteps faded into the buzz of the cicadas and chirping of the tree frogs. Promise and me sat, our backs against a tree, leaning on each other. Promise slept like a child, curled up, her head on my shoulder and both hands folded under her chin. I slept some, but mostly clutched Booker's knife in my lap and spent the night listening for animals, human or otherwise. As the sun's yellow glow lit up the horizon, I fell asleep.

"Wake up, Maisy." Promise gently shakes my shoulder. Pain shoots through my whole body and my eyes pop open. A groan rattles out of my throat.

"Don't. Don't," I whimper. Then my eyes close without my even wanting them to.

"We got to get going. The sun's straight up," she says holding the tin can up to my lips. "Drink this and eat this chunk of bread. You'll feel better."

The edge of the can nicks my lips and I push it away. Promise insists, so I sip and swallow the water trying to pry my eyes open. She holds a bite of bread against my mouth and that swallow of water shoots out of my belly and all over Promise's hand and down the front of me.

"You're looking mighty poorly," she says, wiping her hand on her overalls then laying it against my forehead. "You're burning up too. You got the fevers and that ain't good."

Finally I get my eyes to stay open, but everything looks wobbly, especially Promise's face. All her features keep wiggling around where

178

they're not supposed to be. She holds the can to my lips but I shake my head. My cap falls into my lap.

"What are we going to do?" she asks.

That's a good question. A really good question but I can't let her be scared. Losing Booker is already too much for her to bear. I can't be a burden. That's just not right. In the stillness I hear the gurgle of the river not too far away. I got to do something to get us out of here.

"This is what we are going to do." I say. I'm standing up and we're walking toward that water. Then we follow it until we find some help."

"You can't hardly take a step." The sun comes through the leaves making the ground all dappled like when I was teaching Promise her alphabet. Up to that moment, my life was so hard that I was never afraid of losing anything. But now that I love her, I couldn't bear to lose her.

"I can take a step. And I will," I say pushing myself forward from the tree and moving my good leg under me. "Help me up."

She stands over me, both hands on her hips, shaking her head. One twisted braid came loose while she was sleeping and it jiggles like a snake.

"You can't do nothing, Maisy Wharton. Not with the fevers." Her voice crackles with disgust.

"I can. Help me," I say lifting my good arm toward her. She lets it hang there until I drop it into my lap. She stands above me with her hands worrying the bottom of her shirt until it's almost tore.

"What are we going to do, Maisy? We're stuck. Just plain stuck." She takes one of them hiccupy breaths. "I should of stayed with Pa. And Booker. I never should of gone with you." She looks at me like she hates me except for the sadness deep in her eyes.

Then her body collapses on the ground beside me, her hands over her face and she cries like a baby.

"'Cept Booker's dead," she stutters.

The fact that I got Booker killed is almost more than I can stand. I don't know what to do except put one foot in front of the other until....

I don't even know what until means anymore. But doing this was *my* dream. My idea. I dragged her into these woods and I have to get us out.

"Promise," I say. "Listen to me. You got to stand up and then bend down close to me. Leaning on the tree and let me put my good arm around your shoulders." She makes a few sniffles then looks at me like I lost my mind. "It'll work. You can lift me up."

"Then what?" she hisses at me.

My body gets heavier and heavier, my back pressing harder against the tree. Truth be told I don't know what. Far as I'm concerned, I could sit here and never move again. Except for Promise.

She stares at me, her eyes vacant and her lips pressed together, probably to keep all them hateful words she wants to say to me inside her mouth.

"We walk to the river and follow it," I finally say. "As best we can."

* * *

We must be a sight. The two of us raggedy girls dressed like boys stumbling along the edge of the woods as we trip over stones and roots. The river moves slow and easy on one side of us and the woods thicken to darkness on the other. My arm is over Promise's shoulder holding our bag of stuff that bangs against her with every step. She walks with the crutch under her other arm to keep her from falling over, and the sun is high and hot with no breeze to speak of. It seems like days that we been struggling along.

"I can't go one more step," Promise groans. "I'm stopping right here, plopping you down against that tree in the shade and jumping in that river."

"I surely can't blame you," I say, watching the sweat run down her cheeks and drip off the end of her chin. As she slides me to the ground, I remember the first time we played in the river together, laughing, teasing and the pure pleasure of touching her skin. That must have been a hundred years ago. I lift my good hand to touch her face as she fumbles through our sack, my fingers aching for her softness. She flicks her eyes, hard as river stones, at me and moves out of my reach. She pulls the tin can out of the sack and turns her back to me. Every time she turns away, her spine stiff and not a speck of warmth coming from her, it's like she hits me in the head with a rock and I remember that Booker's dead. *Run Booker, run.*

"I'll bring you some water," she mutters barely looking at me. She walks a few steps then whirls around, her hands on her hips, and sparks flying from her eyes.

"After I get out of that water, we are going back to Ashland."

"We decided—"

"You listen to me. It don't matter what we decided. I ain't dragging you to Detroit or any other place than Ashland. They gots doctors there."

"I'm not going back."

"You're a stupid cow," Promise yells. "You can't do nothing and you're going to be dead soon." She flings her body toward the river, stops, and turns toward me.

She stands still as a stick with her eyes cutting me like razors. When she talks, her voice is cold and low, sending chills through the humid air.

"I am going to the river. When I come back I am going back to Ashland. You can come or you can stay and die."

She walks away and hollers over her shoulder.

"And I mean it."

"I don't believe you," I mutter.

She staggers toward the river over all them rounded rocks, drops the can and plunges in the water, clothes and all. Her sigh skitters through the air, as she lies on her back, feet floating and her head bobbing on the water.

"That coolness is nothing more than you deserve," I whisper to myself as she pours water over her head with the tin can. I mean to watch her, but my eyes close and I'm drifting to where it don't hurt so much. In my dream, my ma's cool hand gently rests on my forehead and she's smiling down at me, her blue eyes asking how I feel.

* * *

"Maisy. Maisy. Wake up," Promise gently shakes my good leg.

I open my eyes and Promise is standing beside a skinny brown-skinned man. I blink a few times and can see that it is Zekial. Zekial? What's he doing here? My hand slips into my pocket and wraps around the handle of Booker's knife. I look close to see if he's got a hold of Promise, but both his arms dangle at his sides.

I wait for Promise to call me names and yell at me some more.

"Maisy. Remember Zekial? He slept up river last night. I saw him when I was floating in the water. He was fishing around the bend and he caught fish with his line. We're going to make a fire and eat them." She looks at me, nodding her head ever so slightly, meaning that he's all right. Or so she says. Me, I'll keep my hand wrapped around the knife. "Real food, Maisy. How about that? We could use some real food, for sure."

"If that's all right with you, Miss Maisy," Zekial says.

"Don't call me 'Miss' anything. Were you following us?"

"No, ma'am. I'm still looking for that town I heard of." He pushes at the sand with his bare toes. "But, as a matter of fact, I was wondering about you two girls and hoping that you was doing all right."

"I'm just great."

"I can see that," Zekial laughs as he lumbers toward the river. He lays his fish down and hollers over his shoulder. "I'll get this fish cooking as soon's I can."

Even though I don't trust Zekial, not that he's given me any reason yet, my stomach growls for joy as Promise gathers twigs and small branches for a fire. Zekial cleans the fish down by the river. Raccoons will be happy tonight. I lean against the tree and sip the water she brought me.

So far Zekial has gone about his business and hasn't done anything sneaky. So far. He built a fire on the rocky beach of the river and now he and Promise laugh as they each hold two sticks with fish over the fire. I don't know what, but something ugly crawls through my chest. Maybe it's how easy they laugh. Promise and me haven't laughed since the night Booker....

The smell of the skin crackling catches on the breeze, making my stomach growl something ferocious and my mind lets go of that ugly feeling. I try to remember how many days it's been since we've been running and I can't. I've been keeping up a good attitude for Promise's sake, but I am weary and I never had pain like this. Not even when Granny Wharton beat me hard. We have to find a town soon. I don't think Promise can carry me much more and I surely can't walk by myself. We got to get to someplace where there's people who can help Promise, not a colored man we found in the woods. Who knows what he'll do to us. Tuscaloosa flits through my mind, the newspaper headlines screaming about them terrible colored boys raping them poor white girls. I slip my good hand under my shirt and fold my fingers around my little sack of coins. $10.36 plus the two dollar bills from Miss Charlotte. We could bribe Zekial not to hurt us if we need to and we got Booker's knife if worse comes to worse.

The money sure won't do us any good unless we find a place with a train stop. I been wondering how much a ticket would be and if we have enough for two. Plus something left for eating. My hand falls into my lap. Those pictures of Detroit from my *Life* magazine fade in and out as chills run through me—which don't make sense seeing as it's so hot out.

Promise shakes my shoulder. She and Zekial hold the sticks with fish. Promise hands hers to Zekial and says for him to sit down while she rummages through our sack, pulling out the last cinnamon bun that Miss Charlotte gave us. Looks pretty sad but nobody says 'no thank you'.

At first we're pretty quiet, as each of us giving the others a good look over.

"I pretty much live on fish," says Zekial holding up his torn piece of the roll. "Good to taste something sweet like this."

"Fish is good," says Promise. "I forgot how hungry I was."

"What happened to your arm?" Zekial points with his chin.

"Jumped out of a moving train," I say taking another bite of fish which I chew slowly.

He nods, his head bouncing up and down like it's on a spring.

"You still headed to Detroit?" he asks, looking at Promise.

"Ashland."

"Detroit," I say.

"Both pretty far," Zekial mutters around another bite of roll.

We eat, nobody saying nothing. The river rolling over rocks and the mourning doves cooing on the branch above us fill the silence. Crows light in the trees in the woods, jabbering to each other and arguing over whose branch is whose reminds me of sitting on our special rocks with Booker in the shade of the trees.

"Eating fish off a stick like this makes me think of the day Booker brought us a mess of fish," Promise says so low I can barely hear her. Then her head flops against my shoulder and she sobs, her fish landing in the sand and my arm screaming so loud with pain I can almost hear it. I place my good hand against her cheek, her tears wetting my fingers.

"I truly wish he was here," I whisper.

"He ain't never going to be anywheres, Maisy. He's gone," she wails.

Zekial sits real quiet in his worn denim work shirt with holes in the elbows, eating his fish I'm wondering if he thinks we're crazy girls. I hold Promise with my good arm, rocking and rocking, humming to her softly until her crying stops. By now the sun is sinking into the afternoon and we need to get Zekial on his way. He probably can't wait to get away from us and our tears. I'm thinking we have four more hours of light. Maybe there would be a town that close.

But then I wonder how Promise and me will manage. She's tuckered out dragging me along and, truth be told, I'm fighting not to pass out from the pain. But I don't trust him. There's no good reason, but I don't.

"So, Zekial. Where you heading now?" I ask hoping he'll get up to leave and, at the same time, hoping he won't.

He pauses, then looks at me and then at Promise.

"It seems you two might use another pair of hands to help you out." He looks straight at me. "That arm of yours is leaking pus and that ain't good."

"I'm fine. Me and Promise have come this far." I sure do sound rude as I say that.

Zekial's head bobs, his lips pressed tight together.

"Don't seem right to leave you two girls out here by yourselves."

"Maisy," Promise sits up from my lap, a crease across her cheek. "I'll do anything for you, but I ain't carrying you one more step. You're sinking and getting heavier and heavier and I'm getting more and more weary."

A freight train roars by on the other side of the trees, filling the air with whistles and the rumble of iron on iron. Promise and I look at each other and, without words, know we're both wishing we were on that train.

"I can't do it anymore, Maisy," she says softly. "And you can't walk by yourself with that busted up foot."

My arm throbs and I know that Zekial is right about me getting weaker, but it kills me to ask. I let my eyes wander to the river and up to the woods. Nothing. No sign posts of roads. Nothing.

"Any chance you're going our way?" I ask, knowing I can't really trust a colored man, but there's surely no other way.

"Just so you understand, Zekial," Promise says, her voice telling me to keep my mouth shut, "our way is going to be Ashland. Least we know there's doctors there."

I open my mouth and Promise gives me a real mean stink eye. I wait.

He studies the ground then gazes out across the river.

"At first I thought you was boys. Lots of them are riding the rails hoping for something better than what's at home." He looks me straight in the eye. "But you ain't boys. You're girls and that makes it real dangerous for folks to see me with you."

Promise's head bobs up and down.

He looks directly at me.

"Especially you. A colored man with a white girl." He shakes his head, pressing his lips tight. "I surely want to help but I don't want to be at the end of a rope hanging from one of them trees." His hand covers his eyes. When he looks up, his eyes are flat with pain.

"I had a brother... it don't matter. You don't need to hear."

"You have to go," Promise says. "We can't ask that much of you. It's too dangerous."

Zekial takes a long breath and lets it out whooshing through his lips.

"The other side of the problem is that I can't live with myself if I walk away leaving you here to die."

"We won't die," I sputter.

He stares at me real hard, his eyes traveling from my arm to my foot, while Promise studies her fingernails. I know he's right, but I'm not going to get another person killed. I already got Booker killed.

"Pack up Promise. We got to be on our way. We can do this ourselves." I look at Zekial. "If you're willing, maybe you could help me to my feet?" I reach for my crutch.

Promise's head falls into her hands, a small groan escapes from her. He keeps staring at me like he's thinking of something, but I don't know what.

"Wait," he says. "I never walked to Ashland, only rode in a box-car. I s'pose that it's about time to see what the tracks look like up close."

Promise raises her head. My hand rests on my crutch.

"If we follow the train track, there's less chance of seeing folks, 'specially white folks." He looks directly at me. "You got to be willing to let me hold you up since you can't walk a step on your own." He pauses. "That means letting a colored man touch you up close."

I nod, but inside I'm wondering if I will mind. The only man who ever touched me was disgusting Elwood. Surely this will be different. Then I remember how much Booker wanted to touch my hair, but knew he'd be crossing some line he shouldn't, even though I wouldn't of minded. Not with Booker.

"And, you two need to look and act like boys, you hear?"

"We can do that," says Promise, life coming back into her voice. "As you can see, we got pants and shirts like boys and we got caps to hide our hair. We tuck it up into the cap and pull the edges down over our ears." She reaches across me and snatches up her cap, slapping it on her head. She tucks her braids inside and tugs at the bill until it fits around her face.

Zekial squints at Promise, his head moving ever so slightly from side to side.

"That cap's too puffed out to look like you ain't got a lot of hair."

An ugly silence hangs in the air. A red squirrel scolds in the tree above us and my fingers travel along the edges of Booker's knife in my pocket.

I grasp the knife and pull it out.

"Sit down Promise. We need to cut our hair."

She backs away, shaking her head. One hand floats up to the cap.

"We got to, Promise. For Zekial." Her head's still wobbling from side to side.

I hold the knife out to her.

"Here. You cut my hair first."

187

Maybe two days go by, then she sits beside me and gently runs her fingers through my hair.

"I love your hair."

"Here," I hold a hank of my hair out and she takes the knife and cuts it close to my head. We do that over and over until my lap is full of blonde curls and my head feels like a soft hairbrush. Promise reaches into my lap, picks up one of my Amelia Earhart curls and puts it in the pocket of her shirt.

"Oh Maisy. You look mighty strange without your gold hair." She tugs off her cap and hands me the knife.

"I know this is a big sacrifice for you girls and I truly 'preciate it," he says softly.

Promise's hair is easier than mine. As I cut off each braid close to her scalp, tight curly hair pops out wildly all over her head. It is surely raggedy but she doesn't look like a girl anymore. I pick up one of her braids and hand it to her. She stuffs it in the pocket with my curl.

We both flop our caps onto our heads and turn to Zekial.

"Much better." His eyes are kind of sad.

I slip Booker's knife back into my pocket.

"You got to walk and talk like boys too. No giggling or being prissy or afraid of spiders." He looks hard at us. "You keep your mouths shut."

I think of how all the men we met so far figured out mighty fast that we were girls but I don't want to tell Zekial that. "How about you teach us to spit like real boys?" I ask.

He laughs, but then becomes serious.

"And," he says, "if we come upon any white folks, no matter who they are, I run for the woods. That means leaving you on your own no matter where we are or who we come upon."

"Yep. Of course," Promise chirps as she begins gathering our things and stuffing them into the flour sack.

He looks straight at me. "Even if you're dying."

Promise gasps but I know what he says is true.

Trying to cover up her gasp, Promise adds "And, we'll swear you was helping us, not hurting us."

"Thank you, but probably that won't make a whit of difference." Something about the way he says that reminds me of telling Miss Charlotte about Elwood. It don't matter what you say, it matters who's listening.

He looks at me to be sure I understand. I nod, a tiny jiggle of my head.

I can't say this, but I'm thankful for the help, especially for Promise, because I'm thinking to myself that I probably won't make it to Ashland.

Or Detroit.

CHAPTER 31

I can't say it's easy but somehow the three of us, me in the middle with Promise and Zekial holding me up, struggle our way over them sharp rocks and up to the tracks, walking slow, bumping into each other and me tripping with every step. I don't complain or make any moaning or groaning as I know it's real hard for both of them. I don't even say that Ashland is surely the wrong way. I figure it doesn't matter anymore. The dizzy, dark spells come one after the other and even though I try to carry my weight some, I know I'm hanging heavier and heavier on the two of them.

"I'm parched," Promise complains.

Sliding me down so I'm sitting on the warm metal rail, Zekial fumbles for the water can and pushes his way into the thick undergrowth toward the river.

"Hope a train don't come," Promise says, picking at the gravel bed of the tracks. Her voice is dull and flat like she moved out of her body and went someplace else. With my good hand, I reach for her knee hoping to comfort her, if only a tiny bit.

She pulls her knee away and shifts her shoulder so it's not touching mine. Useless words tumble in my head but not a single one that will bring Promise back to me. We might as well be a million miles apart. I hold my head with my good hand and wait, the sun beating on my back. *You might as well of pulled the trigger. Run Booker, run.*

Zekial bursts through the bushes, drops of sweat glistening on his face and his clothes stuck wet to his body. Looks like he took a dip in the river.

"Here," he hands the can of water to me. I take it and pretend I'm drinking my fill. I pass the almost full can to Promise.

"Thank you, Zekial," I say.

I'm pretty sure Promise will insist that I drink some more water, but she don't. She swallows every last drop then taps the can against the metal rail.

"So why were you headed to Detroit, of all places?" Zekial asks Promise.

"Maisy's ma had a dream to go there. She told Maisy that was the place for a better life." She practically rolls her eyes.

"Just look at *Life* magazine and you'll know for sure that you want to be there instead of here," I say wishing I had more water.

"Anything be better than here. You know if there's jobs for colored folks there?" He looks at me.

"There's a Mr. Ford that's got lots of jobs in his car-making factory. And good money too."

"But for me. Or Promise?"

"It's hard to imagine it would be true," Promise says. "Seems us colored folks get the leftovers and there ain't many of those these days."

I open my mouth to say there's got to be jobs in Detroit for colored people. There's everything there. But I run out of steam and I can hardly hold my head up. Truth be told, I'm not really sure.

"We better get going," he says. "We got to get you some help, Maisy. You look like you're half dead."

Promise stuffs the can back into the flour sack and stands. Zekial stretches and looks at me.

"You ready, Maisy?" he says. I can't answer, so I don't. He wraps his arms around my waist and lifts me to my feet. Promise takes her place on my good side, her arm around my waist and my arm over her shoulder. Zekial tenderly holds my bad side. I don't know how, but he holds me without causing me much pain. The trees shimmy like they're dancing and they turn a brilliant green with yellow flickers. Gnats fly around our heads as we shuffle along the tracks, breathing hard and grunting now and then.

"So where you from Zekial?" Promise asks.

"Was born in Georgia, but right now I'm from nowhere special."

"Sounds like you had a brother?" she says.

"I did, but he got hung by a gang of white men."

"What'd he do?" I mumble. "To get himself hung?"

Both Zekial and Promise stare at me, then their eyes find each other. Bitter judgment passes between them, but I'm not sure what I said wrong.

"He was a colored man." Zekial's voice is hot and his grip on me loosens. "That's what he did."

"I'm sorry," I say. "I didn't mean anything bad."

"You can't help it," Zekial's tone is cool. "Most you folks don't understand. Not really." His arm tightens around my waist again as he hitches me up.

"That's true," Promise mutters, looking straight ahead so as not to catch my eye.

"You got family?" he asks Promise.

"I had a brother, but he's dead."

"Hung?"

"No. Shot," her breath hiccups. "In the back."

Run Booker, run.

"I'm real sorry," Zekial says.

We straggle along the tracks in silence, my shoes scraping against the gravel.

"So," Promise says, "what brought you from Georgia? There ain't nothing here."

"In Georgia, all my life, I worked the fields every day but Sunday from dawn to dusk."

"Was it hard work?" I ask.

"Break your back and kill your spirit."

We're all quiet, our feet stumbling three in a row. Zekial speaks again.

"Seemed like I wasn't doing any better than my Grandpa done as a slave."

I can't think of a word to say. Seems Promise can't neither.

"So I walked away, looking for something better. Heard about them colored towns, but seems that was just a lie."

Promise's head makes tiny bobs up and down.

"So," she says, "where you headed now?" She swats away a swarm of gnats getting in our faces.

Zekial looks at me and grins.

"Maybe to all the wonders of Detroit."

* * *

We stop for a breath and to wipe the sweat off our faces. The mugginess presses down on us, making each step a chore. Promise reaches across me and touches my forehead.

"You are burning up." She looks up at Zekial. "What are we going to do?"

Zekial hitches me up, jolting my arm. Pain shakes my whole body.

"Just keep going. There ain't nothing else to do."

It's quiet except for our feet crunching on the rocks between the tracks.

Without warning, footsteps shuffle across the gravel bed of the rails in front of us. Promise gasps and Zekial loosens his hold on me. Feels like he's getting ready to run. First thing I think is 'now we're dead'. I struggle to lift my head, holding my eyes open so I can see who's going to kill us. My cap slips off my head and falls onto the tracks.

Standing smack dab in front of us is an old colored man, his back bent and gray hair curled tightly against his head. Beside him is a woman, looks like a granny, her skin the color of hickory nuts and eyes that could rock you to sleep. The man shuffles toward us leaning on a cane, his eyes sharp as a hawk and his face set looking for prey.

"What you two boys doing carrying that white girl down our train track? You want to get yourselves hung?" he asks, his voice not very friendly. He looks at me real hard. I try to look back except his face is wavy and sparkles burst inside my head. "You up to no good?"

"No sir," Zekial says. "She's hurt."

"Can't you walk on your own two feet?" He says staring straight at me. He waits a minute for my answer, but I'm too stunned to talk. "We don't carry white folks on our backs around here. You understand?"

He points, his ancient finger shaking in the air, and then speaks to Promise and to Zekial.

"Let go of her. She can stand on her own two feet. Us folks have carried enough white people already." He pauses for half a second. "Put her down, I said."

The woman steps beside him and lays her hand on his arm that holds the cane.

"I'm Etta," she looks at me with those eyes. "And this here is Mr. Isaiah Potts. He's mayor of our town and is big on keeping the peace and providing justice." She squeezes his arm, nods her head at me, but she speaks directly to Promise and Zekial who are still holding me up.

"Let that girl stand on her own two feet," Mr. Potts orders. "It's not right for you two to be holding her up."

Both Promise and Zekial loosen their grips on me. Zekial lets go completely and Promise keeps her hand around my elbow. I stand facing Mr. Potts, my body weaving ever so slightly and the sparkles in my eyes flashing.

"That's better. Stand by yourself. You don't need Negro people to do your bidding."

I wonder what 'negro people' means as Etta examines me from head to foot with her dark eyes.

"You, however, look like you took on a locomotive," she says to me. "And what happened to your hair?"

Promise slides her hand down my arm and latches her little finger with mine where no one can see. She takes her cap off with her other hand. Both Etta and Mr. Potts stare.

"She needs a doctor," Promise says to Etta. "I know her wrist is broken through the skin and might be her foot is broken too." She touches my forehead with the back of her hand. "And she's got the fevers."

"There ain't no doctor here for you," Mr. Potts says to me waving his finger again. "Closest town is Ashland."

"With great respect, sir," Zekial says. "She is very sick. Close to dying, I'm afraid."

"I'm sorry to hear that, son. But many of our people have died at the hands of her people and we are not, not now, not ever, taking care of white people. That's what this town is for. For us."

He jabs his cane at Zekial.

"For the Negro people."

Zekial gasps. Not a gasp of fear, but of surprise. He mutters something that's hard to hear but I think he says something like 'it's true'.

Mr. Potts isn't done yelling, I guess.

"You white folks got the whole of Kentucky and Tennessee as well as every place else. You leave us be."

He smacks his cane against the metal track.

"This is our town."

The ground under me sways and little flashes of light flicker in my eyes. Etta steps up against Mr. Potts and pulls him aside, whispering furiously in his ear.

"Nope. Not our town," he says loudly. "You two are welcome, but not you." He pokes his cane in my face. "That's the law."

"Mr. Potts," Promise says, "surely a doctor could just look at her. Please."

"No. Not her. That's not possible and you should understand."

195

Me? Why not me? My knees feel squishy and them stars are flickering in my eyes again. I need a doctor real bad. If Promise can go into town surely so can I. And Zekial. He's not even hurting.

"Please," begs Promise. "She won't hurt no one. Just help her. Then we'll go."

"You let one in and they all come in," Mr. Potts hollers. "No. Only Negroes." His lips are pressed in a straight line. "No."

Etta steps away from Mr. Potts and looks straight at me. I try to focus on her face.

"We got a doctor. He'll see you, but then you got to leave. You can't stay."

"I said no. Not her. No crackers here," Mr. Potts yells. "We're not wasting our doctor's time — "

"You're the mayor, Isaiah. You're not God." Etta's voice slices the air.

Mr. Pott's face is grim but he stops yelling. So that seems to settle it. Etta hands Promise our bundle that's been lying on the tracks. She puts my good arm over her shoulder, stretching me upward seeing as how she's taller than me. She hands my crutch to Zekial. I take a step and the train tracks wobble, the rails looking extra shiny.

Isaiah Potts grumbles as he follows us down the track bed and onto what seems like a well worn path. Branches whisper against my face and my pain becomes bigger than me. Sweat runs down my neck, making my shirt stick to my back. Promise's footsteps shuffle behind me. Trees waver in front of my eyes. The leaves turn a funny color. Them flashes of light come again. Etta hitches me up, but my knees collapse and my body slides out of her arms right to the ground. Then everything goes black as pitch.

CHAPTER 32

I stretch my eye lids. But they don't open. There's a creak-creak, creak-creak and a tiny cough that sounds like Promise. I try again, willing my eyes to open but they must be glued shut. I try to pucker my mouth but it won't move either. Nothing works. I tell my finger to wiggle, but it just lies still. Maybe I'm dead.

"She ain't staying here in this town." That sounds like that crotchety old Mr. Potts from the railroad tracks.

"Um hum, that's right. She ain't staying." A woman's voice.

"Her foot's hurt, her arm's broke and she's got a fever. If she don't die it'll be a miracle. She stays as long as she needs." That voice is the woman Etta.

"She don't belong here," a low, slow voice says. "She's got to go."

"None of them crackers belong." That's Mr. Potts.

Creak-creak. Creak-creak. A little faster. I try to pry my eye open just a crack, but it won't budge. My arm is on fire, pain shoots every which way.

"I won't have nobody be saying 'yes ma'am, no ma'am' to no cracker." Mr. Pott's voice is harsh. "This is our town. The only whites welcome here make their deliveries and keep on moving."

"That's right. Our pas and grandpas made this town. This is our town." The woman's shrill voice almost makes my eyes jump open.

"Amen," the deep, gravelly voice says.

Creak-creak. Footsteps pad across the floor and it sounds like a door shuts. The voices are muffled and I can't make out the words but it sounds like there's a bunch of them. Somehow I know the footsteps are Promise's as she walks back toward me. The bed sags and her cool hand slides across my forehead and onto my cheek.

"Maisy. Can you wake up?"

I try real hard to make my lips move and my voice work. A tiny groan slips out of my throat.

"You can hear me, can't you?" She hugs me. Wild fire pain burns through me as she leans against my arm. A long, low moan fills the air.

"I'm sorry. I'm sorry. Oh Maisy, I'm so sorry."

When the hurting stops, I open one eye then the other slides open. Not all the way but enough to see her. I'm hoping the smile I'm feeling inside is on my face.

"I knowed you'd wake up. I just knowed it." Her big brown eyes pull me in and rock me.

I try to talk, but my mouth is parched and my tongue is stuck to the roof of my mouth. Promise reaches for a glass full of water, lifts my head slightly and holds it up to my lips. That water trickling across my tongue and down my throat must be what rain feels like in that Sahara desert place. The coolness travels down my chest and spreads into my stomach. It's the first time I felt anything except pain.

Promise takes my good hand in hers, our fingers intertwine with each other.

"You've been out for two days. Doc George had to cut your arm open to fix the bone and cut out some infection. He said that's the worst thing. The infection. He put some sulfur powder on it before he sewed you up. Must be working 'cause it ain't climbed up your arm." She touches my upper arm and shoulder. "I been checking for red streaks all the time. That leg of yours wasn't broken but it's mighty banged up. That's why it's wrapped up tight like that."

I squeeze her hand. The last thing I remember is standing on the tracks, Promise's finger linked with mine and that old man yelling at me.

"You just got a splint on your arm instead of a cast so's Etta can get at the infection."

"You been sitting with me?"

"Every minute. Etta bringed me food so's I could sit with you." My eyes wander the room. Plain muslin curtains hang at the two windows and the walls are made of logs. A mirror hangs near the door and a rocking chair sits beside the bed.

"Etta's been taking real good care of you. Got you to swallow some soup even though you was stone cold out." Her voice warms as she talks about Etta. "And she moved to a little bed in the living room so's I could sleep beside you at night. She's a midwife, so's it's almost like a doctor. She been putting that sulfur cream on your arm every day."

She holds up the glass of water, letting me sip the coolness. "I'm so happy to see your eyes wide open."

We sit, me sipping water, and her squeezing my hand every so often. I can't help but feel joy from her holding onto me. Makes me remember how scared I was about her not loving me anymore.

"That mayor man don't want us here, sounds like," I say turning my head toward her. She gazes out the window.

A long silence stretches across the dust motes floating in the slice of sunlight.

"It ain't *us*," she pauses. "And it ain't really that he don't like you. But…"

I try to remember exactly what he was yelling about.

"It's just that there ain't no white people that live in this town," she says barely loud enough for me to hear. "And they don't want that to change."

If she smacked me in the face, I couldn't be more shocked. I strain to sit up, but the pain in my arm won't let me budge. I turn my head, my mouth hanging open, and stare at Promise.

"I can't be here because I'm *white*?"

She lifts one shoulder and lets it drop, all the while studying her toes like they was some miracle.

"But I never done anything to them. They never even met me. So how can they hate me?" She picks at a tiny scab on her knee. "Anyway, what's so bad about being white?"

She looks at me then out the window again. Her shoulders droop.

"It matters to them."

"Does it matter to you?"

I expect her to say something like *don't be silly*. The voices jabber in the other room and I wait, my nerves pulsing through my body.

"It's real complicated," she whispers.

She might as well of slammed my fingers in the door.

* * *

The bedroom door flies open. A tall woman, brown skinned, her black hair flecked with grey and pulled tight in a bun, smiles at Promise in the rocking chair. She squeezes Promise's shoulder as she walks by holding a bowl of soup. Setting it on the table near me, she glances back at Promise.

"You doing all right? You must be tired."

Promise hesitates. We haven't said a word to each other since Promise said *it's complicated*.

"I'm good," she says. They smile at each other like long lost friends. I don't know what, but something ugly jitters in my chest.

The woman looks at me, eyes worried. She seems familiar. She must be Etta.

"How you feel? It's been mighty rough on you."

"I'll be heading out probably tomorrow." I'm surprised that popped out of my mouth, but I sure don't want to lie around here not being wanted. Her eyebrows flicker and she looks to Promise like they got a secret code. The rich aroma of soup hits my nostrils, making my mouth water.

"What's her problem?" she says to Promise who doesn't really answer, just fiddles with the edge of her shirt. The woman studies me, shaking her head as she holds a bowl of soup out in front of me. Turnips, a bite of chicken and some okra float in a thick broth. My shoulders relax a little.

"Can you eat this yourself or should I feed you?"

"What should I call you?" I ask not wanting to offend anybody else.

"Etta," she smiles. "Just call me Etta."

"I'll feed her," says Promise taking the bowl. Her face lights up as their eyes meet. Etta pats her back, her hand resting on Promise's shoulder.

"Just thought you might like a break," Etta says. Promise smiles as if no one ever asked her if she wanted a break. Then she scoots beside me and sits on the bed.

Etta lowers herself into the rocking chair, humming. Promise spoons the soup into my mouth. The warmth spreads clear down to my toes.

"How's that pain in your arm?" Etta studies me.

"I'll be ready to travel tomorrow. I won't be bothering you but one more day." I surely can't stay here.

"You'll get up when Dr. George says you can. Got it?" She looks at Promise. "She always like this?"

"Pretty much." They both laugh like I'm not even here. Promise and me got to get out of this town. There's no way I'm staying where I'm not welcome.

"Where's Zekial?" I ask.

"He's staying with Mr. Potts for now," Etta says.

"The crotchety old Mr. Potts?" I ask. "The one that wants to throw me out?"

"One and the same." Etta laughs.

"*He* took Zekial in?"

"Um huh," Etta straightens the cover over my feet.

"But he wants to throw me out?"

201

Etta taps her dark arm. "You ain't got the qualifications."

"That's not fair," I practically yell. I turn my head away and stare at the wall. A long time goes by as I slip into a dream about walking up to the door of my little brick house in Detroit. My home. A place where I belong.

"Maisy," my shoulder jiggles and I pry my eyes open.

Promise spoons me another bite of soup. It soothes me as it moves down my throat. I'm grateful to have something in my body besides all this pain.

"Dr. George left some aspirin. That arm's going to hurt so you got to take sulfa pills twice a day for the infection now that you're awake. That's what just about kilt you. The infection," Etta says, opening an envelope and rolling two yellow pills out into the palm of her hand. She stands and holds them out to me. I never took pills before so I'm not sure what to do.

Etta waits, her hand stuck out in front of me. I finally pinch them pills with my fingertips and slide them into my mouth. I chew but the bitter taste makes me spit them out into the palm of my hand. I flinch from the sharp pain in my other wrist.

"Put that all back into your mouth and wash it down," Etta says holding out the water glass. "Ain't you ever taken pills before?" She sits on the edge of the bed.

"I think she might not of," Promise says. "We were mighty poor and...."

"Course I have," I interrupt Promise. "I just thought they were a different kind."

Etta's forehead wrinkles and her eyebrows pull together as she looks at Promise who has moved and made herself comfortable in the rocking chair. Etta rubs her hand over her face and Promise hides a smile by looking away. Soon's as I can get out of this bed, we are on our way to Detroit. Or Promise can just stay here with good old Etta if she wants, but I'm not staying where I'm not wanted. I sure don't belong here and it seems no one wants me to be here anyways. The tiny brick house flits through my mind. My ma said we were heading for Detroit, her and me. That's where I'm going.

It's not that I'm not grateful for Etta's help but Detroit is where we belong. Well, maybe it's where I belong. Promise looks mighty comfortable sitting in the rocking chair.

"Here," Etta says. "Take these three aspirin with this shot of whiskey. Help you get some sleep and it'll make that arm stop hurting so much."

"My arm's fine." I don't mean to sound snotty, but more than my arm, it's my heart that hurts. I want Promise to smile at me, to touch the palm of her hand against my cheek and kiss me with her soft lips, all the time telling me she's excited about Detroit. She's been pulling away and hiding inside herself. She says no, but surely she blames me for Booker getting killed.

I do.

Etta holds out the three white pills and a small glass of whisky. She flicks her eyes at Promise and winks. Promise grins back at her looking like she belongs right there in Etta's chair.

CHAPTER 33

Streaks of sunlight shoot through the bedroom curtains where the two halves don't quite meet, while Promise drags the rocking chair across the wooden floor from the bedroom into the front room. I don't know how many days it's been, but this is my first day out of bed. Next, Promise holds me up around my waist while I lean on Etta's cane and we shuffle like a couple of old ladies into the front room. The sun's real bright coming in Etta's big window. I squint against the light and see a huge garden outside.

"That's where Etta gets all them vegetables for soup," Promise points to the garden.

"Yup," I mumble, wishing Etta hadn't stopped giving me whiskey as my foot truly don't like me stepping on it. I'm still taking them bitter pills and aspirin, but I like the whiskey best.

Promise helps me sit in Etta's rocking chair, then hands me a big chunk of corn bread. "Etta made this in the skillet this morning," Promise says, proud like she made it herself. Crumbs tumble down the front of the sling that's holding up my bad arm.

Promise laughs, picks the crumbs with her fingers and pops them in her mouth.

"What's your best friend Etta doing?" I ask trying not to be a snot. But I am. I'm still hurting and I hate lying around. Makes me feel real weak. Weak like when I couldn't protect myself from Granny. Or Elwood and his creepy hands. And now it's people coming to the house every day, yelling and arguing about me being here. Etta hasn't complained yet, but she must be real tired of standing up for me.

"Etta?" Promise snorts, looking at me with squinty eyes due to the tone of my voice, I suppose. "She's working at her store today. Had to catch up from the days she missed taking care of you."

Now I'm embarrassed that I said that, but I'm not really sorry. So instead of apologizing I let my eyes wander around the room. In the far corner is a kitchen with a wood burning stove. The iron skillet with corn bread sits on top. Looks like a sink and a refrigerator. A real small one, but definitely a refrigerator, not an icebox.

"They got electricity here?"

Promise stands up and pulls a string. The room lightens and I look up at the ceiling. A light bulb hangs from the ceiling right over my head. Electricity. Here?

"They have electricity." I am incredulous.

"That nasty mayor, Mr. Isaiah Potts, went to Ashland and somehow got the electric company to run a line to Hope. Sometimes it flickers and sometimes just turns off for a while, but it is electricity."

"Hope?"

"This town. I forgot that today is really your first day here 'stead of your fourth."

My eyes continue to travel around the room while Promise talks.

"They're working on getting telephone lines here too."

Looks like Etta's couch serves as her bed now. Despite myself, I admire the patchwork quilt and the three stitched satin pillows against the wall. There seems to be a table and four chairs that are for eating at and a good size chest by the bed that's stacked with books and what looks like magazines. An oil lamp sits on the table and a picture in a gold frame. The wooden plank floor's covered with the biggest braided rag rug I ever saw. Makes me miss my rug. Probably just a pile of ashes now. Wish I could have saved it. *Run, Booker. Run.*

Shaking my head, I close my eyes to get rid of them words, but Booker stares at me kindly in my mind. I whip my eyes open and bump my wrist against the arm of the rocking chair. The sharpness shooting up my arm brings me back to Etta's room. Just near where we're sitting is a shelf with more books and newspapers. I look again. A radio. Standing right against the wall in the middle of the table, its knobs and cloth front are real grand. Promise studies me looking at the radio. There's so much confusion between us now that it's hard to know what to say. She takes real good care of me but I can tell her heart's not in it. Almost anything one of us says riles up the other one. I know I'm grumpy as hell, and I imagine she wishes she could just sit and think on Booker.

I wish we were already in Detroit and this was our little house. I wouldn't be the only white person where everybody hates me and Promise would have a home. I look at the radio again.

"You and Etta listen to the radio?"

"Of a night. We listen to this program called Little Orphan Annie."

Jealousy creeps under my skin and invades my whole body. I try to stop it. I even know it's crazy. But listening to the radio together. *I* should have been doing that with Promise. I rock and huff at the same time.

"You can listen tonight. You can sit in the rocking chair."

I don't answer. What's the matter with me? Maybe it's them little yellow pills.

"Let's turn it on now," I say.

"I don't think…"

"Etta? We wouldn't want to upset Etta now would we?" I rock harder. The floor creaks. What's the matter with me? Why am I mad she listens to the radio? I kilt her brother. I don't deserve nothing.

"This *is* her house."

Promise sits on Etta's bed and runs her finger along the path of the patchwork stitching on the quilt. I rock, ashamed of myself, but not enough to apologize.

"Want something more to eat?" she asks me her eyes wary. Her face tells me she wishes she could run right out the door.

"I'm fine," I say even though I'm starving. I point with my good hand. "What's on that chest over there? Magazines? Maybe she's got a new *Life*."

Promise wanders over to the table and shuffles through whatever's on the chest.

"What's the picture of?" I ask.

"A woman. Pretty, but sad eyes. Maybe Etta's ma or sister."

She cradles two books and several magazines and what looks like newspapers in her arms and lays the stack in my lap. She walks away from me and I don't blame her. But then she pulls a table chair over beside me and takes most of the pile as I leaf through what looks like a magazine. It sure's not *Life* or even *Good Housekeeping*. I never saw this magazine before. It's called *The Opportunity*. I turn the pages, surprised at what I find.

"Everything in this magazine is about coloreds," I say. "Not so many pictures as *Life* but every one is showing colored people." I flip through a few pages.

"Look. This story's about a play in New York City."

"What?" Promise leans against me, her chin on my shoulder.

"It's called 'Green Pastures'. It's a musical, and everybody in it is colored."

Promise pushes in close to see. She traces her finger across the picture, stopping to touch each face.

"Everybody *is* colored. Is this 'round here?" Wonder floats in her voice.

"Up north in one of them big cities. In a place called New York."

"I never knowed coloreds could do this. Turn the page."

I do and there's a picture of a bunch of colored men in baseball uniforms. Promise stops my hand from turning the page. She stares for the longest time then lays her finger on each man standing in the line. Each holding a bat.

"My pa said once that he heard there might be colored baseball teams, but we never believed it."

"I never heard of them."

"Booker would've played, you know. He could spend half a day hitting rocks with a stick 'til Pa told him to grow up." Her hand lies flat against the page gently holding the whole team. "He would have loved knowing about this."

Her breath is warm on my cheek. *Run, Booker. Run.*

"Read me the name of the team."

Blinking real fast to clear my head, I move her hand to see the words, holding it for a few seconds. "Says it's the Pittsburgh Crawfords."

"What's Pittsburgh? And what are Crawfords?"

"I don't likely know. Probably something in the North somewhere."

She spreads her hand on the team again, her head on my shoulder. Her wanting to tell Booker about this fills the room. I leave the magazine open and we just sit side by side for quite a while.

My cranky feelings lie down still for a bit.

* * *

Promise and me are stretched out on the big bed where we sleep. All that sitting up wore me out. She leans against me holding up a newspaper while I read to her. With my good hand I run my finger across her forehead and down her nose, heading for her lips. She turns her head away, dropping the newspaper in her lap.

"I just want to show I love you," I say.

"I know. I don't know what's wrong with me. Since Booker…" Her voice fades into the afternoon shadows.

"Since Booker what?" I imagine she's going to say she hates me. That it was all my fault. Or that she wishes she never met me and she's leaving as soon as she can.

"I'm just all besides myself. I keep thinking he can't be dead. One minute I'm myself and the next I can't stand nobody talking or looking at me. My heart hurts every minute. When you was so hurt I could take care of you 'cause you just lied there, not saying a word. You didn't ask nothing of me."

"But you won't even let me touch you to comfort you," I say, my voice whiny.

"That's just how I am right now."

"That's not how you are with Etta. You let her touch you. How's that different from me?"

Even though she don't move, I feel her body shrink away from me. "The difference is she don't want nothing from me," Promise says. And I do. I want all of her.

I try to roll over, but it hurts me too damn much. I lie half on my side, my body limp and my face turned away from her. She's sniffling now. I know I made her feel real bad. But she hurt me too. Since we been in Hope, we've done nothing but hurt each other. Seems like two or three days go by, but then her arm gently snakes around my waist and she rests her chin on my bony shoulder bone.

"Maisy. I'm so sorry. I just need time."

Truth be told, I'm hurting about Booker too. I keep it all locked up inside me though. Like with my ma.

The best I can do is take her hand in my good hand. We lie like that, just breathing. A ray of sun from the window streaks across us both.

The front door flies open, its bottom corner scratches against the floor, and there stands Etta, a bag of groceries in her arms. She looks straight into the bedroom at the two of us on the bed. I'm thinking we don't look like sisters, holding hands and leaning on each other.

She don't say hello or nothing. Just moves toward the kitchen. The paper bag crinkles and cupboard doors bang. The refrigerator door opens. Then finally closes. Promise moves away from me and sits up on the far edge of the bed. I roll onto my back and try to look real innocent.

Etta steps into the door frame, practically filling it all up, being taller than most women and with her elbows stuck out like chicken wings.

"You listen and you listen hard. Both of you." She waits until we each nod. "Don't you two be hugging and touching in anybody's view." She stabs a finger three times at us. "This ain't a town that will let you push who you are in their faces." She turns to leave. Her shoes squeak as she spins back around.

"Even though these people have suffered, some still got hate inside them. You two got enough trouble without.....without. This."

Her eyes stare hard then she stomps toward the kitchen.

I slip my hand across the bed and press a single finger against Promise's arm.

CHAPTER 34

P romise leaped off the bed like a frog on fire after Etta scolded us,
and we barely even looked at each other all afternoon. Now Promise is stirring the lamb stew Etta made from a little hunk of meat
and vegetables from her garden. Etta opens the front grill of the stove
and throws in a chunk of wood.

The knock on the door startles me. Promise makes a tiny gasp
in her throat. A knock these days usually means trouble.

"Who's there?" Etta hollers as she walks toward the door, wiping her hand on her apron.

"Me. Zekial. Can I come in?"

"Sure," she pulls the door wide open. "Just in time for lamb
stew."

"I could smell it from the street," he says. Etta laughs and slaps
him lightly on the shoulder.

The four of us squeeze around the table, the sweet and sharp
smells of basil, bay leaf, carrots and lamb float in the air.

"This is delicious," Zekial says, a corn bread crumb falling from
his mouth.

"Sure is," Promise and I say at the same time.

"So, Zekial. How's Mr. Potts treating you?" Etta asks.

"Miss Etta—"

She raises a finger. "Just Etta."

"Etta. That Mr. Potts is a little cranky but he's been real nice to
me. Let's me sleep in the back room and yesterday I started working at
his grocery store."

"The old man's not all bad," Etta says around a mouthful of stew.

"You could of fooled me," I say.

Zekial stares down at his lap, his spoon in his hand.

"I didn't mean to be rude," I say. "It's good he's helping you."

He keeps looking at the floor.

"What's up?" Etta asks.

He taps his spoon against the bowl and we all stare at him, waiting.

"Something's wrong." Etta's voice says that he better speak up.

"Some folks... I mean, at the grocery store..." He looks up, worry creases his face. "I didn't agree, but being new it's hard to –"

"Spit it out," Etta slaps her spoon against the table.

"They want to make a town meeting to vote on throwing Maisy out," his eyes travel to mine, hold for a second, then fall to his lap, "on throwing you out of town."

Promise gasps.

"That ain't right. You can't even walk."

"Throw me out?" I say. "They don't need to go to all that trouble. I'm leaving tomorrow anyways." I flash a glance at Promise, my jaw locked tight. "I know I didn't tell you, but I'm going. With or without you."

Etta stands, waving her arms like some big bird. She jabs her finger at me.

"Over my dead body. You ain't going nowhere." The expression on her face dares me to disagree. That is, if I want to take my life in my hands.

Zekial wipes his mouth with a napkin, puts his bowl in the sink and bolts for the door. He thanks Etta and yanks the front door open.

Turning, he mumbles 'sorry', not even looking at me.

* * *

211

Promise, Etta and me are in the living room, but none of us say a word to each other.

I'm sitting in the rocking chair reading one of the newspapers. Promise leans toward me, pestering me to read it out loud. Etta lights the oil lamp, even though the electric bulb is on above our heads, then she picks up a book that's got a book mark half way through and stretches out on her bed. It says *Not Without Laughter* by Langston somebody. Her fingers cover the last name.

The newspaper crinkles as I open it and read to Promise. She stops me and points at a word.

"That letter looks almost like the K in Booker's name."

"It's a Z. Her name is Zora Neale Hurston."

"That a picture of her?" Promise taps the newspaper. "She's colored too. Read it to me."

"Tomorrow we have to teach you some more letters so you can read for yourself," I say.

It's the first time since Booker got kilt that I've seen her really smile. I think to myself *if I'm still here tomorrow.*

"But read this now."

"You won't believe this," I say reading ahead. "This Zora's a writer now, but in 1925 she got to Harlem—I think that's in the North somewheres."

"In New York City. It's a mostly Negro part of the city," Etta says.

I flick my eyes at her wondering how she knows so much. "Anyways she came with $1.50 in her pocket."

"That's like us," Promise's eyes light up.

"She went to college and then… Listen to this. She drove a *car* by herself, taking a gun with her for protection. She drove all around talking to, it says here, those Negro folks asking about their stories and folklore." I don't know what those words mean. Promise waits for me to explain, but I can't.

"It's like the history of a people through their stories," Etta says from the couch. "She talked to Negroes about their lives and their history."

"What are Negroes?" Promise asks. Etta's eyes pop wide open. I vaguely remember Mr. Potts using that word when we were standing on the tracks.

"That's us. You and me are Negroes."

"That the same as colored?" Promise asks.

"Where you been?" Promise's face sags. "Never mind. Yes it's the same, just more modern. Shows a little more respect."

"'Bout time," Promise mutters.

"Amen," Etta says looking at the clock, tick-tocking away on her table.

"Hey," she says. "It's eight o'clock."

"Tonight is Little Orphan Annie with Daddy Warbucks and her dog Sandy," Promise says.

I wonder who all them people are. I listened to the radio at Elwood's all day but never of a night. But to me it doesn't matter much what it is. I'm excited to hear any-thing from the radio. It's like reading my magazines or the newspapers and them taking me anyplace but where I am. Etta stretches and walks to the radio, making that little dial click on. Guy Lombardo and the Royal Canadians play *Too Many Tears* right now. Almost like he can see out of the radio right at us.

Etta turns to Promise.

"So tomorrow, I'm going to ask you to go and help out at the store."

Promise's eyes flick to me and I see the worry in them.

"I'll stay home with Maisy," Etta says, "but it's time you got out and did something useful." She gathers the bowls and puts them in the sink, pumping some water over the stack of them.

"I don't even know where your store is or what to do," Promise says. I can tell she's nervous.

"I'll walk you there and Asa—Asa Blackwell—will show you what to do." Etta says.

213

"I don't need nobody to stay with me," I say as indignation swells in my belly. "I'm not a baby."

"I won't be staying with you. I'll teach you how to make soup one handed and to weed the garden." She looks at me. "Time you got out of bed and did something useful too."

I don't know how to answer her. I know she's right, but my arm still hurts me something awful.

"Pull the rocker closer to the radio. Orphan Annie is on in a couple of minutes," Etta says.

Promise helps me stand as she scoots the rocking chair across the wood floor toward the radio. I flinch at the hollering coming from outside our door.

Splat! Then loud voices. Shouting. *Splat!*

Promise and me both freeze.

"Get out of our town!" the voices jeer, louder and louder. "Get out of our town!"

I grip Promise's arm.

"*Cracker. Cracker. Cracker.*" They chant.

Etta leaps toward the door and flings it open.

The remains of two raw eggs slither down her front door, egg shells slipping to the ground as voices disappear into the night. Laughing and chanting.

"That's for me," I say. "They hate me. I can't stay."

Etta slowly closes the door and pivots on one foot, her eyes burning and her face like stone. She points at me and her finger shakes.

"You," she says. "You will stay here in this house, in this town, for as long as you need to."

Her arm drops. "Do you understand?"

I don't. But that don't seem the right thing to say at this moment. Instead, I stand real still looking at my light skinned hand holding the newspaper picture of that Negro woman in Harlem.

CHAPTER 35

"I can't move any faster," I mutter. My foot kills me with each step as it drags across the floor. Etta loaned me her cane but it's too long and it flops around, tripping me. I grit my teeth against the sharp pain zapping up and down my arm.

"I thought for sure you'd be on your way out of town today." Etta looks at me with one eyebrow raised and that fake smug look on her face.

"I'll hop a train just as soon as I can." I say lightly, but I'm truly serious.

"Until then you got to earn your keep." She waves me over to the small counter by the sink. Vegetables are piled on a folded flour sack, little drops of water sparkling in the sunshine streaking through the window.

"Cut off the stems, roots and anything spoiled and put them in this pot of boiling water." She taps a knife about half the size of Booker's against the counter. "There's some chicken parts already in the pot."

She hands me the knife and I stand there.

"How am I going to hold them down while I cut them?" I ask.

"I don't know."

"You don't know?" I pull my voice back to friendly, given what Etta said last night. "I thought you were going to teach me."

"I never made soup one-handed." She pats me on the back. "But I'm sure you'll figure it out."

She goes right over and turns on the radio, picks up her book and sits in the rocking chair reading. While I do all the work. Well, not quite yet. But I'm gonna.

I start with a carrot. That can't be too hard. I lay it out then cut at the raggedy tip. That damn carrot flies onto the floor. I reach down to pick it up forgetting about my bad arm.

"Ow. Ow.Ow. Dang that hurts." I stand and eye the carrot still on the floor. I peek at Etta. She's rocking and reading. A real good idea comes to me. I feel a little cocky as I lean down and stab the carrot with the knife. Ha. Got it. I put it on the counter top with the knife sticking out of it. Taking hold of the knife, I tap the carrot against the counter top. It flips off the knife and lands right back on the floor. She's still rocking.

I pick up the carrot with my good big toe and next toe. Ow it hurts to stand on my banged up leg. Ow. I grab the carrot and look up to see if Etta's smiling at me for being so smart. She's not. Now that dang carrot's got pieces of dirt stuck to it. I put it in the sink and give it a pump of water. I did that one handed, but for the life of me I can't figure out how to hold the carrot and cut it. I'm getting madder and madder at Etta. She said she'd teach me and she's reading and rocking to her heart's delight listening to music on the radio. Old Fred Astaire sings *Night and Day*. That's what it's going to take me to do all this. I need a bigger knife. I look around the kitchen. It seems I have the only knife clutched in my hand.

Then an idea strikes me. Booker's knife. I hobble into the bedroom, moaning and groaning every step of the way because it hurts so much, and I want Etta to know I'm suffering. She doesn't even ask how I'm doing. Once I get his knife and get myself back to the kitchen, I figure out that if I stab the vegetable with the kitchen knife I can steady it with my bad hand fingers — though it hurts like crazy — and cut the stupid vegetable with Booker's knife. It takes me until lunch time to get all them vegetables into the pot.

But I do it, damnation. I do it.

I slap my behind down on a kitchen chair and let out a long, long sigh. Etta rocks for a minute or so, then smiles at me, places her bookmark and closes her book.

"How about some lunch? You and me?"

"That'd be real nice," I say. I think to myself that it's about time.

"You done a good job, Maisy. Thank you for making supper."

I don't know whether to keep on being mad or to be pleased with myself.

Maybe both.

* * *

I thought maybe after lunch we'd nap or at least stretch out and listen to the radio. But it seems them weeds in the garden are growing so fast they can't wait an hour to be ripped out of the ground. For a minute I wonder if Granny's been weeding our tiny garden back in Paine Hollow. That was always my job. Least I'll know what to do with Etta's weeds.

Etta holds the door open while I struggle, the cane slipping one way and then another. What I really want is to sprawl out on the bed and have Etta bring me tea and honey along with that last piece of corn bread. Of course if she did, knowing me, I'd be sure she thought I'm a cripple and get all mad. She probably can't win right now seeing as how I'm not liking myself so much this minute. This pain twists my insides around so's I don't even know who I am. And Promise is scaring me to death.

We round the corner of the house and a bunch of chickens, pecking at the dirt, don't even move. I swish Etta's cane, but they look at me and keep on pecking. Just like Granny's chickens. For half a second I think about Granny and wonder who is cleaning the outhouse for her. I truly hated that she beat on me but I hope she hasn't drunk herself into the ground. I'm sure that Elwood's making sure she's not starving to death. If nothing else, he always made sure Granny had something to eat, even if it weren't much. That wondering gets pushed out as I remember my ma had chickens too. A long time ago. The mama hens would let me hold the fuzzy chicks. They were soft in my hand, making tiny pecks on my fingers, like my ma kissing my forehead.

I walk around the chickens and follow Etta down a small rock path to a wide open clearing with trees far enough away not to throw their shade on the garden which is bigger than two of her houses, spread across the land with bean poles, beets, rhubarb leaves, peas and rows of lettuce, okra, turnips, tomatoes, hills of corn and a raised bed probably for potatoes and yams. A chicken wire fence is staked all around the garden with a rickety gate. Marigolds, daisies, and some other flowers I don't recognize stand in rows outside the fence. No wonder she's always making soup.

Etta grabs a hoe that's leaning up against the chicken wire fence.

"I'll hoe, seeing as how that takes two hands. You do the picking up." She hands me a gunny sack. I'm about to ask her how I can hold the sack and pick up weeds at the same time, but I know she'll say she never picked weeds one handed.

I figure out how to put the sack on the ground wide open, dump in my handfuls of weeds, and then pull the sack along on the ground with the cane. Ha. I didn't even have to ask for help.

"So I know you got a granny somewhere. You got a ma or pa?" she asks as I pull the gunny sack close to where she's hoeing.

"My pa's dead and my ma..."

Etta stares at me. "....she's waiting for me. Somewhere."

She leans on the hoe, expecting me to say more, but I pick up weeds and shake the dirt out of the roots.

"How'd your pa die?"

Nobody except Promise ever much cared about my ma or pa.

"My pa died of the influenza when I was two years old. All I got of him is a tiny picture."

"What happened with your ma?"

I don't really want to say about my ma seeing as how I don't remember much about the day she got shot and, truth be told, I don't believe she's dead anyway. But I don't say that to nobody seeing as how I'm seventeen and all.

"You got a picture of your ma?" The caring in her voice soothes my edgy nerves.

"Nobody ever took one that I know of."

"Not even your granny?"

"My granny hated my ma." I shake the weeds extra hard thinking about how mean my granny was to my ma. And me. My whole life got filled with meanness when I went to live with her. She probably still sits in her chair drinking hooch 'til she falls over. I suppose I do hope she's not dead.

"So what did happen to your ma?" She glances at me, her kindness wrapping around me.

Flashes of light flicker behind my eyes.

Etta waits.

"She got shot in the head." I know that because Granny told me. I pick up the sack, shuffling as I move it.

"I am so sorry to hear that." Her hand rests on my shoulder. She squeezes and waves of tenderness float through my body. "It must have been awful for you. It sounds like you really loved her." Her eyes look straight into mine.

Her kindness explodes something in my chest and there's them tiny lights in my eyes again. But I ignore them.

"I'd like to hear if you can tell me." Her voice is a hand brushing hair off my forehead.

Them damn lights again. I blink, but they still flash. I look at my dirty fingernails and decide to tell her what I know.

"We were going to go to Detroit to get away from Granny. But. But." Something weird happens inside my head. The garden sort of fades and wobbles and then my ma's face is right before me, true as life, smiling, handing me a biscuit across the table in Elwood's restaurant. Then the door slams open and Sheriff Judd walks toward us. My ma's hands flutter in front of her face, her eyes open wide. He holds out a gun, that big black barrel hole pointed right at me and my ma. There's a flash and the loudest noise I ever heard smashes in my ears. Ma flies backward out of her chair and her brains and blood splatter all over Elwood's floor as sure as if I was sitting there right this minute. Her eyes are still wide open like she's surprised to see me, but there's not a bit of life in them. Just those bright blue eyes staring at me.

I blink to erase these pictures, but they stay lodged in my memory. This has never happened before. I only knew what happened from my granny but I never remembered for myself. I see my mother's blood slowly seep through the cracks in the floor and her arm is flung out towards me, her fingers curled up so I can see that her nail polish is the same color as her blood. There's lots of yelling and screaming in my head, then someone squeezes my shoulders and squats beside me just as my mother's blood reaches my white sandaled toes. Miss Charlotte pulls me to her and picks me up. I keep looking over her shoulder, pounding on her back, as she takes me away. I keep looking.

Hoping.

Waiting for my ma to smile at me.

To say my name.

I realize I been waiting all this time. Waiting for my ma. Waiting for her to say my name.

But she's dead. Really dead.

The garden gets fuzzy and I feel turned inside out. But even still, a kind of relief creeps through me. The waiting's over.

"Maisy? You all right?" Etta's voice pierces through the pictures in my head and I'm back in the garden.

"You're shaking, child. Your face is so white you'd think you saw a ghost."

I let myself sink to the ground, rhubarb leaves brushing my cheek.

"We'll finish this tomorrow." Etta reaches out her hand, brown and no finger nail polish.

Tears push at the back of my eyes then dribble down my cheeks. I never cried since she was shot. Etta leans down and wipes them from my face with the back of her fingers. She holds her hand out again, waiting for me to grab it.

"I'll just sit here for awhile," I murmur. I lie down on my sack of weeds.

My ma's really dead.

Etta looks at me for what seems like a long time, lowers her hand and let's me be.

Finally I cry, sobs shaking my shoulders. I hug that sack of weeds, dirt mixing with my tears. I haven't cried since the day my ma got shot. I never allowed myself. But now them sobs keep falling out of me, one after another. I don't know for how long.

My whole body stutters and the tears barely dribble. Embarrassment shakes me as I lie on the ground, snot and tears smeared on my face. I look around and it don't seem as though anybody's looking. I wipe my face with my arm and turn onto my back, the sun warming me through and through.

I feel different. I study the clouds trying to figure what just happened. My whole body is solid and peaceful, not so skittery and on the edge always looking for trouble to get me.

Pictures of me and my ma float through my head. Ones I never remembered before. Us at the moving picture show in Ashland. Cupcakes for my fourth birthday. Her waking me every morning with our sweet chickabiddy song. Somehow capturing that painful memory gave me a bunch of good ones too. Makes me feel real strong and all stuck together in my body. It seems I gathered up a piece of myself that had been lying around waiting to be found.

CHAPTER 36

We are in Etta's living room and Promise is getting ready for her second day at the store. She is all a twitter. She hasn't smiled like this since before Booker died. I want to tell her what happened in the garden about me remembering about my ma, but something about her don't feel right. Recalling about my ma is too new to take a chance.

"Asa showed me how to check each shelf and how to stock it. Is that the right word? Stock?"

"It is," Etta says. "Many customers yesterday?"

"Oh yes," Promise grins. "So many Asa said good thing I was there. He couldn't of kept up." She turns to me, her eyes gleaming.

"Tonight will you teach me money? Then I can use the cash register." She leans down in front of me with a jar of cream she got from Etta. "Will you make my wild hair lie down some?"

I rub some cream into her hair and press the tiny curls down as best I can. She looks more grown up with her hair like this. I miss her braids.

"Can you imagine," she looks up at me, wonder across her face. "I'm gonna press them buttons—ching, ka-ching—and take money from all these peoples? Me. Asa says that's a real important job."

I'm happy for her and her sparkling eyes make me smile, but I don't like how she's talking about Asa this, Asa that. Gives me the willies her chattering on and on about him especially when she still sleeps with her back to me.

"I never dreamt this could be me. I always thought I'd be cleaning white ladies houses all the rest of my life." She and Etta exchange a private glance. "But," Promise spreads her arms wide, twirling around two times, "there ain't no white ladies here."

Her eyes land on my face. Her shoulders droop and she bites her lip instead of smiling.

"I don't mean that as an insult, Maisy."

"I didn't take it as one. I thought we'd be heading on to Detroit real soon. Not stuck here so you could work in a store."

She looks at her toes, tapping them against the wooden floor.

"I could work in a store in Detroit, I suppose," she says. "This'll be good practice. Right?"

I rock harder in the chair, staring at the magazine in my hands like I'm reading. I don't even say goodbye when she leaves. Just keep rocking and rocking, halfway listening to the radio about this Franklin Roosevelt that's running for president and his promises to make times better. Don't think there's anybody can make things better for me.

Rap! Rap! Someone's knock cracks the quiet. Etta gets up from her paper work at the table and opens the door.

"Come in Isaiah. Mary. And Reverend Blackwell. I'll put on water for tea. I made some biscuits for breakfast." She gathers her papers from the table and puts the pile on her bed. "Here. Sit."

"No tea. Thanks." Isaiah nods at me. Mary looks as far in the other direction as she can without breaking her neck.

I never met Reverend Blackwell but he doesn't introduce himself or look into my face. "We came to talk," he says crossing his arms on his chest making his tie double up under his chin.

Etta motions again for them to sit. They don't.

Reverend Blackwell studies me, his head shaking from side to side ever so slightly.

"So I seen you," Isaiah looks at me with his eyes all squinty like maybe I stole something from him, "out in the garden working yesterday. Must be feeling pretty good, missy." His voice is loud and thin like when someone's trying to sound sincere but they're not.

"Yes," Mary's brittle voice snaps through the room. "Now you can be on your way."

"Surely Etta's been more than hospitable," Isaiah says, "but it's well past time for you to be moving on."

Etta steps between them and me, her hands at her waist and her lips pressed together.

"I'll decide when Maisy can leave."

My jaw drops ever so slightly. No one ever stood up for me before.

"Now, Etta. Don't get all uppity. I'm simply saying as mayor that the girl needs to leave our town. We can't be having white girls here that will make false accusations like with those Scottsboro boys."

Etta's lips press tight together. "That's not who Maisy is."

"Still, a promise is a promise," says the good reverend, his voice deep and his long fingers tapping the Bible tucked under his arm. "You said she'd stay a short time."

"You ain't got no power over me." Etta points at Mr. Potts. "You may be mayor, but I'm a free woman and I'll make my own decisions."

Etta turns and looks at Mary real hard. "That's what this town is about."

Water from the faucet drips into the sink and a flock of chickadees twitter outside the window. Isaiah coughs into his hand.

Reverend Blackwell takes the Bible from under his arm, licks his forefinger and flips through the pages. He squints at Etta, then at me before he goes back to leafing through his Bible.

"You were always headstrong. But people are talking, Etta. You, of all people, know how that goes." Isaiah's voice gets real meaningful. "You want the town against you again?"

Goosebumps creep up both my arms.

"Feelings are real high and things will surely get real ugly," Mary pipes in. Her lips purse into a mean old pucker.

"You mean like throwing eggs at my front door?" Etta's says.

Nobody blinks an eye.

Reverend Blackwell stops flipping through his Bible. "You have gone against the word of God before," he jiggles his finger at her.

"People always talk," Etta's voice is steady. "If I was afraid of talk, I'd be dead a long time ago." She levels her eyes at Isaiah. "I make my own decisions. If you don't remember."

"Yes, you did," Reverend Blackwell speaks like he's preaching in church. "Your *soul* is still in grave danger." He thumps his Bible.

Isaiah unfolds his arms and stands with them hanging for a minute or two. I wonder what they are talking about. Her *soul*?

"There's agitation and talk of the whole town being against you—again," Isaiah warns.

"And you deserve it," Mary says.

The good reverend's head bobs up and down. "Time to move that girl along."

The air stands still and the clock tick-tocks. Everybody's either flicking their eyes at each other or staring at the floor.

"So," says Etta. "You want to be civilized and have some tea? Or, do you want to leave."

* * *

"They couldn't get out of here fast enough," I say around a peanut butter sandwich that I made for Etta and me for lunch. She cut the apples up.

"I'm sorry—for you and for them— that they acted that way," says Etta. "It ain't like you're going to tear the fabric of our town apart."

"I don't know what you mean by that."

"They ain't willing to give you a chance to be trustworthy solely because you're white."

"Does this whole town feel that way about me?" I'm getting more and more ready to get going to Detroit. "I mean, even when I was lying on the railroad track with broken bones Mr. Potts didn't want me here."

"You have to see their side too."

225

"Why? They're just plain ornery. I didn't do anything to them." She looks at me.

"No you didn't personally. But you got to remember that many, but not all, of 'your' people have hurt them and their families real bad. In the past and surely still now." She looks out the window, her hand lightly skimming across her brown skin. "Being a Negro under white people's laws and attitudes is surely a painful thing."

Booker lying on his face in the dirt, blood spreading on his shirt flashes into my mind.

"And, their granddaddies worked hard to make this town a place where Negroes were safe. To have someplace that was our own and where we could live with dignity. So some of the townspeople are afraid. Also," she looks me full in the eyes like she's looking into my soul, "not many people, including us Negroes, has learned yet to judge each other for who a person is rather than judging out of their own anger and fear."

My heart races.

That's exactly what Elwood done about Booker and me. And Booker's dead.

* * *

"So wash the peanut butter off your face and comb your hair. Do you have a clean shirt?" Etta says as I clear the table. "I got a job for you."

"Me?" I'm shocked. "Here?"

"No in New York City," she laughs. "Get ready."

I don't have a clean shirt, but I straighten out my clothes, wash my face and comb my raggedy short hair. I'm sure walking around with butchered hair don't help make a good impression.

We step out the door and walk down her short path, me leaning on the cane. This is the first time I've seen the main street.

Etta points up the road. "My store is straight up that way. *Etta's Dry Goods Store* it says on the sign across the front. Not just dry goods but my extra vegetables too."

"Hey!" a familiar voice hollers. Zekial waves to us. We wait for him to catch up then we all walk in the direction opposite of Etta's store. We pass an apothecary. A tall thin man opens the door and a little bell like Elwood's tinkles.

"Morning Moe," Etta smiles at him. He gives her a big grin but then his eyes slide to me and he shakes his head, lips pressed together.

"Gotta run, Miss Etta." His back is stiff as he enters a door that says *Law Office* next to the apothecary. Etta squeezes my shoulder and we all three walk past a house that looks a lot like Etta's except the shutters are red.

The main street is a lot like Paine Hollow with small red brick buildings with white trim and older wooden houses like Etta's. The big differences is that the road is in better shape and everybody, except me and one white man delivering a bundle of newspapers to the barber shop down the street, is colored. Negro. I find myself looking real hard for another white person. But it's just me and the delivery man. Something lonely and, yes, fearful shivers through me. I've never been the only white person anywhere. Now that I am, everybody hates me and wants me out of here.

"Guess where we're going?" I say to Zekial.

"To Mr. Potts' store?" he laughs. "You going to walk me to work?" He waves across the street. A young man waves back as he opens the door of a store with a big black sign with gold letters a foot tall that says *Pott's Grocery*. It seems like a nice looking grocery store. Not at all like that Isiah Potts.

"Hardly," I say. "I don't think he'd even take my money." My hand flutters lightly against my little bag of coins around my neck under my shirt.

"Oh, he'd take your money. Don't doubt about that," he says. "Then he'd run you out of town." Etta and Zekial chuckle. Not me, though.

"Etta," a deep voice drawls out her name and a tall, man with skin like cream in coffee crosses the road and heads toward us.

"Jeremiah, it's good to see you." I hear caution in her voice as she reaches out and touches his arm.

He nods to Zekial. "Welcome to Hope. Is old Isaiah treating you well?"

So far I am invisible and something in my bones keeps hoping I'll stay that way.

"So." Jeremiah turns face to face with Etta. "As a member of the town council I have to register my opinion to you." Harshness sits in the air.

"There's no need for you to speak," Etta snaps. "I know the exact words and tone you will use."

He reaches toward her and rests his hand on her arm. She moves backwards a step.

"I admire what you've given to this town, Etta. But, this. *This.*" He points to me.

"She's not a *this*, Mr. Johnson. She is my guest and she will remain my guest for as long as she wishes." Zekial nudges the dirt to the side of the wooden walk with his toe.

Mr. Johnson turns to me, menace creeping into his eyes. "You know what they say: Fish and guests stink after three days." A long pause hangs in the sultry air. "Then it's best they both be thrown out."

"Excuse us Mr. Johnson." Etta takes my arm. "You interrupted our business."

I'd be lying if I said I wasn't scared, but Etta's hand guiding me keeps my heart from jumping out my mouth. Zekial nods at Mr. Johnson and follows us as we move along the walk. Nobody says anything. Seems we're all paying attention to where we set our feet.

"Don't you listen to any of that talk," Etta finally says. "You hear me?"

"Pretty hard not to."

She squeezes my arm.

"So where are you going?" Zekial finally asks.

"Etta got me a job." My voice hiccups.

"Where?" he asks and points to the barber shop. Two Negro men, wrapped in white cloths, sit in big chairs. "There?"

Etta rolls her eyes.

She and Zekial walk and I stagger with the cane and my bum leg down the wooden sidewalk, past some more houses that look like Etta's and down a side street. There's a building with a bell in the steeple and I'm thinking it's the church, but there are children in the yard and I realize it's the school. A tire hangs on a rope from a big chestnut tree in the yard.

"So." Etta stops and looks at me. "We only have one teacher for all the students. The youngest are five and the oldest are thirteen and fourteen. As you can imagine Eliza has her hands full."

"You're going to be a teacher?" Zekial sounds disbelieving.

"She is," Etta replies.

My heart is racing. I can't be a teacher. Number one, I don't know how and number two, they'll throw me out.

"I can't," stopping, I stare at Etta. My insides jump into my throat.

"You will," she walks toward the school.

"How many children in all?" I stammer.

"Thirty-six. Some of the older ones help out with the younger ones, but that takes away from their education. So. I volunteered you to Eliza to teach the very youngest since you know how to read and can do arithmetic." She steps back and looks for my reaction.

"I only ever taught Promise." My fingers tap against the cane and my good leg jitters. "I never taught a bunch of little children. Especially in a real school."

"But you've been to school and you remember what your teacher did. Right?"

"I guess. But that was a long time ago."

"You can do it," Zekial adds.

Etta squeezes each of my shoulders and looks me straight in the eyes. "From what I seen you can do this." She smiles. "Even one handed. I trust you with these children. And this town needs you even if some don't realize it yet. Besides you'll be earning your keep."

"Sounds more fun than the grocery store," Zekial laughs.

Nobody ever trusted me with anything important. Not really. Maybe Promise does. Some. But even her, she won't let me close when she needs me the most. I'm happy that Etta trusts me, but I feel pretty shaky too. I don't know nothing about teaching little children. Especially little colored. No, Negro children. Besides, they probably all hate me just like Mr. Potts and his friends do.

CHAPTER 37

Eliza, she's the teacher and real nice too. She reaches right out and shakes my good hand when Etta introduces us. Zekial's as well. She holds his hand a moment longer and gives him a long, slow smile. Her skin is a lot darker than Etta's. I wonder if that matters to the people of this town. It sure does in Paine Hollow. The darker your skin the worse off you are.

She leads us down a narrow hallway then settles me at a table with some pencils and paper as Etta and Zekial leave. Zekial winks at Eliza, a grin stuck on his face. I think she might be blushing as she goes into the other room then comes back with three little kids, two boys and one girl.

"This is Miss Maisy," she says. My breath catches. No one ever called me Miss Maisy before. Well, except Zekial and I yelled at him. "This here is Thomas." She touches his shoulder then rests her hand on the little girl's head. "And this is Annalee. And Elijah."

"Hello Miss Maisy," all three say to me. Two sets of wide dark eyes and Annalee's hazel eyes stare at me.

"She ain't white." Elijah sounds surprised. "She's just kind of pink."

"Hush now. I said we don't talk about that." Eliza's voice carries an apology. I'm not sure why. What color everybody is seems to be on all our minds.

"Each of you pull a desk up close to the table here so's Miss Maisy don't have to stretch." They stand like little statues, all three of

231

them. Annalee's mouth hangs open a little bit. "Go on. Get those desks."

Thomas hesitates, his forehead wrinkled.

"My pa said not to talk to the cracker girl if I saw her on the street because she don't belong here."

My body twitches, wanting to bolt out of the school and keep on going until it reaches the Detroit city line.

Eliza bites her bottom lip and I can tell she's thinking hard.

"This is school, Thomas. Not the street, so I think you can talk with Miss Maisy here." Her foot taps nervously and her lips are pressed tight.

After considerable scraping and bumping, the three are settled in the desks, their hands folded and their solemn faces stare at me.

Eliza turns to go into the other room, then stops, her hand on her hip the same as Etta.

"You be sure to help out Miss Maisy. She hurt her arm."

Each child bobs their head up and down. Smiling, Eliza leaves.

I am alone with these three children. I think what to do but my mind is blank. They are surely waiting for me to do something. Annalee's feet bump against the leg of her desk and Thomas wiggles in his seat. I wish Eliza had told me what to do. Or that I had asked. Thomas squirms back and forth in his seat some more. He raises his hand. I am certain that he is nervous about disobeying his father.

"Miss Maisy," he says cautiously. "May I be excused?"

"We're not even started, Thomas." Fear shoots through me that he will run home and tell his father about me.

"But Miss Maisy...."

I shake my head no.

"I got to go to the outhouse."

Burning creeps up my neck onto my cheeks. I turn to Annalee.

"Is that allowed?"

She giggles.

"I mean by himself?"

Now all three laugh out loud. Elijah looks at me shyly.

"There's only room for one in the outhouse," he says.

"Go on Thomas. We'll get started." I race around in my brain for what to get started on. Then I think of teaching Promise and Booker to write their names in the dirt under the shade of the oak tree.

"All right now," I say and hand each one a piece of paper and a pencil. "Do you know how to write your names?"

Both Annalee and Elijah shake their heads.

"I know mine starts with an A."

"Good. Let me have that paper back." She hands it to me and I print her name at the top in big letters. "That's your whole name. Now you copy what I wrote right under that." I do the same for Elijah and for Thomas when he comes back.

All three work real hard to copy the letters and they do it. Sort of, that is. Elijah got the Elij on the paper and Thomas' S is backwards. Annalee done real well except her name goes from corner to corner on the paper.

"You done real good. Do it one more time trying to make the letters exactly the same as mine."

This time it's a little better. Elijah got his whole name on the paper, but forgot his J.

"Now. We're going to learn to read." Excitement sparkles in the air.

"Read? How can we read when we can barely write these letters?" Thomas asks.

Mister smarty pants. "Annalee. Run your finger across them top letters and read me what them letters say."

She does, and Thomas waves his hand like crazy. Thomas and Elijah both sit up real straight as they each read their names.

"Now, I want you to write your name again under the last one. Try real hard. Then wait and we'll read each word you wrote."

My chest is all full up watching the three of them with big grins on their faces as they grip their pencils and lean their heads over their papers. I never knew I could do something like this.

* * *

Eliza let me go before school was out saying that was enough for the first day and that I did a good job with the little kids. Tomorrow she's going to add two more to our class and she told me to come early so's we can talk about what I need to do with my class. She said *my class.* My very own class. I'm only seventeen and I got my own class.

I hobble with the cane up the road toward Etta's house thinking that I'll take a nap. Them kids wore me out. Then I remember that Etta said her store is on up the road and to the left. Excitement bubbles through me and I might burst out of my seams about teaching them children. I got to tell Promise. She'll want to hear about *my* class, begging me to tell every detail and pestering me what each one said. I surely hope I don't meet Thomas's father on the way, though. Imagine. Teaching a little kid not to talk to white people.

Chills shiver through my chest about being on the street alone seeing as how we don't know who threw the eggs, but it's broad daylight. Nobody's going to throw an egg at me when everybody can see. Even though my arm aches and my foot hurts, I can imagine Promise's hug.

She'll throw her arms around me and squeeze me tight saying what a good job I done. As I make my way up Main Street, there's a lot of people walking on the tarred road and wooden sidewalk. All Negroes. Not even the white delivery man. I am the only white person in sight. I imagine that each of them knows me *and probably hates me* for being in their town, but I don't know any of them.

I stay on the tarred road, close to the wooden sidewalk but not in anybody's way. As I pass the apothecary, with the glass jars and knobbed lids lined up on the shelves across the front window, a woman with a little kid studies me kind of curious like. Most of the people look away from me like I got a bad disease or their eyes catch on fire if they look at me too long. The rich smell of bacon and grits floats by in the air. My stomach growls as I squint through a big window with the gold letters CAFÉ on the glass. Some people sit on them round stools lined up in a row in front of the counter. Two people point at me then whisper to each other. Then, in front of the bank, the name hanging on a sign above the door, a man in work boots comes towards me. I smile a tiny smile. He bumps his shoulder into me and hisses.

"Get out."

I step backwards, catching my balance. My bad arm throbs, but more than that, prickly fear ripples through me. My foot squishes in something mushy. I look down. Manure. Horse manure seeps into the toe of my shoes and between my toes. Shaking my foot real hard, most of it flies off, but it sure does stink. I scrape it on the edge of the sidewalk, getting the last bit of manure off.

Etta's house is set back on the right. Maybe I should hide inside. But my excitement about them children rushes through me and I got to tell Promise. Trudging on, a very skinny man driving a Model T rumbles down the street and waves at someone he knows almost running over my toes. I back up real quick and step up onto the sidewalk as he hollers something at me that I can't understand. He don't even know me and already he's decided I'm a hateful person. I didn't do anything to him — or anyone. It's just not fair. Then a small wagon filled with what looks like furniture being pulled by a mule clomps by. The driver smirks at me, spitting a big goober on the road in my direction then turns his head away and pulls his cap down over his forehead. Chills wash through my body.

Being the only white person in sight, I can't help but be afraid with all this hate jumping around me. My nerves sizzle through my whole body and I look around for just one other white person or Promise or Etta, even Zekial. It's real strange being so different. Especially in a place where I'm not wanted. Hollowness settles in my chest, making me feel lonely and, more than that, afraid. I wonder if I should head back to Etta's, but I really want to see Promise. I know for sure that Mr. Potts and Miss Mary, and even the reverend, are saying bad things about me. But I can't tell who believes them and who doesn't. Is every person walking past me thinking hateful things about me? The sweet smell of fresh bread floats in the air mixing with the ripeness of horse manure from the road as three women together pass me, watching their feet real carefully as they go by. Like I'm not even standing right there. Then a woman carrying a baby in her arms, comes out of the stationery store. She smiles and nods, but doesn't stop just as two women walking by me whisper to each other and give me dirty looks. I trip on the uneven boards of the sidewalk, but catch myself before I stumble.

As I pass the hardware store, I peek in the window hanging with saws. Sitting in the doorway on a stool is an old man with gray-brown wrinkled skin. I steel myself for rude words, but his head bobs slightly as I walk by. My shoulders relax a little. At the corner, a woman charges out of the milliner's shop which is painted a bright yellow and the front window is crowded with hats stuck with feathers. She barely stops before bumping into me. My breath leaves my body making me dizzy.

"Oops. Sorry. I was rushing." She looks me up and down. Everything turns blurry as I wait for her to attack me. "Ain't you the one staying at Etta's?"

"I am," I say bracing for her to say something nasty or to slap me.

"I'm Dinah," she sticks out her hand. As my heart beat slows down, I lean my cane against my leg and shake her hand.

"I'm Maisy." I don't know what to say after that. The touch of her fingers is still in the palm of my hand.

"Etta's a good woman. She's done a lot for this town." She smiles, orangey lipstick is moist on her mouth. "She delivered both my boys. Brought them into this world." We look at each other for maybe three hours and I still can't think of what to say. "Gotta run as I'm already late," she says. Taking a few steps, she stops and turns to me.

"You take care, you hear?" And then she's gone.

I watch her back as she strides up the sidewalk and turns a corner. Unreasonable joy fills me up because someone talked to me. At least a little. I reach for my cane and walk past the post office. It says U.S. Post Office on the front. I'm surprised they're allowed to have a real post office here. I avoid looking at anyone until I see the sign for Etta's dry goods store. Crossing the street, I step smack dab in front of a husky man, his skin the color of night.

"Sorry," I say.

He stops and stands right in front of me his feet planted wide. He doesn't move a speck. His faded blue shirt with them white pearly buttons you sew on making that tiny x of thread is right where my eyes fall. I'm surprised he's standing so still, seeing as how I have a cane and one arm in a sling. I expect him to step aside.

He doesn't. He crosses his thick arms on his chest and glares into my face, his eyes blazing.

"Excuse me," I say wiggling my cane to let him know I'm crippled. He doesn't move a tiny bit and now he's looking at something over my head. His fists are clenched. I don't think he sees me even though I'm right in front of him.

"Excuse me," I try again, holding up my cane and wiggling my slung up arm, but he don't blink. Now I'm getting angry. I have the cane. I have the gimpy leg and the broken arm. What's the matter with him? He should be stepping aside to let me pass. Maybe two weeks go by and I don't know what to do. My breath stutters and sweat pops out on my upper lip. The memory of Elwood attacking me in the middle of the street flashes through my mind and waves of fear wash through me. I got to get across the street. Now. I tap my cane once more but the man studies something down the street.

"Ahem," I say clearing my throat, but he stands in front of me, solid as an oak tree. Out of the corner of my eye, I see a handful of people stop and gather on the sidewalk, whispering to each other. A woman in a bright red dress steps toward us but another woman grabs her arm, stopping her.

Everything is quiet. No footsteps, no talking, just a few whispers. Sweat drips down my rib cage as I wait, noticing the raised veins that run up and down his arms like ropes.

Something shifts inside me and my stubbornness explodes. I stare back at him. What right does he have to stand in front of me blocking my way? My leg aches and that makes me madder.

"Excuse me," I growl at him. But nothing. He's still as stone, a pillar planted in the road. My anger burns and nasty words crawl on my tongue whiles an ugly realization worms its way into my brain. *No. No. Not true.*

I shake my head to chase the thought away. But it won't go. It's stuck in my head. *It can't be true. Not me. I love Promise.*

The words shout, echoing. Filling my brain. This isn't about my cane and my gimpy leg. Or my broken arm.

No. No. Booker was my friend.

The realization won't go away, the ugliness clogs my mind like pitch. My stomach hurts.

Even me. Me.

The understanding pounds in my brain. I expect this man to move because... I can hardly breathe. Because he's a colored man and I am white.

No. No. No.

Shame crawls over my face like maggots.

Yes. It's true. Even me.

My stomach lurches. I study the people gathered on the sidewalks. *They* know what I expect and they're waiting to see what I will do. Time passes like molasses on a winter day.

My mouth is parched. I bring spit onto my tongue, then lick my lips. I have no idea what to say. There are no words inside my head. I wait, then open my mouth. I wait for the words to come.

Finally.

"Excuse me, sir. I didn't mean to impede your way."

Clutching my cane with my sweaty hand, I step aside and walk around him, keeping my eyes to the road, staying as humble as I can, hoping he doesn't grab me.

I nod as I step around him, but his eyes are focused inside his head.

I am behind him. His footsteps against the road go the other way and my shoulders relax. Once I'm past him, I walk as fast as I can around the small crowd who stare at me, fingers pointing and whispers flying like sparks.

No one says hello or anything. And I don't blame them.

* * *

A half block and ten years later, I breathe slowly as I stand in front of Etta's store, my head still buzzing with the notion that I believe I am better, that I deserve what I want because of the color of my skin. No one ever said them exact words to me, not even Granny, but somehow I always believed that was true. That being white was better. My stomach turns over and acid crawls up my throat. I didn't even know that about myself.

I stand in front of the cartons of Etta's vegetables that sit every which way, some on top of others while I calm my nerves, taking a deep breath. The prices are written on a piece of cardboard stuck on a stick reminding me of Booker knowing his numbers and wanting to make a sign for his fish. I surely miss him. His hand reaching, then pulling fast away from my Amelia Earhart curls, slides through my mind making my heart hurt. *He* knew what I am beginning to learn. He understood his *place* even though I considered him my friend.

Reaching down, I pick up one of them shiny red tomatoes. Probably one I picked. Putting it back in the box, my excitement gathers to be surprising Promise and I push my other thoughts out of my head. I imagine the smile on her face, her eyes all lit up, as I walk through the door. She'll laugh and hug me as I tell her about my class. *My class.* I can hardly believe it. But it's true. I have a class. A woman holding a bunch of carrots sees me and says *humph* before she heads inside the store. But I'm too happy about seeing Promise to let her bother me.

I stand on the sidewalk in front of Etta's store and peer through the big window. Bolts of material are lined up against the wall. Maybe I can sew some new shirts for Promise and me. I'd make her a lemon yellow one. Rows of shelves go clear to the back of the store. Then I see Promise. My heart does a little dance. She waves her arms while she's talking and throws her head back to laugh. Then a young man steps up close to her, laughing too. Must be Asa. He's handsome with his long face and mahogany skin. He talks and points. Promise looks serious for a moment then puts her hands on her hips, laughs and shakes her finger at him.

A real sick feeling crawls up my throat and something bitter settles in my mouth. Part of me wants to rush in and yell at her. Part of me is glad to see her laugh. But another part of me is mad as hell she's not laughing with me. That she's laughing with that handsome dark-skinned boy instead.

I step backwards and turn away.

What I do know is that I kilt her brother. So why would she laugh with me?

Besides, surely it's easier to love someone whose skin matches yours.

Maybe all we got now is pain between us.

CHAPTER 38

I must of fallen deep asleep. Voices wake me and I pry my eyes open. I'm lying on my bed. Then I remember I was only going to rest and read one of Etta's magazines. Promise's laugh floats on the edge of an afternoon sunbeam as it cuts across my room.

After a struggle, I get myself up and out into the main room. Promise and Etta are fixing dinner. Promise is chopping vegetables and Etta's making another one of her soups. Zekial's fiddling with the radio and settles on someone talking about Mr. Roosevelt, everyone being out of work, and something called the New Deal.

"Sleepyhead," Promise smiles at me. She lays her knife down, skips toward me and takes me in her arms. No kisses, but one great big hug.

"Here," she pulls the rocking chair near the kitchen area. "We're almost done."

"So how was school?" Etta asks.

My chest fills up and I can't help but smile about them three little kids and them writing and reading their names.

Zekial tips his head. "So how was Eliza?" He says her name with a lilt in his voice.

"School was great and Eliza's real nice. She's going to help me tomorrow and give me more children."

"She really needs help, but there's no money for another teacher. I'm sure she's very grateful." Etta stirs the soup, tasting the broth.

"How'd they like a white teacher? The children, I mean?" Zekial asks.

"They seemed fine. Mostly they were excited to write their names." I decide not to mention Thomas. I'm sure Thomas' father will be yelling at Eliza tomorrow.

I want to talk about what happened in the street and how that changed me inside but as I study the three brown faces I know it is my job to figure out my confusing feelings, not theirs. I never even had these thoughts or feelings before. I never had the tiniest idea that my white skin let me do what I want and go where I want. But, truth be told, I was taught that it was better to be white than dark. Not directly, but between the lines and in the tones of voices. Or Granny shaking her head and clucking her tongue.

I flick my eyes at Promise. "So, how was your day at the store?"

"I worked the cash register," She is almost giddy. "Asa done the money part, but I pushed them number keys." A picture of the two of them laughing and their arms touching up against each other slams into my head. My head aches and something real ugly twists in my chest. I rock faster and try to think about how proud Annalee was of herself. And Elijah wiggling in his chair.

"While the soup cooks, I need you three to help me pick the extra vegetables for the store," Etta gives one last stir and lays the wooden spoon on the counter, untying her apron.

"Wait," Etta says. "I got you a present Maisy."

"Me?" My ma and Promise are the only people who ever gave me presents. I should be jumping for joy, but there's a big lump like a watermelon in my throat.

She walks to her bed and there's a big brown paper wrapped bundle tied with a string. It crinkles when she picks it up and puts it in my lap. My stomach leaps as I hold it.

"Open it," Promise is almost as excited as me.

I tug at the ends of the string with my good hand, but it ends up being a tinier knot.

Zekial and Promise both step beside me to help.

"I'll do it," Promise picks at the knot with her finger nails. The string falls off and I slide my hand inside the brown paper and feel something soft, soft, soft. I grab whatever it is and hold it up. The brown paper slips to the floor.

"What is this?" I hold a roll of cottony material.

"Batting," Etta says.

"Batting?" And then I understand. For my quilt. So I can finish it. I squeeze it tight up against my face then hug it with my good arm against my chest.

"Thank you. Thank you, Etta."

"When you finish your quilt with this, it will be warm and cozy this winter for you and Promise." She grins at us. My mind flashes on holding Promise up against me, her softness against mine. But then I think probably that will never happen now. I don't blame her for not forgiving me. But I sure wish that she still loved me like she used to. I miss her touch and kisses something terrible. It hurts that she laughs so much with Asa. I don't begrudge her laughing. But when I see it with Asa, it bruises my heart and makes me real scared. So scared I want to slap her. I'm not proud, but that's how I feel.

Probably me and my quilt will be headed for Detroit by ourselves. I don't want to go by myself but it feels like all her affection is shifting away from me. And surely being in a Negro town is easier for her than for me.

"Come on Maisy," Etta says. "We still have vegetables to pick for the store. Let's go."

By the time Zekial helps me hobble over to the door with my cane, Etta and Promise have gathered up three large baskets and are halfway out the door. I grumble to myself about being so slow, but Zekial gently takes my broken arm and walks beside me.

I never had a brother. But that's what Zekial feels like. A big brother. My stomach contracts so hard, I double over. Zekial grabs me, stopping me from falling on the floor.

"What's the matter?"

I want to tell him that he's like a big brother. But I can't. Not with Promise's big brother dead.

243

Outside, Promise drops the baskets on the dirt and turns back to me. Her eyes smile at me all warm and welcome. Now I think I'm being stupid and all this worry about Asa is me being a fool. I probably let my jealousy run away with me.

"How's that arm doing?" she squeezes my good arm.

"Better," I say. "Mostly it don't hurt unless I bump it or move it too fast." Etta and Zekial are talking with their backs to us and I lean into Promise hoping for a quick kiss. I wonder if she was thinking about us under the quilt making love like I was.

Instead of a kiss, she presses her forefinger across my lips. Letting go of my arm she skips to catch up with Etta. Snatching up a basket, she picks vegetables near Zekial, chatting a mile a minute and smiling every time she says Asa's name. I stand still, the rough ground under my feet. My head feels like that Ferris wheel I saw in *Life* magazine—just going round and round. Nothing makes sense to me anymore. I don't know what's up or what's down. I don't belong nowhere and Promise changes every two minutes.

"You do the tomatoes," Etta's voice snaps me back to the garden. "Just be gentle not to bruise them." She thinks maybe I'm going to juggle with them? I scoot my basket closer to the tomato plants.

"Me too," I hear Promise say. "I feel like I really belong somewhere for the first time in my life."

"Walking down the street I held my head up, not shuffling my feet and looking at the ground," Zekial says.

"And people smiled at me in the store instead of frowning all suspicious like or yelling at me to get out," Promise adds.

Etta keeps on picking squashes, but I know she's listening to every word.

Zekial nods vigorously. "I went into every store on both sides of Main Street just because I could." He stretches. "Then I walked into that little café and they let me sit down. If I'd of had a cent, they'd of fed me. Every person I saw said *hello* instead of *get out of here.*"

That's sure not the Hope I know.

"Right. And not one sign saying **No Coloreds Allowed**." She turns to me, smiling sadly. "I wish my Pa could have lived here. He'd have been a different man." She pauses. "I know being hated helped make him so mean."

Her shoulders relax and somehow she seems to stand a little taller.

"We could make a good life here, Maisy."

I drop a tomato and it splats on my foot.

"We're not living here. Everybody hates me. I'd sooner die than live where no one wants me." I'm practically yelling. "We're going to Detroit as soon as I can walk."

"Maisy," Promise's voice pleads, but it has a streak of steel in it that I never heard before.

My hand shakes as I set two more tomatoes into the basket. I can't stay here. This is not a place where I can belong and surely not a soul wants me here. Etta coughs. I raise my head and she's standing, as only she does, with her elbows out like wings. Her eyes brim with pain, but I don't know why. She tips her head at me, then goes back to picking squash.

Our baskets are full and Etta stretches out her back and looks up at the sun as it moves toward the horizon. Zekial lifts a basket in each hand.

"I'm on my way now," he says. "But I'll bring these up close to the house." He smiles at Promise and Etta, but looks at the ground as he passes me.

"Thank you," says Etta. "See you soon. And give Mr. Potts our best." She grins and chuckles to herself.

"Sure will," Zekial says heading for the house.

Etta clasps her hands behind her, stretching out her back.

"The soup's still got some time to go," she says. "You two come with me."

We follow her down a worn path and into a grove of trees. The light's dappled and the leaves near the top of the trees glow with a golden sheen from the setting sun.

Etta steps into a clearing and I see weathered head stones. Like for graves.

"This is my family cemetery," she says. "For as long as we've been in this town."

Promise and I walk slowly through the headstones, me reading her the names and dates.

We stand in front of three side by side:

LIBERTY   **LIBERTY**
Evaline   **Joseph**   **Simon**
1853 - 1899   **1855 - 1909**   **1871 - 1891**

"Who are these people?" Promise looks at Etta.

"The two together are my ma and pa. And that one," she points, "is my brother."

"How old was he when he died?" Promise asks. She kneels down and touches the stone. The shadows of the leaves dance across her shoulders.

"Twenty," I say doing the arithmetic real fast.

"How old was Booker?" Etta asks standing behind Promise.

"Seventeen." Promise sits, her knees folded under her for a while, praying, I would guess. She touches the stone one more time then stands. She slips her hand into mine. I squeeze hers and her fingers tighten around my hand. When she does that I know we belong together.

There's a larger stone and Promise and me stand in front of it still holding onto each other. I know these graves are Etta's family, but they make me think of my family. And probably Promise feels the same way. Especially Booker and her ma. Promise squats and runs her finger along the letters. She looks up at me.

"What's this say?"

"Forever."

Promise touches it one more time.

FOREVER
Etta Liberty   **Lena Monroe**
1873 -   **1876 - 1927**

I look back at Etta.

"That you? Etta Liberty?" I ask.

"It is."

"Is that Lena your sister?" Promise asks slipping her hand back into mine. "The one in the picture on your table? She's real pretty."

"No. Not my sister," she pauses like she's thinking deep inside her head. "Lena. She was the person I loved most in the world."

I remember Isaiah Potts' nasty voice in Etta's living room. About how Etta knew the hurtfulness of the town talking against her. And the reverend saying her soul was in trouble.

"So she was..." I don't have a name for what she must have been to Etta.

"Yes. We lived in this house and made a life together for almost thirty years."

"It must not have been easy," I say thinking of how Isaiah and Mary treat me.

"At first, many people in this town gave us trouble, calling us vicious names and committing harmful deeds."

She makes a point of looking straight at me.

"But when they got to know us together, most of the meanness stopped. Not all, but most. But you're right. It wasn't easy. What really mattered to us, though, was who we were to ourselves and to each other." She glances at the sky. "Come on, we've got soup to eat."

Promise and me are still holding hands walking slowly toward the garden. Etta's words lay in my mind. I wonder who we really are to each other because it seems to change every ten minutes.

And then, for the first time, I wonder who I am to me. I never thought about that, really. It's strange to think only about me. Mostly because ducking granny's broom stick and dodging Elwood's hands took up all my energy. No one cared about who I was, so neither did I.

That might be changing. Maybe remembering the day my mother was killed gave a piece of myself back to me that will help me figure out who I am.

CHAPTER 39

We get to the house and Zekial is sitting on the back stoop, his elbows on his knees and his face to the sun.

"I couldn't listen to Mr. Potts just yet. I mean, he's doing me a big favor. I know and appreciate that. But. Well. Sometimes he makes me weary. Could I stay for a while?"

Etta laughs and pats him on the back as she pulls open the screen door.

"You are always welcome. Besides it will be time for Little Orphan Annie in a bit."

We settle into our chairs with our soup bowls in our laps, ready to listen to Little Orphan Annie. I don't know how they get that dog Sandy to bark at exactly the right times.

"When I'm listening I can see them all in my head," says Promise. "Like one of them moving picture shows you told me about, Maisy."

"And we don't even have to buy a ticket," I laugh. Booker poking at the ground and wanting to hold my hand in the movies flashes through my mind making my heart hurt. *Run Booker. Run.* I give my head a quick shake.

"Mr. Potts plays his radio from early morning 'til he goes to bed," Zekial says. "Sometimes I long for a little bit of quiet."

"What's he listen to?" I ask, realizing I never thought Mr. Potts was interested in anything but getting rid of me.

"He listens to a lot of talking, but toward the afternoon he likes his music."

"Does he listen to Little Orphan Annie?" I ask.

"He does. And that Dick Tracy show with all the shooting, too." Zekial grins a funny, lopsided grin. "By the way, how's Eliza?"

"Ahh. Hah!" Etta's laughs, bobbing her head up and down.

"She's happy to have some help," I say. "She's got her hands full at the school."

"I wish I could read," Zekial says. "I'd be *very* happy to help her out." His eyes sparkle in a way that makes me smile.

"Well," says Etta. "That old school building needs some fixing up. Go talk to her about that."

His spoon clanks against his soup bowl.

"Maybe I will." He grins. "I surely will."

"Soup's real good, Etta," Promise says as she slurps a spoonful into her mouth.

"And I like the poke you put in the salad," I say. "Granny used to pick poke for us."

Etta looks at me. "You miss your granny?"

I think for a minute to see if I really do or not.

"I miss having a granny. But I don't miss the granny I got."

Etta keeps listening to me even though I stopped talking. So I say some more.

"She was real mean. To my ma and to me. It's true she took me in and all. I know that wasn't easy, but she kept getting meaner the older she got and the more she drank."

"You've had some hard times," Etta says.

Something about her saying she understands makes me warm and solid. Like she really cares about me. In the garden she knew I hurt bad about my ma. But this time her kindness doesn't make the lights flash and memories come. Instead, my shoulders relax and there's no buzzing in my head.

"Seems like we all have had hard times," I finally say.

"Amen," Zekial says.

Promise reaches over and squeezes my hand. Sandy the dog barks and pulls all of us to the radio. Little Orphan Annie's going to get herself in trouble again.

A tap, tap, tapping on the door startles us. Who would it be with Little Orphan Annie just starting? Etta pushes out of the rocker and opens the door.

"Asa. How nice to see you. Everything all right?"

Promise jumps out of her chair and flies across the room her toes barely touching the floor.

"You did come to teach me money after all." Her face is a sunbeam.

"Everything is fine, Miss Etta." His gaze shifts to Promise and a smile creeps across his face. His dancing brown eyes and his eyebrows like dark commas on his forehead make him look real handsome.

"Yessiree," Zekial whispers. "Someone's sweet on Promise."

I cringe and remember Promise asked me to teach her money, but I was so dang tired that I forgot. I guess she gave up on me. She seems mighty happy with my replacement.

"How are you feeling, Maisy?" Asa asks.

"Better. Still can't use my arm, but I'll be strong enough for us to be on our way pretty soon."

"You and Promise moving on?" His comma eyebrows pull together in alarm.

Promise steps behind me skittery as a rabbit. Then she places a hand on my shoulder.

"Maisy don't feel so welcome here," Promise says.

"I can understand that," Asa says. "Mr. Potts and Miss Mary can be a burr in your side. But I'm glad you two are here." He grins at Promise.

"Anyways," I say. "We're heading for Detroit pretty—"

"Shhh," Etta says as she turns up the volume on the radio.

I move my chair closer to Etta while Promise and Asa settle at the table. I try hard to listen to what's happening to Little Orphan Annie, but what truly has my attention is when Asa pulls out some coins and bills then leans close whispering to explain them to Promise. Especially when he lays his hand against her arm.

* * *

Me and Promise are snuggled under my quilt top. I'm excited to have the batting and I might spend some of my money on a nice piece of backing for the quilt. Maybe bright red cotton. Then I can finish it up. I imagine how pretty it will be all put together. Promise is on her side with her back to me. I'm a little afraid but I wiggle up close and slip my good arm around her waist, wanting to hold her close to me. Heat rises between our two bodies and I want to kiss the back of her neck where her short fuzzy hair ends. But I don't. I let my arm be around her gentle as can be. She don't say anything, but her body stiffens, her shoulders hitching up close to her ears.

"You hate me touching you that much?" I sound pitiful, but I can't help it.

She doesn't turn over. "I don't hate you. I tole you."

"I know. Booker. But how long is he going to come between us?"

A long impatient sigh escapes from her. She shifts onto her back. I think she's looking at me, but it's too dark to tell.

"Maisy," she uses that *I told you a thousand times* voice. "When Booker got kilt something inside me shut down. I don't understand. I don't blame you. Maybe I blame myself, I don't know. But when I even imagine turning over into your arms and kissing you, my body turns to stone. It's like I'm dead too." It's real quiet for a long time.

"Maybe," I say, "you don't want to love me that way anymore. Or maybe you plain don't love me at all." Accusation rides on my voice. I wait for her answer. Asa's hand on her arm flashes through my mind.

The silence hurts my ears.

Maybe she wants a boy to love her the way I do. Maybe she wants to hug and kiss where everybody can see instead of having to hide and sneak around. Maybe it's not just Booker dying. Maybe a different part of her is waking up. Maybe it's her and me that's dying.

"I miss you," she finally stammers as she turns toward me. "But I can't promise you anything right now. I'm too mixed up."

Fear ripples up and down my body. I've never been so scared in my whole life. Not even fighting that man off Promise. I can hardly breathe and I'm shaking like crazy. And I'm mad. I'm not proud I'm mad, but I am. We were going to make our life together in Detroit. And now? That dream seems like a glass shattered all across the floor. My anger gets the best of me. I press my lips shut to keep the words inside me. But some of them escape.

"You're hoping to kiss Asa, aren't you?"

"I'm not even talking such foolishness with you. Go to sleep." She rolls onto her side, faces away from me, and, nears as I can tell, falls right asleep.

Me? I lie real still while fear shoots through me. Pictures of Asa and Promise flip through my brain. Jealousy makes my teeth ache.

When the sun peeks over the horizon I finally fall asleep.

CHAPTER 40

"**I** will not allow no stinking cracker to teach my grandchild. You hear me." That finger points and pokes up and down.

"Miss Mary. Please hush. There's children here. They don't need to hear such language," Eliza says, glancing over her shoulder in my direction.

"I'll say what I want. It ain't nothing they haven't heard already."

"I'm sure," Eliza mutters.

"Everybody in this town wants her out. How dare you let her teach our children." She stamps her foot. "Our Negro children. They need Negro teachers."

"With all due respect, Miss Mary. There aren't any other Negro teachers in the town besides me."

Miss Mary harumphs.

"We can't pay nobody anyway," Eliza mutters. "You barely pay me."

I'm in my little room getting ready for those very same children to come in, and I can see Miss Mary through the doorway. Eliza wants me to do numbers today with the six children. I was real excited, but now I think I better sneak out the back and head for Detroit as fast as I can.

"I got the mayor and half our people behind me, missy." She shakes that finger again. "I'm starting a petition for the Town Meeting. So if you think this is the end of it, you are wrong." It's real quiet and then a door slams.

Eliza's head peeks around the door jamb. "I am truly sorry that you had to hear that. Please remember that she's not everyone." She smiles like she truly means it. "There are folks glad to have another teacher here at the school."

"She's got a big enough mouth for everyone," I say. "Maybe I shouldn't be here. It's only causing trouble. There's plenty more people who feel the same way as her."

"Don't you even think that for a second. You were able to do more yesterday with those kids than I can do in a week. Besides they're all real excited about doing their numbers today."

"But is it worth causing all this trouble?" I ask.

"You listen, Maisy. When these parents see what their children are learning, they'll kiss your feet."

I burst out laughing. "That'd be a sight. I can't picture Miss Mary ever shaking my hand let alone kissing my feet."

Eliza rests her hand on my shoulder.

"Just teach the children, Maisy. That's all."

Something moves deep inside me, but for the life of me I don't know what it is.

Little feet shuffle outside my tiny room. Annalee and Elijah lead three other children into my room while Thomas straggles behind. With my good hand and Eliza's help, I pull the desks up close to me jammed into a jagged circle. After a little scuffling and arguing, they get themselves settled.

Eliza smiles and waves as she leaves me with the children.

"Annalee," I say, "would you please introduce our new students?"

She stands up real important like and points to each new student.

"This is Abraham. And this is Sarah. And this here is Langston."

"I'm named after a real famous Negro poet," Langston says puffing his chest out.

"Well I'm named after my granny," Sarah says.

"I'm the most important because I'm named after the Bible," Abraham juts his little chin out.

"Each one of you got a real important name," I say. "It's important because it says who you are." They all beam like they won the grand prize. I look at those little faces and wonder which one's Mary's grandchild. How can so much innocence exist in the face of such hatefulness?

Eliza told me some ideas for teaching the numbers 1 to 10. First we count out loud then use our fingers to match the numbers I write on the board. After all that, it's time to write the numbers but Elijah and Langston wiggle so much I know they all need a break.

"Now. Listen very carefully. I'm going to give each of you a special number. Then I want you to go out to the play yard and find that many little rocks or twigs and bring them back to your desk."

Elijah's hand waves back and forth as he grunts for my attention.

"I'm going to start with whoever is sitting tall and still."

Suddenly six little faces look up at me and six little bodies are still as stones. I whisper a number to each child and off they run.

After they count out their rocks and twigs, write numbers, eat lunch, play outside and write their names — with Annalee, Elijah and Thomas as my helper teachers — it's finally time for them to go home.

Eliza's older students are in the yard for recess so she slips into a chair next to me.

"Maisy. You are a natural teacher. The kids love you and you've done more than I've been able to do what with all the older kids needing so much teaching. Annalee thinks you dropped from heaven."

The warmth of pleasure rises in my cheeks and I let myself imagine maybe I could belong here. Maybe I could do something good here. I might even be happier than the children to be teaching them. But Mary's voice echoes in my head. She hates me and this is her town, after all.

"Thank you," I say. "I really like teaching them. I never imagined being a teacher, but I feel real happy when I'm doing it. Even when that little Elijah wiggles his rear end all over his chair."

Eliza laughs. "He's a hand full. But he's got a good mind if you can keep his attention." She lays an arithmetic book on my table. "Tomorrow you can do numbers again and more writing like you did before. Also, I brought you the books we have for the little ones," she taps a stack of three books she holds in her arms. "It's good to read to them."

She hands me the tattered books. I look at each one. *Millions of Cats, The Little Engine that Could, and Winnie the Pooh.*

"We only got three books, but they love each of them."

For half a second, I remember leaning up against my ma reading *Winnie the Pooh.* I shake my head and focus on Eliza's face.

"I got a couple of magazines. Could I bring them in and show them the pictures and read the stories?"

"That'd be great to teach them some about the rest of the world."

I hesitate. "They're all white folks…"

"Ain't they all."

My shoulders droop.

"Wait," I say. "Etta has a magazine with pictures and stories about Negroes. Even an all Negro baseball team. I'll bring that."

She gives me a smile that reaches clear down into my chest.

* * *

The sun is hot and the breeze is still but that don't stop me from walking as fast as I can to Etta's store. I ignore the stares and head shaking, smiling instead at each person on the street. I am so filled up with joy from teaching my class. I have to tell Promise about my six children. She'll be so excited and probably have some good ideas too. Maybe if she has some time, she'll even come and help at the school with me. I'm

256

imagining that Promise could teach them about money. And maybe even take them up to the store to ring a real cash register. They would love that. And maybe I could dig some of Etta's vegetable plants and start a little garden in the yard with the kids. My mind races and I haven't felt this happy since before Booker was lying on the ground. Dead.

As I pass Etta's house I look sideways. I don't know why. Maybe to see the garden. Or wondering if Etta's home and I can tell her my ideas. Or just because I live there. I'm starting to think of it as home. But there on the front step two people are standing real close. I squint to see better. Actually they're kissing. I look real hard. Then I look again to be sure.

It is Promise and Asa.

She steps away, her hand lingers on his chest. She says something, opens the door and goes in the house. He stands on the step with his hands hitched in his pockets.

Then he turns and heads toward the road and before I know it, he is walking toward me. The tarry road shifts under me. And there we are, staring at each other. Our eyes glued together and him with a big goofy smile. My body shakes and my fingers freeze like ice. I hate him. I want to hurt him. To throw a rock at his head. To scream in his face. To rip them comma eyebrows off the front of his forehead. But he can't even guess how much I hate him because Promise and me are a secret.

We might as well not exist. We don't count for nothing to the world.

He grins and waves at me. He has no idea who I am to Promise. Or used to be.

I turn away and hobble up the street as fast as I can, not even noticing who's staring at me or giving me dirty looks. I see Etta's sign and, even though my leg is killing me, I fling myself through the door. Tears crawl down my face and drip off the edge of my chin.

CHAPTER 41

E tta says 'excuse me' to a customer and wraps her long arms around me. I don't even care about all the snot I get on her dress front. I hiccup and cry and try to talk at the same time.

"Is Promise all right?" She interrupts my sniveling.

I nod.

"Is anybody hurt?"

I shake my head no.

"You sit down on this barrel and let me finish up with Harriet. Okay?"

I nod.

After Harriet leaves and the door closes, Etta puts one arm around my shoulders and wipes my face with a handkerchief.

"I never seen you cry except when you remembered your mama being dead. What in heaven's name is the matter?"

"Promise."

Etta waits.

"She was kissing Asa on our front door step." Tears choke me. I stand and pace back and forth across the wooden plank floor. "*She was kissing him.*"

"Are you sure?"

"I got eyes don't I? I seen them. Right there." I whirl toward her. "And she touched his chest and let her hand rest right there."

"Calm down. I believe you." She holds the handkerchief out to me.

"I knew something was wrong. But I didn't think that. I mean she laughed a lot with him, but I didn't think they were kissing. And touching." I collapse onto the barrel and some horrible sound bursts from my chest.

"She don't love me. Not anymore. Not even a tiny bit."

Etta's warm hand rubs circles on my back as she croons. No words. No shushing. She softly croons to me. After a few minutes, she steps to the front counter and grabs a Hershey bar. Tearing the wrapper off, she breaks it in half and hands one piece to me.

We munch on the chocolate, no one saying a word. Finally Etta speaks.

"I'm not saying she wasn't kissing Asa, but when my brother died everything was out of kilter for a long time. I was confused and things didn't make sense to me." She takes a bite of chocolate.

"But I kilt Booker. He didn't just die. So she's got plenty to be mad about. To even hate me."

She nibbles on the chocolate, thinking.

"Very interesting," she says. "You blame yourself for Booker's death. And Promise blames herself. And no one blames the man that actually kilt him."

"I do, but still…"

"You are two confused girls."

"But I'm not going around kissing any old body that's got lips."

"True. I think you need to talk to her." She slips the last bite of chocolate into her mouth.

"About this?"

"No. About the weather."

My fingertips are covered with melted chocolate from the candy bar. I lick each finger and nibble on the candy thinking about what Etta just said.

"And give her time," Etta says.

"Time to what?" I snarl. "To fall in love with Asa?"

Etta lets out a long breath and taps her foot.

"Time to heal. To get herself back. Give her time for that and then you'll know she loves you."

Promise needs to stop being an ass. But I don't know if people heal from that.

Etta squeezes my shoulder and heads for the front counter. Another customer comes in and Etta helps him. I sit on the barrel thinking it's good I'm mad because being afraid would only wear me out. My rear end gets stiff sitting so I wander around her store. I ping my finger against the stack of metal buckets and run my fingernail up and down the glass grooves of a washboard. If these weren't Etta's, I'd kick the washboard across the room and throw them buckets against the wall.

Etta takes care of several customers. Ka-ching, ka-ching. I picture Asa and Promise laughing and pushing the keys on the cash register. Ka-ching. I walk through the aisles shaking. Not knowing what to do with myself I pick up a pair of socks and look at the underwear. I should buy myself a new pair. I touch the little pouch of my money around my neck, but I really don't want to spend my money on underwear. Now I'll need every cent for travelling. I hate her right now. I didn't know loving could hurt so bad.

A tear drops down my shirt front. I wipe my face with the back of my hand and let myself be drawn to the fabric. All the colors are lined against the wall, like at Miss Charlotte's. I walk past the needles and spools of thread and run my hand along the sides of the bolts of material. I remember that my mother sewed dresses for me. A little blue one I loved best of all and a frilly pink one that I hated. I think about wanting to sew for Promise and my chest hurts so bad I can hardly breathe.

I don't hear Etta walkup behind me until her hand runs down a bolt of bright red cotton right in front of me.

"This would be beautiful for the back of your quilt," Etta says. My breath stutters.

"It would match my red satin." Maybe this is what I would spend some of my money on.

No. I'm saving every penny to get us to Detroit. Except now it's just me. A stab of pain shoots through me into the balls of my feet. I lurch into the bolts of material all lined up, my face against some blue gingham. Pulling myself upright, I shake my head.

"Here's what I'm thinking," Etta says, like I didn't just do something really strange. "Let's cut a piece for the back of your quilt."

"I can't buy it."

"It would be payment for the work you've been doing at the school."

My heart does one big thump against my ribs.

"I thought working at the school was for my keep with you."

"You're working real hard. I think you need a raise. Besides, I got a special interest in your students."

I look at her curiously.

"I delivered each and every one of them. Brought them into this world."

I remember the woman who shook my hand on the street.

She pulls the bolt of red cotton off the shelf and spreads it on her cutting table.

Even though I'm furious at Promise and I know I'll probably have to move on to Detroit by myself, it makes me unreasonably happy as Etta cuts, then folds, then hands that piece of bright red fabric to me.

* * *

Promise is on her knees pulling weeds in the garden when Etta and I get home.

"Thank you," Etta hollers, and waves at Promise as she opens the door. I don't even look at her. But when we get inside, Etta turns to me, her head cocked.

"Now put that material down and go talk to her."

"I don't even know what to say."

"Go. You'll figure it out," she says and pushes me out the door.

Promise stops weeding and turns her face up to me. She smiles but I can see guilty, guilty, guilty written all over it. I want to say something

261

really mean or kick her in the knee, but I remember Etta's voice, take a deep breath and sit beside her on the ground.

She doesn't ask me how school went or how come I came home with Etta. She just waits.

"So," I say not really knowing where to start. "When Etta's brother died, she was really upset and acted crazy like you are."

"She told me about that." Her voice bristles as she tugs on a weed and shakes out the dirt.

"Did she also tell you that she came back from being crazy and got better again?"

A handful of sparrows bicker and flit through the garden. Promise doesn't say a word. Just pulls at some more weeds. She looks up at me, her hand shades her eyes from the sun.

"That was Etta. But me? I don't know if I'll ever come back. It don't seem like I can." Her hand drops into her lap and her shoulders slump.

"If Etta can, you will. Probably pretty soon," I say as kindly as I can even though I want to slap her. Hard. Really hard.

She looks at me with needles shooting out her eyes.

"The difference is that it's my fault that Booker's dead," she says. "Etta didn't kill her brother."

I wait, standing over her, my hands on my hips.

"I don't know how a person ever comes back from something that bad," she says Little specks of spit fly into the air between us.

I look at her real hard, biting my bottom lip.

"Then it's my fault too." *Run Booker. Run.*

She picks a daisy, pulling the petals off like she's deciding whether she loves me or not.

"Yes. It's your fault too."

I knew she'd never forgive me and I don't blame her. Maybe neither one of us will ever get over Booker.

But then I think that kissing Asa isn't really about Booker. It's about not loving me anymore and being real excited about him. I breathe real slow and think carefully about what I want to say. I want to say it right so we don't end up yelling and being mad. Well, madder than I am already.

"What we're talking about now isn't really about getting over Booker."

Her eyes flash at me. I wave my finger in her face.

"It's about Asa."

She makes a funny little noise in her throat and looks just past the top of my head.

"I seen how you laugh with him. And smile real happy. Like you're flirting." Blood rushes through my ears. I have to say it. "I seen you on the porch today."

Her eyes meet mine for half a second then drop to the ground.

"I seen you kiss him."

She's still as a brick and doesn't make a peep. I can't even tell if she's breathing.

I wait, shifting my weight so my bad leg don't hurt.

What I want to do is yell and spit at her, but I talk real soft. "Are you falling in love with him?"

Her lips press real tight together. "I love you."

"But why Asa then? Why does he get all your attention and smiles and, yes, kisses? You won't let me touch you let alone kiss you because you feel bad about Booker, but..." My anger rises to a dangerous point. I breathe.

I wait some more, breathing slowly. It's all I can do not to turn and walk away from her.

"Why, Promise? Why does Asa make you so happy and I make you so sad?"

Maybe days go by. Or even a year. Finally she sighs and reaches up for my hand. I pull it back.

"Maisy. Please understand."

I wait. I might be past understanding.

"When I look in Asa's eyes, I see Booker's eyes and when I hear his laugh, I hear Booker's laugh. Everything he does reminds me of Booker. It's almost like I'm talking to him again."

For a second that makes sense and my shoulders relax a little. But then the picture of them kissing flashes before my eyes.

"And kissing him?" I snap. "You didn't kiss Booker that way."

My heart hardens.

She studies her hands in her lap as if the answers laid in her palms. She don't say nothing. Not a word.

"Why did you lead him on to get so sweet on you?" My temper rises. "Maybe you've been waiting for a *boy* to come along and love you." My words slice the air.

"That ain't true...." Her head snaps up, her eyes wide open like circles.

"Well, it sure looks true from where I stand." A gnat buzzes in my face and Promise stares into the empty air. "Is that what you want?" I yell.

She tugs at a weed, shaking the dirt out of the roots.

"Listen to me. I can give you love deep from my heart. And I can give you friendship that you can lean on." I shift my weight off my throbbing leg. "But I can't give you Booker back if that's what you think you'll get from Asa."

"I'm not asking for that. Nobody can give me that. I only ask that you to be patient. For a while."

Anger courses through my whole body. I might be on fire.

"So." The ice in my voice cracks. "You want me to be patient while you laugh and flirt and kiss Asa to see if you love me or him better?" My voice rises. "That ain't going to happen. Not now. Not ever."

"No." She rises to stand, her hand reaching up to me, then she sits back on the dirt.

"No what?" I yell. "No. I'm not watching you fall in love with someone else in a town where I'm not even wanted and everybody hates me."

"Maisy. Please." Her voice disappears back down her throat.

"Don't *Maisy. Please* me." I gulp in air. Surely I'm drowning. "I'm leaving. I'm leaving for Detroit tomorrow."

She reaches for me but I step away. Pain slices through my body and her face blurs.

"My ma used to say 'enough is enough.'" I take a deep breath. "And I've had enough."

CHAPTER 42

"Etta," I lean against the tiny counter where she's chopping vegetables. She looks up at me and smiles.

Promise rocks in the chair, her eyes closed and lips frozen into a frown.

"I got to tell you something."

Etta's silent as she slices a yellow squash. Then she washes dirt off three turnips.

"What?" she says finally.

"I'm leaving." All the air whooshes out of me.

I expect her to grab me and wrap her long arms around me but she slams the knife down on the wooden counter. Slowly she turns to me, her eyes like razors.

"You're what?"

I look down at my bare feet. The creaking of Promise's rocker gets faster.

"I'm going to ask the man who delivers papers for a ride and go as far as he goes. Then I'll figure the rest out." I never asked him and don't even know his name. But I decided that's what I'll do.

"You're giving up and running off because things got tough for you?" She huffs and slaps her hand flat on the counter near me.

"Is that it?" Her jaw jumps like a jittery frog.

I don't know what to say, so I lean against the counter, my mouth hanging open a tiny bit.

Her face comes up close to mine, our noses almost touch. I look at the ceiling and then the floor and out the window but I know she's staring at me.

"I expected more from you."

She turns and walks out the door, slamming it hard behind her.

The door flies open and Etta's finger wags at me.

"Don't you dare leave without saying a proper goodbye to those children. They are counting on you." I think she growls at me.

Promise rocks and rocks, no expression on her face, tears dribbling down her cheeks. I huff past her on the way to the bedroom. She doesn't say a word to me and I got nothing to say to her.

In the bedroom, I shake out my flour sack and stuff my batting and red cotton cloth in the bottom. Then I pack everything, except my toothbrush that Etta brought from her store and my two pair of dirty underwear. I carry them out to the kitchen sink. Pumping some water, I rub them with soap with my good hand until I figure they must be clean. Little splats of water drip on the floor as I drag a chair near the stove and hang them over the back. They're full of holes, but at least they'll be clean. I hope they're dry tomorrow. Be a shame to have to travel in wet underpants.

Promise keeps rocking and rocking, not saying a word, as I limp back into our room.

I planned to leave at the first light tomorrow morning, but Etta's right. I got to say goodbye to them children. And to Eliza too. The weight of them all counting on me makes me tired. I wonder if, maybe hope, Promise and me can figure us out, but it don't seem possible. Least not with Promise rocking and rocking with her mouth shut tight as a tick.

Anger snaps in my chest and I snarl at Promise.

"I could of waited while you figured out all them bad feelings about Booker. I could of understood. I *do* understand that."

She turns slightly toward me, not quite looking at me.

"But I can't watch you kissing and falling in love with someone unless it's me."

267

I wait for her to jump up and say she's sorry or she was wrong or it's all a mistake. But she keeps rocking. Back and forth.

I got to go. That's all there is to it. But truth be told, I think I was settling in even though I didn't know it. It's not perfect in this town. And a lot of people aren't happy that I'm here. But some are and I was finding my way. And Etta. She's doing her best to make me a home and them kids really love me. And Eliza too.

I wait some more for Promise to talk. She don't.

Besides now that I rode them rails, I'm mighty scared to do it by myself. Shivers crawl up my back as I remember that man pulling Promise across the dark boxcar by her leg. I'm not so sure I can do it.

Booker's knife. I know it's all she's got left of him but I have to take it. She don't need it. She's got Asa. I'm the one that needs it. I decide I'm taking it. I need it to be safe out there all by myself. She's got this whole town to keep her safe.

I go into the bedroom to put the knife in my sack. I know it's wrong. But I don't care.

She keeps on rocking.

* * *

Etta is stretched out on her couch, with the electric bulb throwing light on her, reading *Book of American Negro Poetry*. Every now and then she reads a poem out loud to us but I don't think Promise is listening as she's got that I'm-not-in-the-room look about her. If she would only talk to me, tell me what she's feeling, maybe I could stay a while or try to understand. What I don't know is if she's chasing Booker in her heart or daydreaming about Asa. But, so far, not a word has fallen out of her mouth. I think that means she wants me to leave.

Loud knocking on the front door makes Etta jump up and fling the door wide open. She looks like she'll snarl at whoever is there. A boy hops on one foot and then the other. He looks to be about eight or nine, but I don't recognize him.

"Etta. You got to come. The baby's coming. Real fast."

"I'm coming, James. Hold on while I get my bag." She looks at me and then at Promise.

"You." She points to Promise. "You're helping me. And you," she looks at me. "You're helping with the little kids. Come on both of you. Now."

We follow James down the main street and onto a side street. The stores are closed but light shines from the houses' windows. I lag behind what with my foot still tender, but I see them turn into a small house with a big tree with white flowers all over it.

As I come up the walk, the door's hanging wide open. I step inside. There's three little kids besides James running around and the most god awful moan I ever heard comes from the other room. Promise is scrubbing her hands at the kitchen sink and Etta is in with the woman making all that noise. I see the husband kneel beside the bed and hold the woman's hand. Her head is flinging back and forth, harsh groans come out of her mouth.

Promise grabs a pot of boiling water and has a stack of clean white cloths under her arm.

"Etta said to keep the little kids busy and out of the bedroom. James can take care of himself." Her eyes meet mine and she looks at me for the first time all day.

"You scared?" I ask. Another moan blossoms into a screech that fills the house.

"I'm shaking. Etta said this is a real hard birth. It's life and death and I have no idea what to do."

"Don't think about your ma. Just get in there and do what Etta says." I give her a tiny smile of encouragement.

She goes in the bedroom, closing the door with her foot just as another scream echoes through the house. I look around and see four sets of big, dark eyes looking at me like maybe I can make the screaming stop.

"James. Has everyone had something to eat?"

"We had dinner and then my ma started."

"Try not to worry. I'm sure everything will be all right."

He scrunches up his face. "I don't remember this much yelling with them." He points to his brother and two sisters.

I don't know what to say. I look around the tidy house. It's a lot like Etta's but there seems to be one more bedroom. There aren't books and magazines lying all over the place. But. Yes. There is a radio.

"James, can we listen to the radio?" I think it's about Orphan Annie time.

"Sure." He moves to the small table where the radio sits and turns it on. The dial points to the same number as Etta's for Orphan Annie, but there's music. Maybe Guy Lombardo. Dancing music. Four faces look up at me. Even though Mary, Isaiah Potts and half the town want me gone, I keep getting pulled into the lives of these people. Especially the children. Even with all the agitation about me being white, it feels real different from getting beat on by Granny or touched by Elwood. Will it be like this in Detroit as well? With Promise I'm sure we'd find our way. But.

It's not going to be with Promise. I'll be on my own again. I was starting to let Etta and the school feel a little like a home, but that sure isn't going to be true now.

I can't worry about Detroit. I got to take care of these children right this minute.

The music surrounds me. I reach down, lifting the youngest one and settling her on my hip with my good arm and take the next oldest's hand with my broken wrist and we dance around the living room. My wrist hurts and my ankle complains, but it seems like dancing with these children right now is most important. Pretty soon James and the boy closest in age to him are silly dancing as well. They shake their heads and wiggle their butts. The song ends and we all fall onto a sofa, piled on top of each other, laughing. A sharp, long scream shoots through the house. Four sets of big eyes look at me.

"She'll be all right," I croon. "It's a lot of work to have a baby and it hurts." What do I know? But it seems to calm them down some. Then the music of Orphan Annie starts.

I stand and carry the baby closer to the radio, sitting on the floor. The other's follow me and we squeeze into a bunch, our shoulders and knees all pressed against each other. We can still hear the screaming, so I turn the volume up. That helps, but not completely. It's still real clear there's something mighty painful going on in the other room.

Promise, her face tight and her eyes scared, dashes out of the room, rummages through a cupboard and runs back to the room with a stack of towels in her arms. A smear of blood runs along her forearm.

We make it through Orphan Annie but then I'm wondering what to do. The music for Dick Tracy starts. I reach to turn it off because I'm thinking it'll be too scary for the little ones. But, it can't be as scary as what's happening right in their own house so we stay in our huddle and listen to the tough talk by Dick Tracy and the guns popping to get the crook.

Just before the end of Dick Tracy, the bedroom door opens. James and I whirl around. The baby's asleep on my lap and the others are too interested in the radio to care.

Promise steps into the living room cradling a tiny bundle in her arms. It's crying. I pull myself off the floor, lie the sleeping kid down on the sofa, and stand beside Promise.

"Her name is Lydia and she's wailing for the thrill of being alive." Tears run down Promise's face as she beams with pure joy. "She and her mother almost didn't make it. I was scared to death. I just knew it was going to be like with my ma. But Etta knew what to do." She looks into my eyes clear down to my soul. "It's a miracle."

I gently rub my finger on the cheek of the baby. Her head turns and she roots around like maybe I'm her dinner. Promise and I both laugh. Then Promise cries again. She leans up against me with her shoulder, jiggling this brand new baby girl.

"Maisy. This is what I want to do." She wipes the wetness off her face with the back of her hand. "I want to work with Etta and learn how to help life come into the world." Her eyes say to please understand.

"I'm trying real hard to believe that I can't bring Booker back." She dips her head. "I know I'm not good at that yet." She rocks the little bundle in her arms. "But I know I can do this. I can bring babies into the world." Her lips whisper across the tiny forehead. Her dark eyes meet mine.

We study each other. This feels like the first time Promise has told me the truth since Booker got kilt. Or maybe it's the first time she ever knew it.

"I never knew I could do something that made a difference before," she says.

My heart sinks and an ache in my chest spreads through my body. There's no hope now that she'll come with me to Detroit. She'll stay here where she belongs. And where I don't.

What's true is that I can imagine Promise living her life here, helping babies getting born. And maybe even have some of her own. But not with me.

CHAPTER 43

Zekial knocks on the door as I'm leaving to get to school. My last day. The day I tell the children and Eliza good-bye.

"Thought you could use some company today," he says standing on the step where Asa and Promise kissed, his bare feet right where they stood.

"Me? Or Eliza?" I tease him, tucking Etta's magazine under my arm.

He grins. "Maybe both."

"You been seeing her?" I ask as we walk to the street and head toward the school in the morning light. The sun is warm on our backs and long shadows walk in front of us.

"I like her," Zekial answers simply.

"You know I'm leaving?"

"Yup. And it's a mistake."

We walk in silence except for the squirrels chattering and sparrows chirping.

"This is a good place to live," he says.

"For you. But everybody wants *me* gone."

"Not everybody. There's—"

A skinny woman, her skin rich as ebony and her grey hair in a tight bun, walks between us and pushes me into the street. I barely catch my balance as Zekial spins around and grabs my arm. Etta's magazine slips to the ground. He picks it up and yells at the back of the woman marching down the road.

"That was wrong. You don't even know her."

The woman slows and almost turns, but then keeps on walking into town.

"That's your hate speaking out," Zekial yells at her back.

"You all right?" he asks as he guides me, holding my arm, back to the side of the road. He passes the magazine back to me.

Tears drip off my chin. Not from what happened but because of what Zekial said. He's a good man and I will miss him.

"Thank you," I stammer. That's all I can choke out, so we walk in silence until the school comes into sight.

Now that I collected myself, I realize that I owe Zekial for the ways he's been kind to me. He didn't have to help us in the woods and I hate myself for taking him for granted. I didn't even know I was doing it. Again, it was because he's colored. Negro. When will I learn?

"Zekial," I tug at his arm and stop on the wooden sidewalk.

He smiles down at me.

"I want," a buzzing of embarrassment clutches at my voice. "I want to thank you for carrying me when I was hurting."

His face is serious.

"I mean, you didn't have to. But you did and I'm grateful. And thank you for you being my friend here as well."

He studies me with them brown eyes then ever so slightly nods his head. Touching my shoulder for a moment, he walks toward the school.

I pull the door open. Zekial looks for Eliza; his eyes dance as he spots her. Giving my arm a quick squeeze, he heads toward her, a goofy grin on his face. I turn toward my classroom, sadness sagging in my heart. Miss Mary stomps toward me in a huff followed by another woman I don't recognize, but her mouth is puckered and bitter. Miss Mary narrows her eyes at me and mutters something sharp and nasty. I don't catch the exact words but something about I'll be sorry. Probably just as well that I'm leaving. Surely moving on is the right decision. Clearly no one wants me here and I don't need a bunch of Negro Grannys and Elwoods in my life. I've been beat down enough.

"Miss Maisy, Miss Maisy!" Annalee flings herself against me, her arms around my hips. She looks up at me with them hazel eyes of hers. They sparkle and I smile.

"Today is my granny's birthday." She grins, one tooth missing on the bottom.

"You lose a tooth last night?" We walk toward our classroom.

She reaches into her pocket and opens her little fist. There in the palm of her hand is her tooth. I'm surprised at how happy it makes me to see that little chip of white in her chubby brown fingers. I pick it up and examine it.

"Very nice."

"So can we," she says taking her tooth and stuffing it into her pocket, "make something special for my granny? I love her so much."

What a lucky granny to have someone like Annalee love her so much. Just for a second I wish my granny had been like Annalee's. I probably would have never left. I wouldn't have needed to.

"Of course we can. Go play with the other kids until school starts and give me time to think." She skips toward the rest of my class.

So much for saying a quick good bye and being on my way. But Annalee needs me to help her. I just got to figure out what to do.

As I lay out the paper for today, I have an idea. I go find Eliza for a pair of scissors, more paper and some crayons. If they have them.

The kids bounce in as I write on the chalkboard.

"Take your seats and when you're real quiet I'll tell you something special."

Elijah gives Thomas a little push, but luckily Thomas ignores him and sits in his chair, back straight and looking at me.

"Today is Annalee's granny's birthday and we're going to make a big surprise for her." Feet shuffle with excitement and little butts wiggle in the chairs.

"Can anybody read what I wrote on the board?"

Elijah's hand whips in the air. "I."

"Great. Anybody else?" They're all looking at the board like the words might jump into their heads.

"It says HAPPY BIRTHDAY. I LOVE YOU."

"My mama's birthday is in fortyteen days," says Sarah.

"Great. Here's what we're going to do. Everybody is going to practice writing what I wrote on the board. Write that whole sentence three times very carefully, making all your letters the same size. Then, after recess I have a surprise for you."

They whisper and giggle with anticipation.

"On the surprise I have for you, you can write these words," I tap the blackboard, "for Annalee's granny or your ma or anybody that you want to make it for."

For an hour all six of them bite their tongues or jiggle their feet, concentrating on writing the sentences. Their letters mostly bump into each other or they're about to tumble off the page.

"I am so proud of each one of you," I tell them, my voice choked up in my throat.

When they take their recess break, I cut out six hearts from the nicest paper I could find. I was hoping for red, but all Eliza had was white, but without any lines. After that I set the small tin bucket of broken crayons on my desk. Then I place a heart on each desk and call them back from recess.

When they see the hearts, you'd of thought I'd given them a handful of candy bars and when they see the crayons, it's like Christmas had come. It makes me sing inside to see them be so happy. How will I be able to say goodbye?

After all the hearts are written and colored – with rainbows, lions, hearts, salamanders, flowers and chickens—each one of the children stands up in front of the class and, proud as punch, reads their heart to the others. I almost cry for being so happy. I burst with pride for them. Then I remember Promise last night, with tears of joy running down her face, holding that baby.

After lunch I decide I have to say goodbye. I can't put it off anymore. I want to take them all on my lap, but, instead, I stand at the front of the class. Like a teacher.

"So I have some not so good news," I say. The rustling and wiggling stops and they all look straight at me, their little mouths slightly open, waiting.

"I really love being your teacher and each one of you is very special to me. But."

But what, I wonder. How can I leave this? These children love me and I'm doing something real important. But. I remember Promise kissing Asa on the front step.

"But I have to leave your town and go to a place called Detroit."

"NO!" Thomas shouts.

"Why?" Sarah asks.

"You can't." Abraham insists.

"I hate you." Elijah pouts.

"That's not fair." Annalee whines.

"I know. But I have to go." I fight back the tears and ask myself how can I leave these children?

"You have to go 'cause you white?" Langston asks. "My mama says you the only white person in this whole town."

"That don't matter," Annalee yells at Langston. "She's our teacher."

"She's still white," Langston says determined to get the last word in.

I look down at my hands. They're white.

I've always been white but, even so, there still wasn't any place where I belonged. Not really. Except with my ma. But my ma's dead. Now Promise is my true home. I belong with her.

Belonged. Was. Used to be. The weight of my desperate heart crushes my chest and I can hardly breathe.

"Miss Maisy," Langston says. "Your face is getting even whiter."

I take a deep breath and rest my eyes on each child's face.

"I will miss each of you. I'm sorry that I have to go."

Little feet shuffle against the wooden floor and Annalee whispers *no, no, no.*

Maybe I can teach in Detroit. But it won't be these six little faces looking up at me. Or Elijah wiggling in his seat. Or Annalee being my helper.

But without Promise, there's no reason to stay. Not in this town.

The afternoon wears on, and it gets harder and harder as I realize each thing I teach them will be the last. I'll never know if Abraham learns to count to twenty or if Sarah's mama really turns fortyteen. Or if Elijah gets his letters to stay on the page. Or who will lose the next tooth.

The day's almost over and everyone except Sarah and Langston decide to give their hearts to Annalee's granny. Annalee says her granny's coming today to pick her up, so everyone is skittery with excitement. Finally the bell in the steeple rings once and school is over. Every-one grabs their heart and we walk out, Annalee leading the line, to find her granny.

I cannot believe my eyes when she and three other children run up to Miss-Mary-crank-and-complain-about-me. Annalee waves her heart in Miss Mary's face and the other's jump and shove to show their hearts to her.

"Happy Birfday," Elijah jumps up and down, bumping into Miss Mary. She puts her arm around Annalee's shoulder and holds the heart up close to her face to read. She takes each of the other hearts being pushed at her and touches each child's head, smiling. Holding the last one up, she lowers it and looks straight at me with her hazel eyes. I'm ready to run, but something changes in her face. She doesn't look friendly or welcoming, but softer and biting her lip like she's thinking on something. She opens her mouth to speak but, instead, looks at me one more time and wraps her arm around Annalee.

While I can, I turn and go back to my classroom for the last time.

CHAPTER 44

My toeless shoes scrape against the pebbles of the path to Etta's door and I step onto the very same porch where Promise stood close to Asa, kissed him and lay her hand on his chest. I fold my fingers around the polished wooden knob of the front door, it's coolness in my palm. Pushing open the door, that still has a few flecks of egg stuck in the grain of the wood, I wonder if my underwear is dry. Maybe I'll have to wait for it. Part of me hopes it's still soaking wet. Inside, I kick my shoes off and there, on the kitchen table, is my quilt top sitting on the bright red cotton backing. I stare. Its vibrant colors fill the room. I never imagined that I could make something that is almost alive as I stitched each square together in Granny's house and in my boxcar.

"What?" I say to Etta who stands by the table. "That was all packed."

"Really gorgeous, isn't it?"

"You had no business..." Her eyes stop me. Not because she's angry but I can see that she loves me.

"You made this out of the scraps of your life. Look at it." She waves her hand over it then touches a row of pearls and a pocket patch. "Just think what you could do if you weren't working with scraps."

She takes a long breath. "Who would you be if you let yourself belong somewhere?"

Biting her lip, she touches my quilt with her finger. The red satin. The flour sack strips.

"I hope you stay," she says.

I run my hand over the bumpy surface of the quilt, tiny beams of sunlight reflect off the plastic pearls Miss Charlotte gave me. My finger traces the red satin edging along the top and I tuck my hand into a pocket for half a second. I want to lean into Etta's strong arms and rest my head against her chest, then collect vegetables, make a soup and laugh with Etta and Promise about how Elijah wiggled right off his chair today.

I drop my chin. My big toe touches the edge of a knot in the planks of Etta's floor.

"I can't stay without Promise being my..." My stomach heaves. There isn't a word for who we were to each other. How can that be?

Etta's warm hand combs through my raggedy hair. Silence sits on us, the shadow of a branch shooting across the floor.

"Like your Lena," I whisper.

Etta nods and folds the edges of my quilt together then folds it into a square. She does the same with the red cotton backing and hands them both to me.

"You look mighty tired. Why don't you wait and leave early tomorrow with a full belly and fifteen hours of sunlight to figure out what you're doing. I'll pack you food and draw you some maps."

All I can do is hitch my shoulder a little and go to our room to finish packing.

* * *

My underwear is dry so I put one on and shove one into my sack. I leave a place for the food Etta promised. I'll need a water jug as well. I don't remember ever feeling so bad. When Booker died, yes. But this is even worse than Granny beating on me or Elwood's creepy hands. Or breaking my wrist. I rummage through Promise's drawer and find Booker's knife in its sheath tucked between her extra pair of denims and her underwear. I slide it deep into the pocket of my over-alls. It feels familiar. I pause. I know the knife matters to her, but right now, I don't care one whit. I'm going to need it and she won't. She's got Asa.

I sit on the bed, lie down and roll over on my side staring at a slice of afternoon sunlight on the wall. I never imagined that first time I held Promise and kissed her that this is what would happen. It seemed we would always be together. But now all my insides are breaking apart.

Footsteps pad across the floor.

"Maisy?" Promise whispers.

I ignore her.

"Maisy. Are you awake?"

"I thought you'd be with Asa." My voice is muffled in my pillow.

The bed dips as she sits down. The streak of light has shifted.

"Come walk with me. Please."

I don't say a word or wiggle a finger.

"Please."

"Why should I? What could you possibly say?"

I long for her hand to touch my shoulder. Or softly graze my cheek. But nothing.

"Walk with me in the woods. Please."

I am silent.

"Please."

I wait for the warmth of her hand on my shoulder, nudging me. Instead she stands.

"Please come walk with me. I know you are angry, but please."

Rolling over, I avoid her eyes. I slap my feet on the floor and head for the back door.

We walk past the garden, the yellow squash blossoms wave in the breeze and white daisy heads bob. She snaps a daisy off and presses the middle against her chin then plucks the petals one by one. I wonder if she's doing loves me, loves me not for Asa. Certainly not for me.

The tiny stones in the olive-colored dirt poke at the bottoms of my bare feet and the almost sweet smell of manure floats in the air. The leaves whisper overhead. The chickens cluck from the bushes where they hunt for bugs.

We walk for maybe five minutes. Promise stops in the middle of the path and grabs each of my arms.

"Please stay." Her eyes search my face but I look away, studying tiny blades of grass, each one fighting its way through the dry soil.

"You know I can't." I shake my arms free from her and walk away.

"I don't blame you for not trusting me. But I want to tell you something." She catches up and slips her hand into mine.

I want to hold her hand, our palms pressed together, my arm soaking in her warmth. Instead, I pull away and stick my hand in my pocket, the roughness of the denim against my skin.

"I'm going to tell you anyways," she says.

"It won't matter." I wonder how far it is to Detroit. "I can't trust you anymore."

Her body jerks as if I slapped her.

"I know that's true. But, Maisy Wharton. Please just listen to me."

I snort.

"I'll take that as a yes."

I think about not forgetting my water jug and wonder if my underwear is truly dry.

"Last night, being so close to death and to new life, changed me." Her voice is somewhere between talking and whispering.

She waits for me to say something, but I have no idea what I could ever say.

"I don't have lots of words yet to explain to you, but when baby Lydia and her ma were both so close to dying, I got to help them live. That changed the part of me I thought died with Booker. It made me...... Better. Like Etta got better."

"That'll surely be good for Asa." I say, turning my back. I walk deeper into the woods.

She chases me and grabs at my arm. I jerk away from her fingers.

"This ain't about Asa," she yells. "I know that for sure now." Her eyes plead with me.

I look away.

"It never was about Asa," she whispers.

"It sure looked like it was about him on the front steps."

"Maisy. I made a terrible mistake." She reaches for me and I pull away. "But it wasn't for not loving you. It was about being crazy with Booker being kilt."

I walk ahead of her. A cardinal whistles from a branch above us and a crow caws passing overhead. It flies off, its black wings disappearing into the deepness of the woods.

"I'm begging you to forgive me."

I turn away from her and walk further into the woods. Her footsteps follow me and her fingers slide down my arm and lace with mine.

I want to pull away, but I let them stay there. The warmth between us rises up my arm.

"I want you Maisy. I want us to be together. Loving you makes me feel alive."

I drop her hand and swing to face her.

"You'll never forgive me for Booker," I say.

"We will always hold Booker between us," she says. "You and me both feel guilty for Booker getting kilt." She studies the blueness of the sky. "But we got to carry that together, helping each other."

Her hand brushes my arm and travels across my skin. Her pinky finger links with mine.

"I should have said to Booker that I didn't love him in that special way the very first time he talked about going to the movies and holding hands. I should have said we were only friends."

We stand facing each other, our fingers linked.

"If I'd said that, he wouldn't have come to see me that night," my voice disappears into a whisper.

It seems like days before Promise answers me. I pull my hand away, letting it flop at my side.

"You should have, that's true. But now he died thinking you might have loved him."

I walk further down the path to the edge of a small stream.

"And me," she says. "I should have told him about you and me. But I was afraid."

"I know."

Promise links her arm with mine.

"Listen to me Maisy Wharton." She stops and pulls me closer to her.

"It weren't us that kilt Booker. It was hate. Elwood's hate is what done that," she says.

I pull away. She grabs my hand.

"Our only sin," she says, her face so earnest, "was loving each other." She gently jiggles my hand. "And surely that's not a sin."

Pulling my hand loose, I step across the stream and lower myself onto a rock, picking at the moss. She follows me.

"What you say is true. But, you weren't simply grieving." I look her straight in the face. "You betrayed me."

Surely she will turn and leave me now.

She stands over me for the longest time. Then she kneels beside me and places her hand, fingers spread, on my back. Her warmth soaks through the worn work shirt Miss Charlotte gave me.

"You're right, I did betray you. I can't ever find words to tell you how sorry I am."

I wait.

"Please, forgive me."

The stream ripples through its mossy banks, lightly gurgling over rocks.

"I love you Maisy Wharton. I want to have a life with you." She takes my face between her hands.

I want to lean into her. To kiss her and feel her skin against mine.

"But," I take one of her hands from my face and hold it, "how can I trust you? What if I'm always waiting for you to love someone else?"

She sits and picks at the moss then her eyes meet mine and she reaches for me. I lean away, ever so slightly. Fear scrambles across her face.

"I can't promise I'll be perfect," she says, "but what I can promise is that I'll surely try to love you like you deserve to be loved."

I start to object but she presses her finger against my lips.

"You can always leave later." Her sadness begs me. "I ain't tying you up with a rope."

We sit eyeing each other, taking measure. A bumble bee buzzes between us and a dragon fly swoops, drinking from the stream. Pictures of who we've been to each other flip through my mind and the memory of the lightness of her touch whispers across my skin. But I need to know about Asa. It's like picking at a scab.

"I have one question," I say. "What was it like kissing Asa?" I want to know but, at the same time, I'm afraid of the answer. What if she describes the way it feels for me to kiss her?

She pretends to think, cocking her head from side to side.

"Well, he's a nice boy. But kissing him was kind of like kissing my grandpa."

Despite myself, I laugh and relief pours off my skin. Then we each laugh and our laughter floats together into a song.

It would be so easy to lean into her arms, press my head against her chest and listen to her heart beat. Then to let our lips touch and to slip my hand under her shirt knowing that she would feel the same joy and electricity as me.

But. There's something else important that I can't find words for. I pick up a stick and poke it at the moss, thinking. I want to roll her on her back and lie along the length of her body, my hands cradling her head.

But I wait. My head and chest lightly buzz with the words *it's not enough.*

"So you'll stay?" She asks smiling her crooked smile. She reaches for me and I pull away ever so slightly. Her hand hovers in mid-air.

I pause. There's more. I want to tell the truth. More than that I want to understand the whole truth.

It's not enough to stay for her.

I barely understand those words. Everything I've done is for her.

But.

Etta's words *who you are to yourself* whisper in my mind.

"I surely love you," I say. "But there's something else." *Not enough.*

"What else could there be?" she puzzles.

I think hard to give this feeling a name. But nothing comes. Only the words *not enough.*

She waits, her hand on my knee, fearfulness sitting in her eyes. I can't find words but pressure fills my chest. Words struggle in my throat.

"I do hope we find a way to be together," I croak. "But..."

A tiny moan escapes from Promise.

But what? This is bigger than Promise and me. It's about how I've changed from when I sat alone in the box car, night after night. Instead of words, pictures tumble inside my head, one after another. Etta's face, kindness in her eyes, wanders through my mind, her finger shakes at Isaiah Potts and Mary. Elijah and Annalee's voices, dance settling in my ears. *I love my Granny.* Eliza's hand reaches out and squeezes mine then hands me three worn books. Zekial's strong arm presses against me, holding me up, beads of sweat running off his face. His words defend me on the street. Excitement tumbles through my chest as six shining faces fill with pride when they read their names, written with broken crayons and stubby pencils, out loud, holding their heads high, little white teeth in wide grins. *Why* Sarah asks. *No.* Thomas shouts. Then Miss Mary's face slips across my vision, ever so slightly biting her lip. Her eyes a question. A tiny slice of hope. Then, finally, the tall dark man in the middle of the street fills my mind. He holds onto his pride, his right to dignity, and does not move to let me pass, even in the face of my broken arm, my cane and my prejudice I didn't even know I had. All these pictures collide and I understand.

I am different now. I am changing in ways I never imagined or even knew existed. It's for me that I want to stay. For me. For my own heart and soul. For me to become who I need to be, who I want to be. For me to be somebody I am proud of.

I sit real still. Promise picks at her fingernail, her breathing shallow. I surely thought I was going to say that without us loving each other, I would head for Detroit in search of my home, the home my mother promised me. I was going to say that surely Promise was my only reason for being here in this town and that I would only stay for her. That I needed her love for me to stay.

But now I understand that simply her loving me would not have been enough. I need to be here for myself. I need to stay to make this town my home even if it is hard. And, mostly, I need to give something to those children.

The brook rushes over the loose stones and shadows flit across my lap.

"So," I say taking her hand, "this is what I know about staying here. I love you deep in my heart, but it will, most certainly, take a while to trust you again."

She whispers, "I know."

"Also, I am different. I'm not sure we can make promises to each other about the future." Her arm tenses, squishing my fingers.

"I hope someday we can. I hope we love each other in a way that lasts a lifetime and that we will grow old together. But." Fear skitters across her face. "Whether we can or not, whether we stay together or not, *I* need to make my home here. I need to be in this town because finding my way here, in Hope, turns out to be my Detroit."

ABOUT THE AUTHOR

Mariellen has had the privilege of working, laughing and crying with teenagers as a school psychologist for many years. Besides writing, she loves to garden, travel the world, and hang out with her friends and family.